DEAD BLOW

Other books by Lisa Preston:

Fiction:
The Clincher: A Horseshoer Mystery (#1)
Orchids and Stone: A novel
Measure of the Moon: A novel

Nonfiction:
The Ultimate Guide to Horse Feed, Supplements, and Nutrition
Natural Healing for Cats, Dogs, Horses, and Other Animals
Bitless Bridles

DEAD BLOW

A HORSESHOER MYSTERY

Lisa Preston

ARCADE
CrimeWise

An Arcade / CrimeWise Book

Arcade Publishing books may be purchased in bulk at special discounts for sales promotion, corporate gifts, fund-raising, or educational purposes. Special editions can also be created to specifications. For details, contact the Special Sales Department, Arcade Publishing, 307 West 36th Street, 11th Floor, New York, NY 10018 or arcade@skyhorsepublishing.com.

Arcade Publishing® and CrimeWise® are registered trademarks of Skyhorse Publishing, Inc.®, a Delaware corporation.

Visit our website at www.arcadepub.com.

10 9 8 7 6 5 4 3 2 1

Library of Congress Cataloging-in-Publication Data is available on file.

Cover design by Erin Seaward-Hiatt
Cover photo credit istockphoto.com

ISBN: 9781510749115
Ebook ISBN: 9781510749122

Printed in the United States of America

Chapter 1

D YING FROM A HIND HOOF GETTING run through my skull would smart, at least for a minute. If this big old girl didn't learn some manners pronto, I'd be finding out if the noggin went numb right quick or if maybe it kept stinging as I flopped around in the barn aisle, landed-trout style.

Or Sandy could behave herself, that'd be an idea.

She and I were on the near side of needing to go take a Pay-Attention-and-Act-Like-a-Lady walk. The barn grunt was off cleaning stalls. He'd just put the mare in cross-ties—I hate working with the horse in cross-ties—before hustling away. Wasn't his horse and he probably had a chore list longer than his hairy arm, so he wasn't about to do extra like mind this horse. Now I was left with a horse stomping, pulling away, and swaying like we were in a hurricane.

I was ready to whack her in the butt.

The horse stood nicely for the two seconds it took me to get back in position under her haunch, then she snapped her leg into my gut and twisted away, hopping on her other hind leg and throwing me onto my toolbox. I got up mad but let that go for now, because anger and horses don't mix well. I gave Sandy a stink eye. She gave

1

me one right back, indicating maybe she hadn't caught up on her kicking quota.

Then something just wonderful happened.

Whatever saint is supposed to keep watch over horseshoers woke up from a nap and cast a quick spell on Sandy. She stood like stone and I finished that hoof like nobody's business. Well, nobody else's business, what and all with this being my whole business. And business was fair near booming. I was still grinning thinking about the phone call this morning. Couldn't wait to go grab dinner with Guy and tell him about my new account.

When the Widow Chevigny rang and asked me to shoe for the Buckeye, it suited me fine. This was a ranch account and I wanted to be Donna Chevigny's shoer mighty bad. Word is, she's been needing a shoer. Her husband had done their shoeing but he died last year, around the time I moved to Cowdry. Being new, I learned about the accident—rolled his tractor, is what I heard—in bits, here and there. I've been needing more clients but hadn't wanted to go pound on a widow's door asking for a job.

"I want rim shoes," Donna told me on the phone. "Getting some of my ranch horses shod for a herd dispersal sale. They've been keeping themselves way off at the back, by the grazing lease." This brought a big sigh and I knew she was thinking about how it'd take her time and trouble to bring the horses in. Guess the area where her excess herd was hanging was too rough for driving to, or she'd have been telling me how long it'd take us to get out there with trucks or four-wheelers.

Real pleased with my new possession, I allowed as to how I could cold shoe out in the tooley-weeds, without need for my anvil and stand. My fellow's folks had gifted me with a Pocket Anvil as an engagement present. It's a portable horseshoe shaper that folds up. What gal wouldn't be completely swept off her boots with such a bonus? That gift selection was surely Guy's doing, because I can't imagine how his parents would have thought up sending us a pasta thingy *and* a Pocket Anvil for engagement presents.

Still, a full shoe inventory would be quite a ball and chain to pack to the far end of the Buckeye ranch, so I asked, "Do you happen to know what size feet you got out there?"

"They're all ones." Donna sounded like a woman who was certain. "All four feet on all twelve horses."

"I won't be shoeing a dozen in a day, ma'am." I mean, yeah, stories go around about old timey ranch shoers whupping out fifteen and twenty shoeing jobs in a day, but I've never known a sure shoer to manage twelve where the work site was remote, needing an hour's ride to get to and from the string. Lots of steel to pack. Chances were, some of those front feet were supposed to be size two, and some of those hinds were aughts, anyways.

"I thought you'd try for half one day, half another." Donna told me the brand of horseshoes she favored. Regular stuff. I had a fresh box in Ol' Blue, my truck.

Thrilled with my new tool, I told Donna all about the Pocket Anvil, this portable gadget that lets me shape horseshoes in the backcountry. Getting by without my real anvil would let me ride out to shoe in remote country. Without my forge, I wouldn't be hot fitting the shoes, of course, but I'm not above cold shoeing when circumstances demand.

"A pocket anvil? Goodness, I've never heard of such a thing." Donna sounded floored, then hopeful. "I wouldn't have to bring the horses in?"

"Nope. We could ride out to them as long as you scare up some saddlebags that'll freight my gear. Just the regular hand tools, a couple dozen shoes, nails, and my Pocket Anvil." *Just*, ha! It was still no small chore. And I'd be shoeing without my good hoof stand all day, so I'd be feeling it in my back and legs the next day. But, on the plus side, without my real anvil, there wouldn't be heavy hammer blows striking steel, so my ears wouldn't be ringing.

Donna's appreciative exhale let me know she was considering my offer. "It sure would help me out an awful lot if we ride out to the stock instead of me having to bring them in the day before."

"We'll do it," I promised. I already had my appointment book out and found a free day that worked for both of us. I used to worry about not having my work weeks scheduled full, then came to find that they tend to fill up just fine.

Donna worked all the hours a day sent, too. "Is six too early for you to be here? I'd have my horse tacked up, with the heavy packing saddle bags, if you're sure we can handle everything you'll need to haul."

Given that it was almost fall, we'd be riding out in the cool dark morning at that time, which sounded kind of wonderful. "I'm sure. Um, the horses needing shoes, they handle all right?" I didn't want to be battling broncs in the backcountry.

"They all handle fine. We won't have any problems with them out in the rough, and there's an old pole corral there. Goodness, Rainy, it will save me hours of pushing stock and eating dust if we can just ride out to where they're pastured."

"You'd need to give me a mount," I told her. "My Red's a good horse and I'd love to ride him out at your place, but I don't have a trailer."

"I can put a good horse under you," Donna promised.

* * *

Soon as I finished trimming this big tough mustang's feet and nodded to the barn guy, I slid Charley over on Ol' Blue's front seat, gave him the necessary kiss on his good gold Aussie face, and went to get something under my belt. The restaurant I go to in town is an outfit that's gone from a good place to get a glass of water to a whole bit better, thanks to my Intended.

If Guy's not there, the Cascade Kitchen is just a diner and that's what it always looks like. Lots of orange caps and vests at the counter come hunting season, sometimes a tractor in the parking lot when the guy who farms the adjacent hundred acres comes in for a hot lunch.

Today a horse trailer with living quarters, hooked up to a dually four-door F350 truck, took the five-plus parking spots a rig that size demands. The pickup's custom paint job read *Paso Pastures*. I didn't know who owned the truck and trailer, but horse people are my tribe. Folks are getting used to seeing me ride Red into town for an ice cream. If the Cascade Kitchen's owner put a corral, or at least a hitching rail, behind the restaurant, it would suit me fine.

Walking in the back door like a boss, I grabbed the mail stuffed in the wall tray to give it a gander. Guy and I started using the Cascade Kitchen for mail after our road mailbox got baseball-batted. Sizzling scents made mail sorting a pleasure.

I waded through way too many cooking and spice catalogs before the mail got good. A horseshoeing supply catalog, an ad for glue-on shoes, another horseshoeing supply catalog, a tack catalog, a different horseshoeing supply catalog, then a couple bills, and some official-looking fat letters: envelopes for Guy and me from the fifth judicial district, whatever that meant, which apparently pulls up a chair in Clackamas County. We're in Butte County, but this fifth judicial deal also claimed to be from the State of Oregon. How many people get mail from their own state? Too early for Christmas, so these would be . . . subpoenas? I thought those got handed out by seedy-looking creeps who tracked you down when—

Whack-whack-whack, whackety whack. Guy's rangy, almost six-foot frame stood at a metal counter in front of a cutting board piled with red peppers. His right arm moved like it was demon-possessed, powering a butcher's knife, whacking peppers into long strips.

Only I could break the spell. "Hey."

Guy put the knife down, turned and squirreled his arms around me. "What happened to you? Are you okay?"

I followed his stare to my dirt-covered legs. "I was working on Sandy's hinds. She's from the Riddle Mountain herd, a big Kiger mare—"

Guy broke in with a solo. "I've got a . . . *Kiger by the tail it's plain to see.*"

Never sings the right words, Guy. Bursting into song is one of his things, like he breathes and eats and sleeps. He knows a gajillion and six songs, but he adjusts the words quite a bit. We'd talked at the house this morning about me going out to work on some mustangs. New clients have a pair of these beautiful, stripey-legged tough duns with the hardest feet any horse ever thought of growing. True Kigers, that band of barefooters, born wild in Oregon's southeast. I'd been tickled to become their shoer—okay, their new trimmer—and tickled to tell Guy about the job.

He tickled me, snaking his arms all over as he dusted me off and went for free feels.

It's a little embarrassing to be fussed over and it'd be best we not get started in the kitchen. I mean, in our kitchen at home, that's fine, but not here at his work. That'd be some kind of food safety violation. Man in his line of work ought to know that kind of thing. I pushed him away.

"Well, fine." Guy kissed me like he meant it, smoothed my ponytail, then brushed again at the dirt on my jeans. "Anything broken?"

See, here he was gathering points. He knows I'd prefer a How's-the-Kit question when he can see plain enough that I'm still standing.

"My chaps," I said. "I've got to cut a long, thin strip of leather to replace one of the leg straps."

Guy grinned and washed my dirt off his hands before scooping up slices of red pepper. "Julienne leather?"

Oh, he seemed to think he was clever with this little . . . was it a joke?

I am new at julienne jokes.

New at a lot of stuff, actually. New at making my way in Cowdry, this town I've called my own for the better part of a year and a half. New at letting someone like Guy feed me love. Sometimes it's too good to be true, like I can't believe this is my life.

Customers seated at the tables and booths and counter gave me a glance as I went through the swinging doors to the front with Guy. I like to act all cool as I go to my spot at the very end of the counter and rack my boots on the rail. That last twirly stool is as good as mine.

As the man who wants to marry me fetched up a tall iced tea—not sweet, no lemon—and put out pie for folks in the far booth, I blabbed bits about me getting a go at the Buckeye ranch account.

The Buckeye ranch is a cattle operation with a few good ranch geldings sold on the side, making little more than enough hay for its own use. Trying to keep the Buckeye going on her own was going to be the death of Donna Chevigny, I feared. More work than a single body can do. I didn't know how she was fixed for money, but I knew that even if her hiring me as a shoer strained her pocketbook, it would take strain off her back. And she picked me, The New Girl, as I'm known to horse folk here.

I hadn't asked for the title. Hadn't asked to be Donna Chevigny's shoer, come to that. I'd bided my time and didn't sniff around for the job like Dixon Talbot, one of the other full-time shoers in Cowdry. Plenty of part-timers would have liked to land the Buckeye account, too. But, there's generally enough shoeing jobs to go around. Most times, we work our butts right off, especially come summertime. Come fall, things taper down. People ride less in bad weather, and hooves grow more slowly up here in the north country winters.

Guy raised his eyebrows and made the right noises, especially at the part about me telling the widow that I could do remote shoeing with my Pocket Anvil.

"Well, fine, you'll like that? Riding out to shoe with this woman?"

"Donna Chevigny," I told him again. "Looking to get some tuck now."

"And that would be?"

Having done my formative eating in Texas and California, my

palate, such as it is, doesn't know what to do with itself with Guy in its life. Hope in my heart, I asked, "A burger?"

He rolled his eyes, as he is wont to do with my cuisine choices. It's not like the Cascade Kitchen is some upscale eatery with wine guys and cheese courses anyways.

"With mixed greens?" Guy suggested. When I gave him a Look, he moved on with, "Fries or potato salad?"

"Tater salad. And an extra burger patty to go, for Charley." I winked. He gave me more iced tea, then bumped through the swinging doors to burn me a burger. As I settled into my stool to wait, something gave me the heebie-jeebies. Eyeballs bore into me from somewhere, quivering my skin like Red's does when he's knocking a fly off his back. In the mirrored part of the wall behind the counter, I saw a gal with a wolf's watch studying me from the first twirly stool at the lunch counter. She flicked her gaze away when she caught me catching her.

Somewhere. I knew her from somewhere.

Well, from around town, most likely. Cowdry's not too awful big and it does seem like the same people are the fill-ins at the post office and bank and grocery store and all that, so probably I just—

There she did it again, checked me out in the mirror. Now both of us knew we were looking at each other and having half a mind at wondering what the other was up to.

She looked a tad younger than me, probably barely drinking age, in sneakers, shorts, and a bright, synthetic T-shirt, with dark hair not prone to summer streaks like mine is. Her build could have helped her make it as a horseshoer—strong-looking but not too tall, and no gut to get in the way when squatting under a horse. But probably, horseshoeing wasn't her career choice. It startles people when they find out how I earn my living.

More motion in the mirror distracted me from remembering where I knew Wolf Eyes from. A couple rose from the booth right behind me. This woman's clothes were my kind, broken-in jeans and an open plaid shirt over a cotton tank top. Her hair dangled in her face, not properly tucked behind her ears or in a ponytail. And him? He was a big guy with a Fred Flintstone haircut. Something about big beefy boys leaves a bad taste in my mouth, probably because the last one I dealt with tried to hang me with my own rope.

Flintstone wore perfect, too-clean jeans and a yoked blue Western shirt with white piping. His cowboy boots bore no scuffs, no caked pucky in the inner corner where the heel meets the sole.

Not a real horse guy, just someone with a costume in his wardrobe.

"Doll, let's go now." He slid a hand across her patooty and gave the left half a squeeze.

She ignored his command and grope, so at least she had that going. When he dropped money on the table and headed out, she turned her tall self around and strolled the other direction, toward the powder room. I just knew she'd be in there a good long spell while he cooled his boot heels, but I guessed her payback would be wasted on him.

Like a horse or a dog, a fellow ought to know when he's being punished for turdiness.

Doll, he called her. Oh, dandy.

She didn't much look like a doll to me, but what do I know about dolls? Dolls and me broke up as soon as I discovered horses. I don't know how old I was exactly but it was before figuring out how to read. Way, way before boys.

Tall Doll brushed aside long brown bangs hanging shaggy over her eyes and winked at me as she passed by on her way to the ladies'. Older than me by maybe five years, she wore those lace-up riding boots that gave her extra height and let me figure her for someone who spent time in a saddle, since the boots were scuffed in all the right places to show stirrup wear. This gal was horse people. Obviously, she used someone other than me for a shoer, but maybe she was from elsewhere in the county since I didn't think I'd seen her around town. And I'd been thinking lately, what with growing new roots here in Butte County in general and Cowdry in particular, that a friend would be a nice addition. Guy and I need people to invite to our wedding, though we're not planning it quite yet.

A real friend, a girlfriend, that's something that might be a good thing to have.

She'd have to be a rider, of course, to be my new best friend.

In the mirror, I saw Fred Flintstone out in the parking lot. He opened up the big Ford truck, letting me view the *Paso Pastures* sign on the door. And I realized Wolf Eyes took it in, too. Something in her shoulders relaxed as she rose to come take a seat on the empty stool next to me.

"Melinda. Melinda Kellan." She hitched her chin in greeting.

I'm five-foot-six on a tall day and I'd say we measured the same. This Melinda's muscles probably resulted from lifting lead, not honest-earned by hefting an anvil and shaping steel.

Guy set a meal in front of me and headed off with a couple of vegetable sides for another table. I wanted to get after my new job—chowing down—with a good business-like attitude, but then I recollected where I'd seen this Melinda Kellan before. And I bet now that I remembered, I was blanching like Guy's vegetables. I felt as smart as a carrot.

She was the police clerk who took something from me during that unfortunate misunderstanding a while back.

My fingerprints.

"You work at the Sheriff's office. The little one out here in Cowdry. You're the one who fingerprinted me." Butte's a small county but Cowdry's a pretty good ways from the county seat, so there's just a small deputy force out here, with office space in the strip mall near the grocery store. I've been needing to check in with them, to see if I'll have to testify. I can never remember the investigator's name. I always thought of him as Suit Fellow.

Melinda Kellan squinted at me all this time I jabbered and rec-ollected. I figured she ought to be able to help me out.

"What's that guy's name, you know, the investigator?" I waved my hands to help her understand.

She smirked, said a name that flew in my left ear, sprinted across the open prairie of my mind, and fell out my right ear. Then she nodded. "He's retiring soon."

I hate it when people answer a question that didn't get asked, not lingering on the one that wanted good answering. Do I really have to see Detective what's-his-name and will he make me go to court? I wanted to scream, but I kept my mouth very shut.

"Will you do something for me?" Melinda Kellan spoke like she wasn't asking, more telling. "Will you let me know if anything, anything at all, strikes you as not fitting while you're at the Chevigny place?"

Made me itch to say something like, "Sure, I'd be happy to spy on my new client—a widow at that—for you, you bored little clerk." Instead, I studied her, trying to get my eyeballs and brain moving instead of my mouth. Melinda Kellan wore running shoes. She's not horse people. I turned away from the little inquisitor, bit my burger and made eye contact in the mirror beyond. "You ride?"

Kellan shook her head.

"Ever make hay?"

She grinned. "Not in the way you mean."

Bristling and not liking her sin-uendo, I turned a little red. I guess I'm a bit of a prude. It figured that she didn't ride and didn't get how tough and dangerous the work of making food is. I don't mean making food like Guy, in a kitchen. I mean making it like Donna Chevigny does, like her departed husband Cameron had. Making feed for cattle and tending those cattle 'til they're ready for slaughter and—

"So, I don't ride. What about it?"

Then Melinda Kellan went quiet as the tall rider sauntered back from her powder, taking the long walk across the restaurant in her sweet time.

There's horse folk and then there's everybody else. With plenty
of people, I can peg 'em for what kind of horse they'd be if they'd
been blessed born. Guy, for example, would be a Thoroughbred,
though a palomino. Sometimes I can tell more than the breed,
I'd know how good the legs and feet would be and what kind of
an attitude is in the eye. It's not always a good thing, this gift of
mine. There's some people I don't take to, but everybody I cotton
to shows up in my mind as a horse. Not Melinda Kellan though.
She wasn't one of us.

Tall Doll and I made eye contact in the mirror as she passed
behind me this time. I winked. We had an instant connection.
She would be an Appendix Quarter Horse, with good feet, if she
were a horse.

Tall Doll, my new friend, paused and said, "Watch yourself at
the Chevigny place."

Turning my stool all the way around, I faced the Tall Doll.

She made a wry, friendly face then dropped her tone low
enough to keep it between us. "Some folks thought she caused
Cam's funeral. You could end up in the ground just like he did."

Chapter 2

WHEN I GOT TO THE BUCKEYE before dawn on the first day of working for Donna Chevigny, two chestnut Quarter Horses stood saddled, with halters over their bridles. They looked to be decent, working horses, a good many weeks into their shoeing cycles. Lead ropes that probably didn't need to be there tethered these good old boys to the hitching rail by the water trough. Both horses had a hip cocked, resting one hind hoof on the toe. The saddle on one gelding was an old fat-horned Wade with scarred fenders. The other horse's saddle was older still, with a way-high cantle and bucking rolls that would curve over the rider's thighs. Easy to stay in a saddle like that, but I'd sure hate to have to get clear of it in anything like a hurry.

Donna was thinner than I'd remembered from seeing her a few times at the Co-op, our local feed store. Her jeans were baggy enough to be inconvenient and her hair had grown shaggy past her shoulders. With most every word, her mouth pursed and puckered, leathery skin showing she'd forgotten to slather shortening on her face in a good while. As much as I'm in the sun and wind, I'll be looking a whole lot like Donna if I don't start greasing my skin.

13

Guy doesn't keep Crisco in the house, so I'll have to use his coconut oil or olive oil or some such.

Batwing chaps went on, covering Donna's baggy jeans and slopping over the toes of her roper-style boots. Neither of us wore spurs, but with gloves stuck in the front string of her chaps and a straw hat on, she looked more like a hand than me with my open top visor and no gloves. My boots aren't the cowboy kind. After my California mama gave me these Blundstone boots, I discovered they're a big thing for English riders. That's okay, since I have clients who use those little saddles, too. And the boots are great, supportive and comfy.

Still, even though I wasn't dressed the part, this ranch work felt right to me and I really hoped this shoeing account would be a keeper. *Zing.* A bit of fur flew by a foot off the ground, ending in a four-paw skid behind the water trough outside the barn doors.

"What was that?"

"An idiot," Donna said, then called to the dog. "Slowpoke, settle down."

Slowpoke wiggled out from his hiding place. He looked like the twenty-pound result of an orgy involving every dog breed in existence. He also looked delighted beyond measure that a horse ride was about to happen, dying to know if he was invited.

Donna had some good, roomy saddlebags behind both horses' saddles and we packed my gear into them without dilly-dallying about it. I'd brought some size aughts and size two shoes, too, just in case she wasn't as squared away as she thought about every one of her horses having all size one hooves. Ranch outfits sometimes like to simplify things and maybe squeeze a horse onto a shoe too small or wangle a too-big shoe onto a small hoof. The only squeezing I wanted to do was getting all the gear into the bags and we did fine as frog's hair.

Then Donna strapped on a rifle scabbard and slid a shotgun—a big mother, twelve gauge, I'd reckon—into place on her old rancher saddle.

I'm actually not a gun handy kind of girl, which is my mama's fault, nervous nelly about the gadgets that she was and is. My gun-learning should have happened when I was living with my ranch-hand daddy in Texas, but that must have been a battle mama won with him, because he kept me clear of revolvers and rifles when I lived with him. Now I turned away from the weapon to the open country of still-dark pastures beyond the Buckeye barn. I wondered what she expected to encounter.

"Packing some extra hardware?" I said.

"That shotgun is the only artillery we've ever had," Donna said with a shrug. "Cameron always carried it with buckshot and slugs in the backcountry."

She swung up ahorseback, so I did likewise and we moved easy as our eyes got better at the low light, her mutt tagging along. Donna carried her reins in her left hand. It's the right way to ride as it keeps us normal, non-Lucifer-possessed people with our right hands free to rope and shoot.

Early sun eked out of cracks in the clouds, making pink and orange strips in the sky that reached out to kiss the few tree tops. I felt pretty pleased to be there, astride, feeling the powerful motion of a good horse beneath me. As we trotted out through hock-high orchard grass, Slowpoke ran laps around us.

From the back pasture, the Buckeye land dropped across a big dry wash then rose again in a long slow way that made for good hay growing as water would neither collect too bad nor run off too fast. The fields went on for a couple of hundred acres, easy.

With more saddle time, we came to a sharp ravine running across the whole ranch like a scar, separating hay fields from rougher ground beyond.

Enough daylight was up by then to see the steepness. The ravine was serious, but the strong horses under us sat back on their haunches, picked their way down the fifty-foot cut, crossed the bottom then climbed back up. The land swept away, rockier. A wire fence came into view a couple hundred feet off and I realized we'd almost reached the back of the Buckeye. The rough pasture we were in, though not hay-growing heaven, offered enough forage to sustain the dozen or so milling horses.

We rode toward a little pole corral, Donna jiggling a small sack of oats. The loose horses got curious enough to head our way.

The sprawling acreage on this far side of the ravine was split in two sections by the skinny reach of a hogback hill that ran almost to the drop off we'd just climbed. That sudden humped ridge looked like a finger pointing at the ravine. Taut electric wire ran up the center of the hogback on our right, but to the squinting eye, it was the natural hogback that marked a divvying point between us and the east field. The electric cross-fencing up the hogback ran all the way up to an open machine shed at the top of the little ridge. The land behind the shed had to be the grazing lease, federal dirt, marked by barbed wire where the Buckeye land ended. Cattle dotted the slope back there, absorbing the attention of Donna and her dog.

She sighed. "I'll have to get them brought in within the month."

I pointed at her pooch, who bristled, staring up the hill. "Can he herd?"

"He can't do anything but get in the way."

* * *

The day came up with a plan. Clear weather like this makes for cool nights but real hot noons. A tractor rusted away at the base of the hogback, though the machine should have been parked under cover. If the shed was empty, it would offer shade to work under.

But, no. Donna dismounted and tied her riding horse at the failing pole corral. By the time she haltered the first loose horse, I had my gear set up. Then my mind was on nothing but balanced hooves for hours. Because she wouldn't actually be working these boys like cow horses, I left them more room in the heels, enough to support them and leave them room to grow.

As I leaned on my shoe shaper's handle again and again in quick motions of rounding toes and turning heels, Donna commented.

"Newfangled, that gadget. But it is the quietest shoe bending I've ever heard."

"Yep. A Pocket Anvil is a nifty tool." Only the sound of tails swishing, nostrils blowing, rasping and nailing. Cold shoeing all day also meant no burnt hoof scent in my hair for Guy to wrinkle his nose at tonight.

"Can't level a bent shoe with it though, can you?"

I showed her how I could make a try at it, moving the shoe ninety degrees in a way that would let me pressure it if it wasn't already flat. "With a bad bent shoe, I'd just start over with a new shoe."

Her silly dog offered up sticks and cow pies, hoping for a game of fetch or keep away. I was on the second horse when Donna said, "Might be too late to start over."

That came from nowhere and no-how for me, so I let it pass, worked her horses, dripped sweat. We had enough to agree on and didn't need anything else.

Donna knew her stuff, it's just that her stuff's from an old tradition. She knew her horses too. I could have stretched to setting them up all in size one shoes, with a couple fit tight, a couple with a bit too much room, and a couple needing the heels beveled off so they didn't cover the commissures of the frog and make picking out more of a chore. But I nailed on some size aught and size two horseshoes that day and was glad I'd hauled them.

Just before I started the fourth horse, I swallowed a bottle of water Donna offered and wiped my mouth on my sleeve, looking out toward the hogback. Definitely a two-sided shed up there, looked to be some equipment in it but surely it had some room available under a roof.

Shade.

We were stuck under the sun and pretty well cooked when we could have worked under a covered area. Summer time, shoeing's always a Stand There and Chat for the horse owner, but a lot of worked muscles and sweat rolling off the nose for the shoer. Even when it's cooler weather, I've been dripping and glowing while my clients hold a lead rope, snuggled up in a jacket. So, it's not like clients think about it and notice, like I do, that one of the two of us is warm from work. But it was extra hot today. I was back under a horse again, working hard to get half the herd done in a day.

"Rainy, sorry. Damn shame it's so hot." Donna shook her head a long while later. "This spell of weather we're having."

"Yes'm," I said, itching for the part where she noticed we didn't have to slow roast.

She rubbed her eyebrows. "So much to get done. Haying. Fixing. Herd dispersal. These geldings being shod might help sell them."

"Maybe we could go up there next time," I said, jerking a thumb over my shoulder toward the shed and its salvation from the sun.

"So much to get done," she muttered again.

Donna half-turned toward that hogback crowned by the shed. "Got to bring those cattle in and they'll be getting a little raunchy by now. I've left them untended on the lease land. Got to sell these horses. Neighbor tells me Cameron made a handshake deal on these back pastures before he died, so he's buying it out from under me. Late on the second hay cutting. I'll be late on the third. Got gear and fences that need mending."

We both swallowed at her list. I got myself a brilliant idea on bringing in her rough cattle.

"They dog-broke?" I asked. No sense getting Charley clobbered.

"What's that, dear?" Donna was awful distracted.

"Are those cattle dog-broke?"

"They're probably not too awful wild." She squinted at the lease land and frowned, finally paying attention. "You got a dog can move them? We'd have to go over to that shed to bring 'em in. It's a run-through, the back end's a big gate. That's what we use to bring the cattle off the federal lease land."

I was finished with the fifth horse and felt half baked. I was about to beg that we make use of the shed next time.

"Fact is," Donna began and faltered. She gave me a worn smile over granola bars and more water chugging. "I ought to get some bosals and braided reins out of the shed. Stuff's going to ruin and rot in that place."

Her tractor didn't have much business being out in the open either, I figured. I wondered how long it'd sat where it was through winter rains and summer sun. If it would start after being idle, driving it back up the hogback and into the shed should have been easy enough. Then I realized I might be looking at the tractor that killed her husband. I felt terrible.

"We can pack a bit more stuff back to your barn." I planned to tie the extra gear to our saddles, turn the good horses we rode into moving storage units.

Good thing I was around Donna hours and hours that day, seeing as how it took her time to move a conversation along. I'd finished the sixth horse and had forgotten what we'd left off talking about when she asked, "Do you think you'd mind?"

"Mind?" I packed my gear, too tired to think. I had a notion she was asking me to behave or watch over something. I tell Charley to mind a gate when I leave it open. No horse or cow's ever come through a pass when my little dog's minding the opening.

"Do you think you'd mind going up to the shed," Donna asked, "and fetching those things for me now? And maybe next time bring your dog, move the cattle?"

"We'll get it done," I promised, feeling good to help her out and for being deep into this job. Charley's at least middle-aged, not a young squirt like Slowpoke, so it would be quite a long trot to get out here from where Ol' Blue sat parked back at her barn, but he'd have hours to rest while I finished the shoeing. "Shouldn't take Charley long to get them pushed through a gate. There's no cattle in this piece we're in?"

"No, right now they're all in the hill country behind the machine shed. The lease land. The bull's in my east field." She swiveled her skull around, looking for a problem that wasn't there. "It'd sure save me some work if you've got a dog that can move cattle."

"Have they been dog-herded before? Charley's older and I wouldn't want to send him on real rough stock."

She still hadn't mounted up, just stood there holding the reins. "They'll be all right. It's Cameron's bull we have to be careful of. The stock tank up at the shed is shared between the east and west pastures. If the bull's up there, steer clear."

I thought I got then her reason for avoiding the hogback hill. "I can see why you wouldn't want to ride near a rank bull even with a fence between you." My riding horse stamped a foot, letting me know he'd thought I should be aboard since I'd tightened the girth, but he'd be good and wait for my say-so.

The wryest sad smile ever came across Donna's face and melted right off again. "Well, it's not for the bull that I don't like being near that shed."

"No?"

"No." Donna looked down with one guilty shake of her head. "I'd have to go up the hogback to get there. That hill was the death of my husband."

Some people seemed taken up with the idea that Cameron Chevigny's tractor-rolling accident was suspicious. Sitting on the Widow Chevigny's horse at the back end of her ranch made for a hard time knowing what best to say or do. Donna was square with sending her horseshoer off on an errand to a place where she wouldn't go. But she also seemed to be coming apart at the seams, her eyes squinty and her hands in fists that she pushed into her underarms.

* * *

I pointed the loaner horse toward the machine shed.

Donna turned her back to me and said, hoarse-voiced, "Bosals and braided reins. Should be hanging right inside the machine shed. There's a gate where the cross-fencing between the west and east fields attaches to the shed. It runs right over the shared water trough. That gate should be shut. You're not safe from the bull if it's open."

Because of the hill, we couldn't see into the east pasture from where we stood. The bull could be close, right over the rise.

But the view improved once I was astride. Didn't take but a couple minutes to ride to the hogback. Slowpoke tagged along, a ready fool.

A stout horse like the one under me could scramble up the steep rock, but with the tractor, the thing to do would have been to drive from the lowest part of the hogback, where it extended right between the two fields, and keep the rig pointed right up in a long, careful climb up the narrow center of the hogback. A little tricky, but surely a thing the Chevignys had done plenty. To drive the tractor up to the shed from where it sat at the foot of the hogback's steep west side would be too dangerous. I shook my head and leaned forward, freeing my horse's hind end to push us up the steep stuff, but pulled him up when something shiny caught my eye on the hogback.

Picking up horseshoes is a habit of mine. Many's the time, it's me who finds the missing shoe in a client's field. I see the lay of the land and I know where those tires get thrown. I look into deep hoof prints out of habit and that's why I saw this shoe, forty yards up the hogback.

Horseshoes, lying loose with their old nails curving around, look wicked, but it's not too often that a horse steps on the wicked-looking thing and gets a problem. Still, a pulled shoe full of nails isn't something a body likes to see on the ground where livestock are kept, so I swung down from the saddle and picked it up. Bad rusted nails, no rust on the shoe, but it was oxidized real good. Aluminum. Hard to imagine the Chevignys ever put such a shoe on their ranch stock. Aluminum shoes conduct heat faster, so they're colder in winter and hotter in summer, but the main thing with them on hardworking horses covering a lot of rock is that aluminum wears out faster than steel.

This shoe had been out there a long time, for the nails to be rusted that bad. It was a double aught but I didn't study on it more, just hooked one branch into my right hip pocket and swung back up where I belonged.

Once up top the hogback, I could see the two-sided shed plain, one wall to the prevailing west winds. Its open back had a full-length gate that would be easy to open from horseback. Baggy barbed wire that looked to be mostly made of rust ran off both back corners of the building, separating the federal lease land from the Buckeye proper. Perpendicular to the shed and barbed wire, electric wire ran up the east slope of the hogback splitting the west and east fields that the hogback helped divide. The cross-fence gate was strung right over a big water trough. The gate was closed, so even if the bull came up for a drink, I should be safe. Having the trough straddle the area under the fence gave stock in either Buckeye pasture access to water. Some of the horses I'd been all day shoeing had come on up to the shed to drink. There must have been water for the cattle out on the federal land somewhere.

Inside Donna's shed, braided reins hung alongside four rawhide bosals on hangers made out of tin cans nailed to the middle purlin. All the leather looked mighty dry. I tied the tack onto my saddle, eyeing the rougher country behind the shed while enjoying the cool shade and draft the open building offered.

Slowpoke romped in from the lease land carrying something disgusting, like a dead bird or a piece of garbage, thrilled with himself.

Donna was mounted up when I got back. She turned her horse just before I reached her, but I heard her sniffle. I reined my horse back to give the lady privacy. Her slumped shoulders shuddered before we dipped down into the ravine and that was the end of Donna's crying spell.

Kind of gave me the heebie-jeebies, knowing I'd just ridden

across the hill that Cameron Chevigny died on. I felt bad for Donna and wanted to suggest maybe laying down flowers or saying a few words would be a help, but Donna seemed to just want to stay away. And anyway, there's no way I'm someone who should make suggestions to anyone else about how to lead her life.

"Drop that," Donna said to Slowpoke, who was still carrying his whatever prize, something dark, not much bigger than a wallet.

Wasn't a surprise when the mutt refused to obey. Instead Slowpoke carried his prize through the ravine.

When we climbed out of the ravine, I said, "I can sure see why you like riding out here. So many ranches use four-wheelers to buzz around nowadays."

"Cameron used one, long time ago. An old three-wheeler. Then it killed our daughter when she flipped it, so we got rid of that miserable machine."

"Oh, no, Donna."

She gave one nod to my sense of it and said, "A truck can't make it through the ravine, of course, so we stuck to riding the back part of the ranch."

When I mumbled sympathy for her, Donna looked away. Said it was nearly twenty years ago her daughter'd died, and closed that subject. I'd never heard talk around town of a Chevigny daughter. I guess it was the decades that kept it quiet.

We rode easy. Soon we were catching glimpses of Donna's barn in the distance. I can keep a silence all right, I guess, but it seems a natural thing to pass a few polite words in an hour beside another body, be that body a dog or horse or person.

"Found a horseshoe out there," I said, half pulling it out of my hip pocket.

Donna snorted without giving it a glance. "There are things to be found out there."

I shoved the funky horseshoe back home in the denim.

Slowpoke, the silly dog, was dying for a drink, having been unable to pant the whole way back to the barn because of carrying that thing in his mouth. He dropped it—a glove—at the water trough and jumped in, mucking it up, spilling water, tickled to death.

After I unsaddled the horse I rode in on, I studied a high shelf in the barn aisle. Broken tools, a glass insulator, a single spur with rusty rowels and a dried leather strap, a cracked mug, a real stiff leather braid piece and a little thing about an inch high, at the end of the row of useless things, a short shell casing. Stacked under the shelf was the stuff of my interest—an anvil on a stump, nippers, rasps, and clinchers.

I realized I was looking at Cameron Chevigny's shoeing tools.

What shoer can resist looking at another's tools? It's not that we covet, exactly, but we want to see what brands the other farrier favors. Cameron had had better than cheapy tools, but far below the best quality nippers. A welcome breeze gusted through the aisle, with the scents of dust, hay, sweat and horses. I stepped outside and almost planted a foot on what Slowpoke had dropped. His prize was indeed a glove. It wasn't flat though. The outside was coated in dog spit. The inside had bits of dried dark stuff on white bone.

The glove held a hand.

Chapter 3

"**A** HUMAN HAND?" GUY ASKED.

"Yep." I was bone tired and so glad he wasn't closing up the Cascade tonight. Way, way better for him to be home twirling handmade pasta in cheesy sauce with smoked tomatoes and peppers, plopping a plump roasted chicken breast on top. Garlic wafted.

Spooky, Guy's stinking shorthair, tripped me as I carried my plate to the dinette. There was a time when my old sheepdog Charley would have made an effort, herded Spooky and any other feline, fowl, or hooved critter clear of me. Or at least to the top of the sofa. Tonight, Charley just winked at me from the old wool horse blanket in the corner.

In the rock-paper-scissors of this house, I can boss Charley around and Charley can boss Spooky around and—get this— Spooky thinks he can boss me around, maybe because he was living in Guy's house before I was. All that cat does is shed. There's no place in this house that chocolate-colored cat hair isn't.

"Arielle Blake," Guy said.

"Huh?" Hard to talk with a full mouth.

"We need a map."

"Please pass the salt. Why do we need a map?" When I ride Red, I never carry gadgets. My horse and I are just out there to see the countryside. But my Intended has a thingy on his kitchen computer that lets him upload runs he's tracked with a cell phone app or on his fancy runner's watch. The program, TrailTime, maps his weekly trail run and tells him how wonderfully fast he is at sprinting track intervals.

"Please really taste food before you salt it." Guy flicked the machine on now and tabbed over to his running maps, but he also pushed the salt and pepper toward me. "How far did that dog go?"

I swallowed. "Slowpoke?"

"What?"

"Huh?"

"Rainy, would you tell me what happened?"

Sometimes Guy gets frustrated with me for no reason, but I tolerate—

"Hello? Rainy? Donna Chevigny's dog found a human hand."

"I expect so. Not many kinds of hands and pretty unlikely to have been a baboon's."

"And then what happened?"

I waved all around the dining table. It's just a little nook next to the kitchen in Guy's little house at the end of Vine Maple road, but it's homey. "This is what happened next. I came home starving and you started feeding me and we told each other about our days."

Home with Guy, mornings or nights, the bits of weekend we don't work, it's become one of my favorite times. We putter. Charley tags along or not. Soon, Guy will be leading his colt Bean on baby trail hikes. Bean's dam is Liberty, who belongs to my youngest client, Abby Langston. Since Guy hired Abby as an under-the-table afternoon dishwasher and I hired her as a sort of helper, we'd seen a lot of her over the summer and pretend we're her aunty and uncle or something like that. Abby asks me stuff and tells me stuff and, well it's got to be said, she looks up to me. No one else ever has. Come to find out, I like to aunty Abby. There's no better way to aunty a pre-teen girl than ahorseback, which demands just a few road crossings from each of us as we make use of every bit of natural land between our homes. When I'm on Red and Abby's aboard Liberty, we can say nothing and understand everything.

When Bean moves into Red's pasture next month, my good horse will finally have a pasturemate. In a few years, Bean will be old enough to ride, then Guy and I will finally be riding our two horses out together on the trails.

This is a good life.

Three hard knocks on the door startled us. Yellow fur flew as my old Charley jumped up, barking and embarrassed. His commotion sent Spooky zinging for parts unknown. Charley never used to sleep so hard a car could drive up without his say-so.

"That would be a Sheriff's deputy," Guy said.

My jaw dropped enough to be bad manners. I snapped it shut, swallowed my mouthful of pasta, and asked, "Why are you expecting the po-lice?"

"I think it's one of their assigned duties to keep tabs on body parts."

Turned out, Guy can see the future, or near enough, because the gloved hand that Slowpoke had packed across the Buckeye ranch from the federal land is exactly what Deputy Paulden wanted to discourse on.

But my pasta was so tasty, and getting cold. "Donna said she'd call the sheriff."

"Miss Dale, Donna Chevigny did call us. That's why I'm here to talk to you."

"Arielle Blake?" Guy asked the deputy.

The sheriff's man pointed at my Intended. "You and one of your buddies went out on the search."

Guy nodded. "Biff. But we were sent over by the lake behind the Country Store."

On the road that runs out of town southeast and connects to

the highway, there really is a convenience store called the Country Store. I scratched my head, way too far behind.

Paulden nodded. "Keeper Lake."

"We were way off." Guy folded his arms across his chest. "Why did we get asked to comb those trails by the lake?"

"The detective had information that Ms. Blake was last near the lake."

Guy frowned toward his computer. "Someone must have seen her."

Getting information out of Guy and the deputy was less fun than shoeing draft horses all day without a hoof stand, but eventually they cleared up that some gal named Arielle Blake had gone missing about a year and a half ago—plus or minus around the time I'd moved to Cowdry. They didn't know if she'd simply walked off on her boyfriend—a wind farmer—or if she'd gotten lost on one of her all-day walks, met with accident, or come to a bad end some other way.

It was the last thing, turns out, because the deputy allowed that they were pretty sure it was her hand inside the glove.

"From a DNA test?" I asked.

Deputy Paulden shook his head. "We won't have the results back for a while, but Arielle Blake had a distinctive piece of jewelry on her right hand, so we have a tentative identification. The detective asked me to have you draw a map showing where you and Mrs. Chevigny's dog went."

"Oh." I fetched a blank paper out of Guy's printer. A couple of inches down from the top, I drew a line across the page. "This line is the ravine that cuts the Buckeye hay fields from the rough pastures we were in today. Her hayfields are below the ravine. Like, past the bottom left corner is Donna's house and barn. The top of the paper, in the middle, is her open shed where I got the bridles and reins for her."

Deputy Paulden rubbed his jaw. "This left side, the pasture north of the ravine that borders the Yates land, that's where you were working today?"

Now that I thought about it, there was one mailbox I passed on that long lonely road through forest land out to the Buckeye ranch. Next time, I'd pay attention and look for the Yates name. "I was shoeing in the west pasture. Her bull was supposed to be in the east pasture, but we didn't see him. Her horses needing shoes were in the west pasture and she's got cattle on the federal range which is north of the shed."

Paulden frowned at my map and tapped the table above the paper, indicating north of the Chevigny shed. "How far onto the federal land did you go?"

I shook my head. "I didn't. I was just in the shed, getting some tack for Donna."

"So her dog went out there on his own?"

"Yeah, he followed me when I rode up to the shed. I wasn't there long. Like, minutes. Slowpoke was carrying something when I headed back down the hogback. I didn't think much about it, but he carried it all the way back to the barn."

Guy put a finger next to Paulden's. "Isn't the Buckeye ranch pretty far from the lake behind the Country Store? Like ten miles or so?"

"More like fifteen," Paulden said. He waved across the table. "Your pepper mill would be Keeper Lake."

Guy shook his head. "We were really looking for Arielle Blake in the wrong place. If she just broke her leg, hit her head, whatever, and needed help out there, we were never going to find her."

Paulden ran a hand over his buzz cut and looked at me. "While you were at the Buckeye ranch, did Donna Chevigny mention anything at all about Arielle Blake?"

"I'd never heard of Arielle Blake until the last couple minutes with you and Guy."

The deputy squinted. "And Yates? He still not letting Chevigny cross his land?"

Some memory tried to niggle up, but it couldn't get a purchase in my hungry, tuckered mind. "I don't know anything about that. I've never heard of Yates."

"Stan Yates. The wind farmer. Arielle Blake's boyfriend. They lived together. His place backs up to the west part of the Buckeye ranch, north of the ravine."

My shrug showed my lack of clues.

"Is that tractor still out there?" he asked.

I nodded. "Hey, Guy and me got subpoenas about the other thing. Is it really going to trial?" That "other thing" involved the murder of one of my clients back in the spring, but that's another story.

Paulden said, "You'll have to speak with the investigator about that."

After the deputy left, Guy repeated the local news I'd paid no attention to back when I first moved to Cowdry. Arielle Blake, a young woman who was known to hike alone for hours, didn't come back one day and no one ever knew what happened to her. When they asked for able-bodied people to hit the trails, Guy and his rugby buddies and other people had joined the search.

"And why were you looking near Keeper Lake?" I asked.

"That's where the police asked us to go. Biff and I bushwhacked circles around it, but never saw a sign of her."

Biff is one of Guy's rugby and poker pals. I twisted my ponytail, whipped tired and still hungry. This was all someone else's sad business, not mine.

"You had a couple messages," Guy said as we went back to the kitchen.

Apparently, a found human hand had trumped talk of messages earlier.

Guy whisked our plates away for warming. I'd have been happy to finish dinner cold, but kept that unsaid. I glanced at the message machine, which was not flashing, so he'd already played the messages. One or two cell towers would not go amiss in Butte County. As is, coverage is just not good enough at a lot of my clients' barns, and it's next to worthless here at the end of Vine Maple road. Guy's cell works at the Cascade, and the app he uses to track his runs works off GPS.

"What messages?" I racked my socked feet on his chair.

"One from the Delmonts, with a lame horse."

I frowned. I'd shod for Earl Delmont recently—using the hooey out of my hoof stand because holding up draft horses' feet is not my back's idea of an afternoon's fun—so his horses shouldn't be needing my care. If the problem was a pulled shoe, he'd have probably said as much in his message.

"Who else?" I asked.

He twisted his mouth and spoke from the kitchen with his back to me. "That vet."

Guy needs to get over his thing about the vet. Neil Nichol is not a bad guy, even though he's good looking, arrogant, and gets under my skin sometimes. There was a time when I considered my options with Neil, but that, too, is another story.

But no one living with Guy wants him in a bad mood for dinnertime, 'cause it could be a long time 'til the roast chicken pasta comes back to the table.

"I'm shoeing for our little helper tomorrow afternoon," I said, by way of distraction. Abby Langston's Arabian needs new shoes every six weeks, the girl rides so much. She lives with her daddy, who's a good guy, but works eight-to-five weekday hours, so Guy and I enjoy kind of putting her to work.

My mention of Abby failed to lighten Guy's mood, so he was still sour about Nichol calling me. I shrugged off Guy's attitude and got my appointment book so I could get Earl Delmont's phone number out of the address section. Spooky helped me dial by playing with the phone cord. I hate that. Makes me want to hit him with a rock and scissors then wrap him in paper.

"Mr. Delmont?" I said, holding the phone with one hand and swinging the cord at the cat with the other. "It's Rainy Dale. Tell me about your horses. Which one's lame?"

The Delmonts are the last loggers hereabouts using horses and they favor Belgians, though they do have a three-year-old by their stud out of a Clydesdale mare. He's a perfect white-socked bay. Just like his mama, a looker, is what I heard about her, though I've never seen her. The Delmonts took the baby in trade some time back and are bringing the colt on as a new hauler.

The youngster's the cutest thing, and I generally don't cotton to cute. But he's a hoot, always asking questions in his horse-way about my tools and whether or not I'd like to play and if I thought a leaf blowing across the yard was likely to try killing him.

Why'd it have to be him, this yet unnamed boy, the one they just called The Kid?

I leaned down to stroke Charley's fur for the comfort the touch brings.

"Seems like it's in his shoulder." Earl Delmont paused and sounded a little embarrassed for both of us, a tone like an apology. "The vet asked when he'd last been shod and I did mention that you'd shod him real recent."

"Right," I said, flipping back through my date book. I remembered he'd wanted to take the boy out to try him at a real logging job. "When'd he come up lame?"

"It was noticeable this morning and it's getting worse. Not real sure exactly when it started, you know. Doc Nichol is coming out late tomorrow afternoon."

So, Neil Nichol would want me at the Delmonts' place at the same time. And I'd thought I was going to have a short day for the first time in a long while. But making sure a hurt horse was, first of all, done right by, and B, not my fault, was more important than knocking off work early, so I promised to get there as soon as I finished Abby Langston's horse the next afternoon. Right now, I didn't know if the vet was helping or hurting me in his attitude about wanting me there. Nichol and I have had our ups and downs and it seems he got a little frosty with me after Guy and I went official.

Chapter 4

WATCHING TWO PEOPLE HAVE A RIP-ROARING fight is an unpleasant occupation. I especially don't care to witness a girl giving her daddy such a mouthful as my second-to-last client of the day, Abby Langston, was doing. They were too far away for me to comprehend the words or the reason for her rage. I've seen her pretty upset before, but she'd generally been one to keep it together. There was, after all, that felony she committed, a theft thing, that resulted in her mare getting with foal, but that got sorted out without the law needing to be involved. Oh, I'd been involved though. To hear Abby tell it, I'd been the inspiration of it all, but that's a story for another day.

Bringing Ol' Blue to rest near the barn, I dismounted, surprised that Abby's mare wasn't tied, ready to be shod. Abby's usually a pretty conscientious customer who doesn't keep her shoer waiting. And this shoer happens to be her boss too, as I let Abby ride with me on weekend work and slip her a few dollars.

Abby ranted in the pasture, holding the lead rope to Liberty's halter but not making any progress to the little barn, just arguing with her daddy instead. I'd never known Keith Langston to even be in the field—it's his daughter's domain. The whole horse thing was just for Abby. Her daddy's just for her, too. He's divorced and the mama isn't around.

But now I could make out Abby's rough talk.

"It would kill me," she shrieked as Keith Langston made calming motions with his hands. "You want to kill me?"

Never had I heard Abby giving such lip to her daddy and I'd never expected him to take it in the face like he did. He's a good firm kid-raiser who doesn't take trash off a kid.

Whatever he said back to his put-out daughter was low and gentle, almost pleading from my view.

"No!" Abby was screaming now. "You can't make me. I won't do it."

My little client-helper hopped on her due-for-shoeing mare and loped away with only a halter and lead rope for guidance. At the pasture's end, she manhandled an old gate without dismounting, then cut through the back neighbor's place to ride away for parts unknown.

Liberty's hoofbeats on the neighbor's dirt road reported Abby was still riding fast.

Plenty of times I shoe Liberty on Saturday morning, then Abby comes with me to work a rodeo or a horse show. She's my horse-holder, shoe-cleaner-upper, and tool-fetcher. I'd be working weekends alone if Abby didn't straighten up. A little help really does help, but also, I like playing like she's my baby sister or something. When I want to piss her off, I call her Doodle-bug and it works every time. Getting used to Abby's company on Saturdays came easy. There wasn't an event on our end of the county this weekend, which was why I'd had Abby's horse scheduled for my last shoeing tonight. I hated to see Abby turn into a teenage demon and she wasn't even due, age-wise.

Abby's daddy looked at me, then studied my truck. He sighed and dropped his shoulders some more. Wouldn't be right to pry, but it didn't seem neighborly to just mount up Ol' Blue and drive off.

"Her, uh, mother has moved back to the States for a job in Portland, the green energy business. She's asked for a change in our custody arrangement. The judge ordered that Abby is to go spend some time with her, think about going to a charter school in Portland."

My jaw dropped while he rubbed his. All the sudden, I didn't much care for this nameless, greenie mother of Abby's. Hadn't I heard something about wind farming lately?

"We're working out the details," Langston said.

Being a country girl at heart, I'm thankful that my daddy got me back from my mama for a while after she took me to California, but then I got stuck with my mama again when daddy hit the road driving truck. When he'd try it as a ranch hand again, I'd get to go live with him for another spell.

Please let Abby not mess up her teen years as bad as I trashed mine.

Langston blinked and looked away. "I'm sorry she's run off on you like this. It wasn't right but she's pretty upset. We both are."

I nodded.

"Shouldn't you be paid for coming out, for the missed appointment?"

I shook my head.

"Are you sure? I thought you charged when people stood you up."

"The second time, I do," I said.

"Abby's never done this to you before, right?"

I shook my head, still getting used to the idea that Abby was going to be yanked from her daddy, home, horse, and happiness because some judge thought it'd be fine. And here Langston was, not wanting the girl to get away with stiffing me by no-showing on a shoeing. It made me smile in the saddest way.

He swallowed and kept up his good work. "You'll charge her for it if she does this again? Promise me you will."

I knew his meaning. He's raising a winner. I promised, "I will."

* * *

On my last call, I pulled in behind Nichol, who, as usual, took the parking spot worthy of his paycheck. The number of digits in our fees and the number of letters after our names, him being a DVM, me being a high school drop-out, is what seems to determine how good our parking is. Leaving me to hump my anvil in from a distance, while he waltzes into a barn, stethoscope swinging.

I do have a like-hate relationship with the only veterinarian in town who sees large animals as well as small. Neil Nichol sometimes acts like he's the end-all-be-all of horse soundness, but we both know he needs my skills. We don't cut each other a bunch of slack. Maybe it's because we once dabbled too close to being interested in each other.

I headed to join the Delmonts at their fence while donning my chaps. The shoestring I'd put on as a temporary patch for the torn leg strap reminded me to buy a piece of leather soon as I could.

But as I approached, I could see there'd be no fixing The Kid.

Some sore horses can be spotted across a field and that's how it was with this sweet big boy.

Earl Delmont had both thumbs hooked into the bib of his Carhartt overalls. The knees of the canvas were so faded, they'd have been white if not for the dirt stains. Only in the bib did the yellow-brown color last. A logger is as hard on clothes as a horseshoer. Earl shucked his hands from the bib, whipped off his baseball cap and rubbed a palm over his balding head. "The limp started a few days after the shoeing, I think."

"Showed as a shoulder lameness right away?" I asked.

"I guess."

Nichol frowned, his gaze on the over-three-quarter ton patient. Interested as always, The Kid came across the field toward us. Dragging his toe as he hobbled, he was wearing away my fitting of the front of his shoe as well as his own hoof.

Wincing, Earl said, "It's much worse this morning than it was yesterday."

Nichol was over the fence, in the field, running his hands over The Kid's body, talking quietly to the huge young half-breed. He asked questions that needed asking but irked. Yeah, I'd shod the horse, 'cause yeah, he'd needed shoes to handle the work.

Delmont boggled back and forth as Nichol and I got each other up to speed on The Kid.

"What have you been doing with him?" I asked.

"Had him hitched with Buster, doing light logging. He worked good, shaping up to be a good hauler."

We could see and hear that Earl Delmont didn't want to lose this young pulling horse. The Kid was a piece of the past and part of their special future.

"What was the land like where you worked him?" I asked, wondering about real wet grass or mud. We'd had a bone-dry summer, but maybe there were some wet spots left alive in the dark hollows.

"Nice piece of property halfway across the county," he said and then shook his head. "Lot of construction going on over there."

True, the building up over on the more populated Gris Loup side of Butte county—people say the name like 'gree-lew' unless they're dummies or new or new dummies, then they say something more like 'grease loop'—is a scary thing. Too much growing is just unsettling.

"But this was a nice piece of land," Delmont went on. "Pond and a pasture, pretty view where I'm sure these folks will build a fine house. Had us thin out the woods enough to pay for their construction to start."

"So," I asked, "it was good footing where the horses worked?"

"Not too rocky or steep."

"And dry?" Nichol asked.

Again Earl Delmont nodded, sure he'd not overworked his horse. "Good ground, just one boggy spot where The Kid slipped but Buster helped him out."

Nichol looked my way at this last bit of commentary. We met eyes, then he went back to the horse, though his hands now stroked the bay's neck in consolation instead of prodding that droopy foreleg in a quest for answers.

Delmont cleared his throat and sounded defensive, insistent. "I didn't push him too hard. That logging was good learning for The Kid."

Still, it was some minutes before Nichol came clean and exited the horse's field. Then he turned to me.

"Well, Rainy Dale, what do you think?"

"Sweeney."

Nichol nodded and glanced behind us. Earl's wife came to join in, wearing sneakers and a housedress. Her hand slid automatically onto her husband's shoulder as the vet put the situation in words that would warrant his bill.

"It's the motor nerve of the supraspinatus muscle. He's injured it and it's paralyzing him. This will get worse before it gets better, if it gets better. In another day or two, he'll be dragging that toe worse. We can't help that nerve. Only time will tell but he'll probably never be normal again."

"The super . . .?" Earl's voice trailed off, no doubt his mind parked on the part about the horse not recovering.

"The supraspinatus," I said, since I did go to shoeing school, after all. It was a ways after that horrible two-year half-try I did for high school. I was better studying something I loved. And it was a super good shoeing school. Supraspinatus was a name I'd have gotten right on a multiple choice test, but not a fill-in-the-blank. The closer to earth—the farther down the leg—things go, the more solid my anatomy is. I'm happiest in the hoof.

But I wouldn't be able to fix The Kid. His hoof wasn't the problem.

He'd have still been okay for breeding, but of course, the Delmonts gelded colts young, plus The Kid was a crossbreed, so a stud's career was already not an option for him. He was about out of options and uses. Shit. Oops, I mean crap. Sort of.

Delmont had an unhappy face pulled across the front of his skull. "You mean you don't think he'll recover to heavy haul?" He scratched his head as he stared at The Kid.

Never, I knew. As it stood, the sweet young fellow would need at least six months, maybe a year, of being a pasture ornament.

"He's paralyzed," Nichol said again. "The suprascapular nerve might repair to a significant extent, and the—"

"But hauling?"

Nichol shook his head and I closed my eyes, fearing what Earl Delmont was going to do with what he was about to hear.

"He will never heavy haul again," Nichol said. "I'm sorry, but he won't."

I'll give him this, Nichol spoke more like a people-doctor, like a vet who cares, than many. Some would sound like a mechanic telling a guy his engine's header was cracked.

Becky Delmont stepped forward, a good woman whose wide face showed its wear in the way of ranch wives. She could probably buck hay bales all day long. Clear enough, she'd try to make things work. "Hitched up with another horse, maybe he could haul?"

I shook my head with Nichol this time. Recovered Sweeney horses can sometimes become light duty horses, pull light loads, but they can just about never be hard workers again.

Muttering out loud the stinking thought that clogged everything up, Earl said, "Can't keep a horse what can't haul. I just can't." He had his hands on his hips and went to shuffling and pacing to work himself all through the bad news he'd been fed.

Nichol turned to me, giving the family a minute to grab on to this sorry deal with both hands. "The Chevigny woman called me this morning about getting some vaccines and she mentioned you were coming out to her place later. You're her shoer?"

I nodded. Earl gave us some frowns. I wondered how much doctoring Nichol was doing for Donna Chevigny or if he was just letting her buy stuff through his office to do her own doctoring. I hoped he was cutting her some deals. She didn't need to be paying fees for simple things like giving vaccines when almost any idiot can poke a needle in a horse's muscle or under the skin, whichever's called for. I bet the Delmonts gave their own shots, too.

Nichol touched my shoulder. "Would you be willing to be a delivery girl?"

Such is not my favorite job, but I'd be looking pretty churlish to refuse to carry vaccines to the Buckeye ranch, since I did have the second appointment scheduled. I nodded again. "I'll be at the Buckeye all day next Monday."

Earl Delmont glared over with as ugly a scowl I'd ever seen on his mug and muttered, "Chevigny got what he deserved," then got back to looking at his boot toes.

Becky waved me over. I eased over to her elbow to commiserate about their promising young horse that was ruined for the logging life.

With a nod toward her husband, Mrs. Delmont told me in a confiding whisper, "Little bit of bad feeling between my Earl and him."

I reckon my face showed my confusion. Again she gave me the conspiratorial whisper. "Cameron Chevigny once made a lady friend out of Earl's sister."

I felt like someone had changed the TV channel while I was out of the room and now I was watching a whole 'nother movie and nothing made sense. Besides, if Cameron Chevigny had stepped out on his wife, it was just another reason for Donna to hurt. She'd surely been hurting with his passing.

Earl Delmont hawked from deep in his throat, spat a wad on the ground and muttered an oath, his back to us.

So, The Kid's lame shoulder wasn't the only thing bugging Earl. Nichol bringing up the Chevigny name rankled our client. This left me working to know what to make of old small-town drama.

"Thought himself a real lady-killer, Chevigny did," Becky Delmont said, looking from the vet to me and back again.

We're the new kids in town, Nichol and me. To these people

who grew up and then raised their own families in Cowdry, we'll always be foreign, needing this town's past explained, since we hadn't lived it.

Then Becky moved on with, "Did you see the paper? Terrible thing, that poor girl they finally found in the backcountry. I remember when she was overdue from a walk and people were out looking for her. Must have gotten lost and died of exposure."

Nichol nodded. "I read the article. It happened before I moved here, but she was a client of Doc Vass. Stan Yates still brings her cat in to me."

"Uh . . ." Honestly, the time I spend waiting for my brain to fire up could be better used for all kinds of work.

Becky gave a good sure nod. "Yes, the boyfriend put flyers up all around town when she disappeared. It's good she's found and can be buried proper."

The boyfriend. Stan Yates. Donna's neighbor. Donna's neighbor had a handshake deal with Cameron Chevigny regarding some of the Buckeye land.

Next time I passed the one mailbox on the road to the Buckeye, I'd pay attention.

There was other stuff I hadn't thought about the first time I worked at the Buckeye. Now I remembered the deputy's mention of Yates not allowing the Chevignys access. My mind circled Cameron making a deal with Yates, Donna having to get her stock off part of the Buckeye north of the ravine. It was like my brain was a herding dog, circling a couple of rank sheep or cattle or thoughts.

When Becky Delmont went to put a hand on her husband's shoulder, I turned to Nichol and asked under my breath, "Does Stan Yates seem like the kind of guy who'd make a handshake deal on something as big as a land purchase?"

"Wow, Rainy. Where'd that come from?"

"A 'no' is what that sounds like."

Nichol exhaled long through his nose. It's a nice nose, not crooked like Guy's. Nichol is built like he'd be cast as the quarterback hero in some sappy movie, not like a mixed-practice one-man vet office.

"I suppose not," Nichol told me, his voice very low. "He seems like a decent guy. Brought the cat in when it was due for shots. Not every guy would take care of his disappeared girlfriend's cat like he does. What's this handshake business you're talking about?"

"Look, I don't know Yates. Never even met him. I just heard that he and Cameron Chevigny had a land deal, I think on the northwest part of the Buckeye."

Nichol cocked his head. "I don't know Stan well myself. But I'd say he seems kind of conflicted. Wants to be a wind farmer, but really more of a city person, you know?"

Earl Delmont whistled long and hard and turned toward us, come to words.

"We'll have to put The Kid down. I'll have to call around, see about the game farm or the zoo in Portland. See who wants him for meat."

Nichol rolled his shoulders around, leaned this way and that, and looked like he'd hoped for more of a conversation before we got to this part about throwing The Kid's carcass out for wolves. My face went string tight and Nichol's fixed a hard blank look, too.

The zoo wasn't going to want a horse with a load of pheno-barb in his muscles, so The Kid was going to get shot in the head after an uncomfortable trailer ride to the big city. He deserved a better death. And he'd deserved a better life. All the sudden, I wasn't tough enough for my job, the things I had to hear. Not tough enough at all.

Chapter 5

DRIVING HOME, A BIG DUMB NOTION came to me. This happens on a regular basis.

How to finesse Guy to the idea was a whole 'nother matter.

But no. No, I couldn't. It made no sense to ask for something I wasn't too sure I wanted myself. Whatever way of warming Guy to this notion there was—if there was a way—ditched me and I was left in snacking mode as a means of helping my thinking.

Him not being home left the kitchen free for my grazing and there's always plenty for the mouth in Guy's kitchen. He's on a bit of an appetizer kick right now, but it itches me—absolutely makes me twist my ponytail into a stick—when he calls the little saucers of food "starters."

With a good double squirt of mustard on the spoonful of mayo I got in a bowl, I stirred up the stuff my dad and I called "holidays sauce" when I was a kid. Usually, I like it on tater tots and chicken chunks but it's also tasty on veggies and I saw Guy had a bunch prepped up in little glass containers in the fridge. I took two of everything so as not to deplete his piles of asparagus, zucchini, peppers, green onions, carrots, and celery.

The sigh that slips out my mouth gasket when I sink into the couch with some snacks after work is an honest one. That relief of my feet going up on the coffee table is a real fine feeling, too.

Guy zipped home in minutes to score part of the last green onion from me and then got mighty interested in my bowl of dipping goo.

I said, "I forgot you were starting the dinner crowd tonight. We work too much."

He frowned, then made faces while sniffing my sauce, finally working up the bravery to stick a pinkie in and give 'er a try. I'd been half thinking I'd catch some static for breaking into all those veggies he'd prettied up, so I waited him out on more talking. And here it came.

He squalled, "What have you done?"

This was one he should have been able to figure out his own self but I suggested right back, "Had a little old snack?"

"I mean, what's that slime you're eating?"

Oh. Well, seeing as how he seemed chiefly weirded out about the sauce, not the vegetable thievery, I explained all about holidays sauce.

"Do you mean hollandaise sauce?" And he looked pale. I gave the shrug he deserved.

"We always called it holidays sauce."

"No way." Guy shook his head.

I tried to help him out. "Big way. Maybe because we usually had it on holidays."

"Look, I think your family was doing a hideously goofy version of a classic sauce. Technically, this has a similar color to hollandaise—and I'll make you some, the real stuff, you'll like it—but I'm sure it was called hollandaise, not holidays."

Guy has some kind of hard life coming on, hitching himself to my wagon. Now he expounded on how he wanted a road trip across the county for vegetables and mushrooms. They have a much bigger grocery store over in Gris Loup and a farmer's market with Friday evening hours. It used to be that if Guy said he wanted to shop, I'd say no thanks. What I'm trying these days is to say yes before I find a reason to say no.

To Gris Loup we would go.

In my growing up years, we'd been on a frayed-string budget, even before the folks split. Now, a shoestring seemed like too much an advertisement about my past life for me to want to mend my chaps with one. And finding a leather goods shop wasn't something that happened in little Cowdry. The co-op feed store sells leather bundles, but I wanted a heavy, flexible piece. My broken chap strap needed mule or buffalo hide.

"I can check at the sheriff's office on that thing and have a gander at the tack store. I think in Gris Loup they have evening hours." I do like to ogle saddles. The fact that I don't own one is a heartbreaker, am I wrong?

On the twenty-mile drive, Guy called his buddy Biff and left a message asking if he'd deleted a TrailTime map. Then I told Guy all about The Kid's shoulder and about Earl Delmont having a case against Cameron Chevigny, and we frowned over this bad blood.

* * *

There's a fancy tack shop in Gris Loup that I'd only been to once, when I first moved here. It's a bit of a drive and since I'm not a window-shopping type gal and can't spend money just to spend it, the tack shop hadn't been honored with my presence in some time.

When we pulled into the open market parking lot in Gris Loup, I gave Guy the same *stay* sign—a spread palm—I give Charley when I don't want him pushing the livestock up to me any faster. It means *take time*, sort of a lazy *stay*. Might as well put some use-ability onto Guy, what and all with us planning on keeping each other.

He grinned. "I'll sort of stay. I'll be here cruising the market. And you? You'll *come bye* and then *away to me?*"

Guy thinks he's so adorable since he learned a few sheepdog commands. Let's see him use them proper one time.

My *take time* hand got busy, thumb to pinky, for checking off my errands, but I counted the scary chore twice. "Tack shop, and maybe the craft store if I can't get a replacement strap at the tack shop, Sheriff Magoutsen. Grub later?"

"Yes, fiancée. Don't call him Magoo," Guy said as we parted ways, like he was being all helpful, just reminding me of something stupid I might do, when we both knew he was sticking a bad habit in my head, setting my mouth up for a mess. Our short bald sheriff does peer over his glasses, but he's a good guy. Not his fault I have a natural disinclination to go to the sheriff's office.

* * *

That humongous *Paso Pastures* pickup truck was parked outside the Saddle-Up tack shop, a nice glass-fronted store where bells rang as I walked in.

The scent of well-soaped, clean leather filtered through the Saddle-Up store's air. With a selection from budget to fancy, they stocked Westerns as well as those saddles that were missing the rope-dallying device. These can't-rope-a-steer-from type saddles had stirrups made of metal and skinny little belts that they call *leathers* to hang those shiny nickel stirrups from. That is to say, they were saddles of the English persuasion.

This end of Butte county hosts a lot more English-style riders.

A gal was repairing a well-used Western pleasure saddle's leather in one corner. A guy, Fred Flintstone—stood over her.

That would make the saddler Tall Doll.

She inserted new lacing in the saddle's skirt, binding the left and right halves together behind the cantle to go smoothly over the horse's spine. Her man hovered in a way that'd get him pasted in the kidneys if I was the one whose style he was cramping. I now remembered that I'd heard somewhere that the Saddle-Up people had Pasos and I could almost remember their last name.

Truth to tell, he didn't look like a horseman, more the Stand Over Someone Who's Working type.

She ignored him, just worked away, pounding now and again at the new leather lacing with a dead blow hammer. Saddlery is a skill I'd like to have. My eyeballs lingered on her swing—farrier-steady style, that would be able to drive a nail just so, like me—and then her tools. I've no need for a lead-shot filled mallet in my line. The most leather working I've ever done is a bit of braiding, but this gal had all the tooling stamps and leather-carving knives on a rack beside her. Basket-weave belts streamed across the counter next to a saddle tree with a Western pleasure rig in-progress, about to get fancy tooled floral designs all along the fenders.

A crackling, odd, electronic voice sounded, followed by squelch.

The counter behind the cash register had a mess of radios—one hissing static and police codes—and an ancient CB scanner, too. One Motorola radio on its side had a cracked case and a broken antenna. The dude moved to the counter and picked up the broken radio and started banging it with a screwdriver handle, pausing to listen when one of his scanners blathered more clipped words and numbers. Those guys that are police groupies, they chafe me, they really do. Figures this know-nothing is one of those.

I studied on the loose leather for sale, picked out a buffalo hide strap, and went to the cash register. *The Western*, Cowdry's weekly paper—Gris Loup's newspaper comes out six days a week—was spread out beside the register, featuring a front page article with a head shot of a smiling woman not much older than me.

"Got a customer, Doll," Mr. All Kinds of Useful said, without moving his muscles.

She was already getting up to help me anyways. We gave each other a look that I'm pretty sure commiserated on her bad tastes in the Other Gender.

I've never developed a taste for bossy men.

I gave her a friendly grin, got one back, then felt a frown coming at me from his direction.

Yep. Flintstone scowled, so that's the expression I handed back. Everything about him looked store-bought, too-clean black jeans, fancy shirt with piping and two bright colors, yellow and red. And this time he was wearing a cowboy hat decorated with a big jeweled cross. Oh, pretty please. There's horse-hair hat band cowboys and there's leather strappers with a concho or two. Both are fine, but I don't even want to talk about these goobers with jeweled hat bands. I mean, what in the world is that all about? And still, his boots weren't dirty. Clearly, he was a neat freak, a town boy playing at country. City-bred types like him leave me shaking my head. What did a talented saddler like her see in him?

Outside a police vehicle pulled up. One of Sheriff Magoutsen's uniformed deputies heaved himself out and paused by Ol' Blue, reading the sign on my truck door: Dale's Horseshoeing, and then the house phone number.

The oaf sauntered out the Saddle-Up's front door, making harness bells on the door jingle. I could hear him and the deputy chatting, though couldn't make out the words. The crew cut deputy was unfamiliar to me. There's more deputies over on this side of the county, but I guess we'll be getting a new one over in Cowdry soon, if they promote one of ours up to fill the spot being vacated by their retiring investigator.

Suit Fellow, the detective on the case of my poor client who died last spring, told me a couple weeks back that I might have to testify in court about that whole mess, but he didn't yet know for sure. And I've heard that trials can go on for weeks. The subpoena—which I did work up the gumption to read—didn't make itself clear about exactly when I'd have to say what. I wanted to firm things up. Guy's after me to settle on a wedding date for ourselves, so I needed to know when and if we'd be in court. And I hoped the "if" would turn out to be a "no, don't have to." Testifying is not my cup of coffee. Even with never having done it, I knew it would not play to my strengths. Not enough shoeing questions, too many people questions. If the deputy here at the tack store could tell me I was free and clear or at least give me a firm testifying-in-court date, I'd be knocking off two errands at once here.

That's when I saw it, hanging behind the register. A size 44 sheriff's department uniform jacket, with a name badge that said *Reserve Pritchard* on it. Yeah, this couple who had the Saddle-Up store, their name was Pritchard, I recalled now, Loretta and Vince Pritchard.

Much as Loretta Pritchard's warning at the Cascade had raised my eyebrows, there'd been talk. I thought about stuff I didn't want to. Earl Delmont's sister having been a lady friend of Cameron Chevigny. Noise to ignore before, but now when it was just us two gals, I went on ahead and put it plain to Loretta.

"The other day, you were in the Cascade Kitchen and you told me to watch out on the Buckeye ranch."

Loretta pressed a finger to her lips. "Sorry. Maybe I talked out of turn. Sometimes I blurt things without thinking."

I felt sympathy for her, because I have on occasion been about the worst at blabbing. I nodded. "But what did you mean?"

"Well, you know, he stepped out on her." Loretta shrugged, like she was just telling the ways of the world.

"You're not saying you think Donna killed him, are you? Over stepping out?" I was ready to take my paid-for chap strap and go deal with my Intended. The world looked different these days, like it had altered or I had. Couldn't set my finger on it, but something seemed to have changed since the morning the widow called me out of the blue, wanting a horseshoer.

She wasn't there to defend herself and it didn't feel right to listen to negative talk on my new old client.

"Eh, what do I know?" Loretta said. "Hey, you ride, right? Do you want to go ride sometime?"

I paused. "I'd like that. But I don't have a trailer."

There's so much stuff I need to save up for. Loretta had some great used saddles for sale in the Saddle-Up store. She had less expensive, but super handy stuff, too. Specialty gear for camping with the horse. Good saddle bags. Really cool folding saws and nifty hatchet-shovel-combo tools that could be handy on a trail ride. I pointed. "Nice saws."

"Yeah, those could cost over a hundred bucks."

I nodded. Horse gear is expensive, sometimes unnecessarily so. A good saw in a deluxe riding catalogue is three-digit pricey, but she wasn't marking up the price too much.

She nodded with me. "Those expensive saws you see at a lot of outfitter stores are really the same as gardening saws. So, I started stocking them here."

"I'll be getting a trail saw from you someday," I promised. "And I'd love to ride with you."

The front door chimed as her man followed the uniformed deputy inside.

I asked the deputy, "Would you know if the Sheriff's around the office still?"

He shook his head. "I can reach him on the radio but he's over on the west end today."

Vince Pritchard nodded like he was all in the know and the deputy turned and said to him, "Taking time with Bill, before the retirement. I think Bill's picked his last day. They'll promote from day shift or swings and hire a new deputy. You could be full-time regular before the year's out."

This chat got a satisfied nod from Vince Pritchard.

If Vince was the likely candidate to quit being a reservist and become a full-fledged deputy, I couldn't help but wonder if he would get assigned to the Cowdry office, which might mean the couple would relocate and move their horses closer to my neck of the woods. I wondered who their shoer was over here in Gris Loup and whether they'd want a new shoer for their Pasos if they moved to Cowdry.

Maybe I should do some advertising, subtle-like. My I-Don't-Shoe-Big-Lick-Horses rule doesn't extend to all gaited horses. Anyone who lets their gaited horse have a natural stride instead of going Big Lick with unnatural shoeing and training that makes horses painful and fearful can be my client. We could have us a fine business relationship, the Missus Pritchard and me. And maybe a friendship. There was something there I liked, and I've noticed my lack of friends—well, I'm new here—and she rides and does cool leatherwork. So, hey.

Cryptic words and numbers played on the deputy's hip radio and the scanner behind the register at the same time. The deputy gave it little mind.

Vince Pritchard gabbed to the deputy, manly-style, talk about schedules and reserve time and staffing some parade. These men-folk were more than I could enjoy trying to window shop with, so to speak. Passing a look over Vince Pritchard, I let my gaze check the attitude on Loretta.

She was inspecting the saddle she'd been working on. I'm like that, able to tune out the bystanders when I'm shoeing a horse. Someday, I'd have to talk to Loretta Pritchard about a good used saddle for my Red horse.

On the corkboard at the back of the store, notes and flyers advertised horses and farm equipment for sale, litters of pups and whatnot. Business cards for yard work and such were pinned up. I fished some cards from my wallet and put 'em up.

The deputy stood beside me and said, "You're the one who found Arielle Blake's…"

I was glad he didn't finish that sentence, and said, "Donna Chevigny's dog found it."

"Sounds like they found the body," Loretta Pritchard said, behind us.

"Processing the scene now," the deputy said. "Trying to get done before dark. Coyotes beat us to it some months back, so the body's not intact."

Vince Pritchard gave an in-the-know nod. "Heard the skull's fractured. Maybe had a fall out there."

The deputy shook his head. "It was not a natural death."

Chapter 6

I BOUGHT A COPY OF *The Western* on my way to meet Guy back at the market. The article said human remains were found on the federal land, but it didn't name Donna, Slowpoke, or me as the ones responsible for finding the gloved hand.

The Western's front page offered a nice picture of a gal somewhere north of my age, closer to Loretta's thirty-ish. Farther down, there was a smaller picture of a gray-bearded guy in a ball cap and flannel shirt captioned: *Stan Yates never stopped looking for Arielle Blake.* The mean part of my mind wondered about those women who pick guys old enough to be their daddy. Right away, I reminded myself it was not a nice thought and not my business anyways who anyone loves.

"Hey." Guy greeted me near the boxes of summer squash. He had both hands full of shopping that looked to be vegetables that never graced my childhood. Eggplant, purple potatoes, purple onions, purple carrots. We were going to be eating a lot of grape-colored, but not grape-flavored food.

"You wanted to drop a deposit in the bank," Guy reminded me.

"I'll pass. Since we're way over here on the east side already," I told him, "let's stop at that country store off the highway. You like their produce anyways."

* * *

The bulletin board at the front of the Country Store had some of the same business cards thumb-tacked up that I'd seen at the Saddle-Up. Lawn care, a realtor, a pet-sitter. There was a hand-written flyer offering free kittens. Someone selling chickens. And there was a dog-eared flyer—half-covered by newer ads announcing a rodeo and a pie social—about a missing woman, Arielle Blake. It was the same photo of her that the newspaper carried but zoomed out, showing her from waist up. She was smiling, her strawberry blonde hair loose and sunlit, her right hand resting on her left upper arm. A funky, clunky metal ring on her right thumb caught my eye.

I'd bet that ring was on the hand in that glove that Slowpoke packed from the federal land all the way across the Buckeye ranch.

Ew.

The guy behind the Country Store cash register noticed me looking at the flyer. "Need to take that down. She's not missing no more."

I pulled the thumbtack and held the flyer, thinking. Keeper Lake was not far from where we stood, maybe a mile behind the store. Another fifteen miles of rough country beyond that, and I could chance upon the shed at the back of the Buckeye ranch, provided I knew the lay of the land well enough, which I didn't. How often did Arielle take walks so long? I've never walked that far, not even when I was homeless, not even after I'd sold my car for food money. On a horse, I'd cover that distance sure, but these people who walk all day, I do not understand them.

"You know," a female voice said, low and slow, right behind me, "when I asked you to pay attention for anything suspicious out there, I didn't mean for you to go find a human hand."

I turned and tried to remember the name of the young woman whispering this aside. She was about my size and age, but darker eyes, hair looked almost black, wearing a sweaty tank top and running shorts.

The guy behind the register called out, "Good run, Melinda?"

She hesitated a second, her gaze on the flyer in my hand, then on my face. She raised her eyebrows and told him, "Sure was. Five miles."

Melinda stepped past me for one of the coolers, picking out an unnaturally yellow-green sport drink.

Guy grabbed a carton of duck eggs from the Country Store's offerings of local goods. Our geese and ducks at home lay eggs in the darnedest places, and we can never get enough at the same time for Guy to work with.

"Can we have a quiet weekend?" Guy asked me as he paid for his eggs at the register.

"Except . . ." I smelled soap. The Country Store stocked local gift stuff on the counter. Whoever thought of scenting soaps with lavender, licorice, or lemon?

"Except what?" Guy asked as we walked out together.

"Tomorrow, I've got to get Charley on some cattle, make sure he's sharp and fresh for when I take him to the Buckeye Monday."

Melinda came out of the Country Store as I opened Ol' Blue's door. That odd aluminum shoe was in my door pocket and she was right beside me, headed for I don't know where, since there weren't any other cars in the gravel parking lot.

"Look," I said, "it's for sure and for certain none of my business and all, but here's a thing, I found a shoe out on the Buckeye ranch and I know it doesn't belong there."

Melinda looked at me with a plank face. "Let's see it."

Like she thinks she's Perry Daggummed Mason.

"Oh," she said, as I pulled the shoe out of Ol' Blue. "A horseshoe."

Figuring her assessment wasn't worthy of comment, I gave her none and racked that double aught, slightly squirrelly aluminum shoe that used to be on a front foot of a little horse back in Ol' Blue's door pocket.

Melinda headed down the road on foot, southbound. I pulled out north, taking my Guy and his eggs and vegetables back home, thinking about a little horse I didn't know, though I knew it had a shoer who marks the outside shoe branch. I'd tried not to wonder which shoers around these parts worked that way. It would have been to the credit of anyone who had the sense to wonder with me, but no one did.

* * *

Owen Weatherby's a guy who'd used me as a pinch shoer a few times but still stuck with his long-timey man, Talbot, for regular shoeings. Weatherby likes roping and reining and he has a dog that pens sheep and cattle like nobody's business. The Saturday evening gathering wasn't one of his regular get-you-all-togethers with his buddies but he said a couple folks were coming out and he was willing to let me run Charley on some cattle. I'd been to one of these deals before but not with my date. I picked at my dog's chest ruff, sprucing him up. Summer and fall are seed season so Charley's coat was giving me fits. Burrs and seeds from wild grasses were digging themselves into him, making him less than smooth to stroke. He doesn't go for a lot of fondling, but I couldn't present him looking uncared for.

"Guy and Charley," I told my host, by way of introduction. The folks, they did make an effort to put a basic set of manners on me in my growing-up years.

Weatherby nodded at my dog and fiancé, in that order, which made me wonder if I should try to cover the Who's Who again just for clarity, but Guy was already moving to the single grub table out to the side of the parked horse trailers. He added a bowl of pasta salad to the offerings. He'd brought food even though I'd told him this wasn't a proper hootenanny, just a chance for me to work

Charley on cattle. But it did seem the proper time of day to feed my face, so I followed Guy. Charley followed me.

Sonny Weatherby—a more bow-legged, less pot-gutted version of his daddy—swaggered up to me near the grub table. Guess he'd heard from his old man that I was at the Rocking B to run Charley on livestock, though he might not know I was warming my dog up for working for Donna Chevigny.

Turns out, he knew.

"Watch that you keep a fence between you and trouble out on the Buckeye," Sonny told me, then took his cowboy self a-swaggering away. No doubt he had to get back to helping sheep over fences.

Most talk around the ice chest of beer and soda was about roping. A couple folks mentioned the Outfitters. Four times a year, every equinox and every time the sun has its longest and shortest days, folks with time on their hands get together and set up teepees and shoot black powder guns and wear silly, fringed clothes 'cause they have nothing better to do. Outfitters just like to hold big old weekend campouts and howl at the moon out in the middle of the forest land.

It's hard to see the point of all that foolishness when what's interesting about a group of horse folk gathered together is their horses, how their feet are balanced, how they move. I'd been eyeing the hooves of every steed present, seeing whose toes were too long, who was kept steeper behind than was helpful to the horse. It's enough to keep the mind busy forever.

Guy wrinkled his nose over some ribs he'd sampled. I elbowed him when talk around us went to where one guy was getting his Hollywood Mountain Man style rifle sling. Apparently, a bunch of them frequented the Pritchards' shop for their kit.

Trying to get Guy noting who's who and what's what is a chore, but it's my chore. If he's going to be in my world and me in his, we'll have to ante up a bit. So it's left to me to get him seeing and putting together anything that's not food. I bumped my hip into him. He quit inspecting the meat. We both know he can't eat and listen. I had to get my words in before his mouth went back to sampling.

"They're talking about the Saddle Up in Gris Loup." My mind traipsed back to the couple who owned the store, him overbearing, her seeming like someone I'd like to make friends and ride with some day.

"They had marvelous onions in the open market there," Guy said, fiddling with a barbecued rib on a paper plate.

How I wish he wouldn't nibble like a girl when there's witnesses.

"That gal in the Gris Loup tack shop, does the leather work . . ." I started, waiting to see if his mind had truly come off the meat.

"What about her?"

"She was in the Cascade the other day. Then at the Saddle-Up, she said she'd ride with me."

"Well, fine." Guy knows I've been hankering for riding buddies, and he's offered to be one.

Mulling on my time in the tack store made me recall driving out there with Guy that evening. "Did you ever hear back from Biff? You called him over something about a map?"

Guy shook his head. I tried the tater salad—lots of eggs in it and someone who used holidays sauce in the recipe—and was about ready to do what I'd come for.

"This was a pointless sacrifice of a steer," Guy said, setting his rib plate down.

All the time, he's whining about other cooks not making good use of meat. Poor presentation and seasoning and accompaniments or some such. It's his main interest, but it occupies his mind way-too much.

Glad I'm not like that.

Soon as I got me a soda, I went to the back pens where Weatherby had his Border collie out for bringing in whichever steer his boss took a notion to wanting.

Word is, Swiftsure came from Scotland proper. Sheep is what

he was made to move. But to that little black and white dog, a steer's just another kind of sheep.

A body standing watching Swift sweep across acreage would wonder how he knew there were more sheep beyond some distant rise. He just knows, though. That's what herders do. They know. Some sheepdogs like to specialize. Swift does dandy at cattle, but the talk said he moved sheep with his stare. A dog with a lot of eye like that doesn't need to push with power, that is, doesn't need to charge and nip.

Over the evening, steers would get moved from holding pens on one side of the arena to the other, each giving up some aerobic entertainment as its pass to rejoining the herd in peace.

A clang, a snort, then dust puffed as a cowboy threw open a gate and loosed a rank steer. It was in the split second that Swift glanced at his person, Owen Weatherby, and in the slice of a minute that Owen was not paying attention, all of which put Swift on hold while this one steer, already way too close to Swift, decided to charge. It was one of those times when everybody can see that a disaster is two seconds from starting and finishing and no one has time to even open their mouths to protest.

That steer was going to catch and kill Swiftsure. We were all going to watch a good dog die.

Chapter 7

"SWIFT!" I HADN'T MEANT TO SCREAM. You should ignore another handler's working dog, and certainly never command or call to it. My shout was a matter of not wanting to see the inevitable killing crush that steer was going to put on that great dog.

Swift flipped and ran when he saw mortal danger about to grind him into the dirt. We'd expected that. But the steer was coming like the devil on a runaway train from Hades. There was only so much spare distance between them. It wouldn't work to our favor. No way. We could all see the inevitable, given the best speed of the dog and the steer, already going.

A fit young dog can summon a next level sprint.

Somehow, in that last half-yard between them, Swift fired afterburners that kept his hindquarters clear of the steer's lowered skull. The dog shot through the arena fence. The metal pipe panels clanged as the steer knocked hard against them.

The hush was our collective swallow.

Guy let out his breath beside me. A couple of good old boys let out appreciative whistles. A few clapped.

"Run that sorry cuss out of there," Weatherby called to the

hands manning the arena gates. Then he said to me, "We'll find some milder stock for your dog."

Being the first into the frying pan after the one before was cooked bad, well, that's a tough break.

"Swift," Weatherby said, "that'll do."

Swift parked himself, looking a little put-out about another dog doing his calling but he honored my Charley, stayed down where Weatherby told him to lie and wait.

The gate man shooed fresh steers into the arena.

Sometimes cattle stay tight. These scattered, one bucking and running deep across the ring, another snorting and turning its heels, the third meandering.

"Away to me," I said, like I was talking about the weather, but my words meant the world to my old dog.

Charley shot into the arena, arcing wide in a counter-clockwise circle. His age always dropped when I sent him to gather. Later that night though, he might be paying for his eagerness with a stiff body. Still, the stock respected him, the two less rambunctious steers tightening up, wary-like about Charley, no longer feeling free to mill around.

The far steer stopped dead, watching with the rest of us as my dog's arc swept closer, closer. Then Charley froze just shy of making any of the cattle feel like they had to move a millimeter. It wasn't just the lone recalcitrant beef with his stare fixed on Charley he was influencing with his eye—the two gathered steers would scatter if my dog pushed the stray to the point of bolting.

Creep. Charley took one step, the other front paw raised in a threat to take another step. The steer lowered its head, able to defend itself from my fluffy little descendant of wolves.

Charley put his front paw down and lowered his head, eyes hard on the threatening steer, giving up nothing. It was a balancing act. They were playing chicken.

The steer broke eye contact, looking to the gathered steers waiting seventy feet away. He broke his pose and trotted to join them. Charley kept a non-threatening buffer as he followed. If I sent Charley to circle the other direction, the balance would be perfect to push them all trotting for the far end of the arena.

"Come bye," I said.

My dog ran in as big a clockwise circle as the arena allowed. The steers gave way and started for the far end. Just before they reached the open gate that would pen them out of the arena, the ornery steer didn't want to cooperate. He broke, wheeling to leave the group. Charley's automatic response was instantaneous, zipping about to push the jerk back, and in the end, he brought all three steers through the gate, with me moving nothing but mouth muscles.

Guy shook his head and went to study the steers in the holding pen.

"That'll do, Charley," I told my good dog, liking my host's nod to us both. Old Charley's no sheep whisperer but hey, he can move cattle as well as woolies. And geese? Oh, Guy'd like him to quit herding our geese around.

No fowl here tonight except the fried chicken someone had out on the grub table.

An old duffer near me gnawed the cartilage off the end of a drumstick. I bet he'd been watching me work Charley on Weatherby's steers. We gave each other friendly nods though I couldn't quite place him. Somehow, I had the notion that even if the old man hadn't given me a nod before I worked my dog, we'd be having a howdy now. But first, he talked without words to Charley, stroking his head, then running both hands around my good dog's ears. I caught his pause when his fingers reached the ear tips but I left it alone. I'm a little sensitive, just for the sake of Charley's feelings, about the ears. The thing is, is they're misshapen, too short. It doesn't hardly show because of his long fringe of hair, but a body can fondle Charley and feel the flaw—no pointy ear tips bent over, just fur grown past.

"That's a real nice dog."

Some cowpoke behind me hollered, "Hollis!"

The old duffer beside me excused himself with a nod and a "Ma'am," before going to see what the yeller wanted.

I hunted up Owen Weatherby's son to talk on the subject the young man had had aspirations of that stupidest of sport, bull riding. I figured he could maybe fill me in on Chevigny bull stories.

He could. It was a Light the Pipe talk and I was fixing to hear plenty.

"Horse hunter. A killer," Sonny began, shaking loose tobacco from a pouch and tamping it in his pipe's bowl. Doesn't he know a guy has to look 170 years old, like that Hollis feller, before pipe smoking looks cool?

"What was that killer's name?" I asked.

"Dragon?" Puffing helped him think. "Dragoon!"

Sonny gave me the whole story, but in a nonchalant way that pretended he hadn't daggummed near died in his effort to sit on a boiling Brahma for eight seconds. Cameron Chevigny had partnered up to try being a rodeo stock contractor and started with his bad-apple bull, Dragoon. Dragoon was a rough ride for those few who'd had a chance to try his back and the bull never suffered anyone riding him the full eight seconds. But not many had a crack at him. Dragoon was the unridden bull of the West, had one great season beating some better-than-good bull riders, but his deal was that often he'd seriously attack the pickup rider after he dumped his cowboy. Because the bull proved truly to want a career as a killer, Cameron Chevigny didn't get a contract to bring him to Vegas for the National Finals Rodeo, so money couldn't be made that way. Maybe Chevigny was hoping to do well breeding that big son of a gun, but then he died under his tractor.

Sonny was yanked out by the fighters and rail sitters who only had free access because the bull decided to charge a rider. Sonny about gave up bull riding, there in Salinas. And when Dragoon tried the same Gore-A-Pony move at a sanctioned rodeo a month later, Cameron Chevigny was told not to bring the bull around anymore. A shaky start and end for Chevigny's side business of providing rodeo stock, rolling in with an extra dangerous animal. Had me shaking my head as Sonny'd told how after the bull pitched him high and mighty, it had just turned and charged the rider. Not that bull riding can be safe by any stretch. It takes some seriously silly boys to try that. Unlike bronc riding, where the pickup rider pulls up alongside the rodeo stock to get the contestant off, in bull riding, it's the fighters, often dressed as clowns, that run up to the bull to help the rider. The fighters—two or three cowboys on the ground—straighten out the bull, protect the bull rider, get him clear. Yeah, sure, there's safety riders in the arena but they about never rope these bulls, because there isn't a horse strong enough to hold a raging Brahma. That day, in Salinas where Sonny Weatherby was bull riding, Dragoon just plain bypassed the fighter and charged the safety rider at the far end of the arena. The safety rider's horse went down, the rider barely escaped, and the poor horse had to screech out of the arena as the bull charged him again. Then the whackjob bull bent the rails trying to go after the horse.

"That's why I told you to watch out for that bull," Sonny said. "If you're astride out there, he'll want your horse."

"I get it." Makes sense. I'd have figured that another rodeo stockman would have bought the bull and made another try of him or kept him for breeding. Either that or he got rendered to fatten up a whole lot of dogs. He was huge scary, that bull, from what Weatherby's son had to say. And yeah, that was the bull Donna had mentioned.

Thinking back, I'd heard of Dragoon before I ever came to Oregon—when I was apprenticing as a shoer in California—but I'd never realized I was living where the little bit famous un-rideable rodeo Brahma was pastured.

Putting his head through a cowboy's chest is understandable enough but we can't have a bull trying to kill horses. A tough bull is a crowd-pleaser, but a horse-hurter is a whole 'nother deal.

And Donna Chevigny had this blasted killer Dragoon out on of her pastures?

"Why didn't they sell the bull?" I asked.

Shrugging, he suggested, "Maybe it's not hers to sell. Chevigny was partners with Hollis Nunn in the rodeo stock business."

"And that never quite got off the ground, huh?"

Sonny shook his head.

Some things in Cowdry weren't making sense. These things were new to me, but old news for others. I waited a piece before asking my host's son, "Ever hear tell of the Chevignys' daughter?"

Sonny Weatherby looked hard at me, nodded and shook his head all at once. "Three-wheeler accident. About broke them. It was a damn tragedy. Everybody loved her. Including me."

My mind went grabbing for straws.

Now it was a question of what and how much to tell Guy. He sometimes gets himself a little exercised thinking I'm going to get myself broken in this job of mine and he's a wee bit of a coddler, truth be told. How much did Guy need to know about Cameron Chevigny's bull?

It was more than enough to think on. I recalled the hot wire fence that had kept the peace between the Buckeye's two back pastures, confining Donna's horses on one side, the bull on the other, then remembered the saggy barbed wire that defined the federal lease land behind the Buckeye ranch where her cattle ranged. I hadn't been wary enough and counted myself lucky I hadn't been killed.

Didn't make me none too excited to go back for a second helping.

Chapter 8

THIS DAY, DONNA OFFERED ME A good stout buckskin.

"The sheriff asked me to not let Slowpoke wander onto the federal land again where he could mess with their crime scene processing. Your dog won't just run around and pester and roll in things?"

"Charley will mind me."

She shut Slowpoke up in her house then mounted a too-tall Appendix Quarter Horse.

With half her range horses shod our first day, I'd still have to do an even six, plus get cattle moved. We rode out back, through the ravine, and scored nicely cooperative horses again. We could both see what was left to be done up at the open machine shed, but still the shoeing happened by the pole corral, same place as the first long day.

I worked in peaceable quiet that morning, but my mind kept moving to the other chore that wanted to be fit in before dinner. Charley squished himself against sagebrush tight enough to win some shade. Over midday sandwiches, we pieced together a plan for Charley to bring the range cattle off the lease land without the bull chancing up to kill us. Dragoon, somewhere out in

65

the Buckeye's east pasture, would likely get interested when we brought the herd in off the federal land and into the west pasture. And the way the gates worked, he'd be less secure when we had the back gate off the machine shed open to let the herd run through from the federal land to join the horses.

"Why don't you get rid of that bull?" I said, even though it was purely none of my blasted business. "Sell him or shoot him, I mean."

Donna had less to say on that than she'd had all day, which is, nothing. She held the horse I was shoeing, fetched the next one, passed me a water bottle regularly and that was all afternoon.

Six full shoeings on, I felt like I'd done a full day's work. I was whipped by the time I released that last hoof, and awful glad to be putting my tools away for the day. We'd be ahorseback while Charley moved the cattle.

Donna sent me to ride right up the hogback to the shed, saying she'd just be a minute. I looked back from the hilltop, just shy of the shed.

She stood her horse by the tractor with her head bowed. I heard her murmur, couldn't make out the words, but was glad, because this was private stuff. I looked away.

Our plan was that Donna would mind the big gate, be the last one through. I wanted my horse fresh, so rode to the water trough.

The Buckeye's solar electric fence, taut across a long row of metal T-posts, divvied the west and east land, marrying up the sections at the shed's front gutter downspout. The hot wire straddled the long oval stock tank. I was waiting for my mount to wet his whistle at the water tank when I saw the serpent yawing away into the east side.

Sometimes I think I didn't come far enough north when I left the Southwest. I hear tell there's no snakes in Alaska, and parts of Washington don't even have poisonous ones. Here in central Oregon, we've got snakes.

Snakes and me have never seen eye to eye. If this one had been going into the shed's shade, instead of heading out for a constitutional, I'd have never looked harder. Guess I gave the stare where the serpent slid out just 'cause I was so happy he left. Between the trough and the shed wall was a concrete block that had been giving the snake a cool hiding place. The tip of something else was cached there.

I dismounted, leaned, extending my chest and belly over the low water trough and avoiding the electric wire that ran across the works. Leaned 'til the backs of my thighs hollered 'whoa' but I could move the block so the snake wouldn't come back.

A leather scabbard was secreted there, holding a knife with a beautiful bone handle. I reached, got it, then eased back into a normal position and mounted up again.

Donna still stood near the tractor, being brave. After a time, she scrambled her gelding up the ridge and moved him through the shed to pin the gate open. We stared around the east side for the bull that was nowhere to be seen but cattle on the federal land to the north looked up as I rode through with Charley.

Somewhere out on that land, Slowpoke had found Arielle Blake's gloved hand. And apparently, the sheriff's men had found the rest of her body. Why did Guy and his buddy get sent fifteen miles away to look for Arielle around Keeper Lake? I wondered about Stan Yates, the wind farmer, who'd brought Arielle's cat to the vet after she'd disappeared, and who was now buying the back of the Buckeye ranch on a handshake deal.

I grabbed my saddle cantle and twisted around to eye the land to the west where I'd spent the whole day. White turbines turned in a lazy breeze in the distant orange light of what would be sunset in another hour or so.

"See something?" Donna called.

"Is it Stan Yates who's buying your land?"

"Only neighbor we have." She waved a hand westward where the Yates land abutted her west pasture out here north of the ravine.

"This is a dying way of life," Donna said. "People hate stock being on the federal grazing land."

Some people did make a lot of noise about private cattle on public land, that's true. These tend to be people who think meat comes from a grocery store, never acknowledging that first it was a steer that, if it had a decent life, grew up grazing somewhere.

Donna rode farther onto the scrub country ready to remind any cattle that picked up speed coming down the hill that they really did need to go through the gate, instead of just coasting on by the shed. Her other job would be to count the stock as they came through the gate onto the pasture where the newly shod range horses were stringing out.

It was nice work, nice land.

Rather than scramble the buckskin gelding up the steepest and rockiest part of the country back of the shed, I rode beyond to where it leveled and turned the horse around there, waiting for cows in the scrub. Past the far brushy area, the land promised enough view to afford me a chance to run my horse clear of the bull if he showed up on the wrong side of the barbed wire.

The brush promised something else, too.

"Come bye," I told Charley.

Would have pleased a few grumpy taxpayers, the way my dog cleared the Chevigny cattle off the federal lease land out back of that shed. He was a while working, but Donna and I just sat steady on our horses, trusting Charley to do the job.

"Should be another five pair," Donna said after a bit.

Charley's posture showed he already knew this. Away he went, soon pushing eight toward us, paralleling the east pasture. The border fences separating out the federal rangeland from the Chevigny ranch were another interesting matter. With our Escape the Bull plan being to gun the horses through the shed after the loose cattle, Donna slamming the gate soon as we were clear, I was not liking that sagging look of the old fence. It surely did look tired.

Donna saw me frowning at the old barbed wire while Charley circled for two final stragglers. Though the Buckeye had the responsibility for the fencing that marked the start of the leased land, fencing efforts had clearly been directed to the home pastures instead.

"Those strands are new," Donna hollered in her defense, pointing in the general direction of the electric wire that ran up the long slope of the hogback, cutting the west and east fields from each other. "He was fixing to keep some stock out here year-round, rodeo stock, and thought he needed something more trustworthy than the old fence here."

"Used to be barbed wire between the two pastures, huh?" I hate barbed wire. And I was about to ask Donna about the rodeo stock business plan that was no more when Charley swooped through the barbed wire fence into the east pasture. He saw the last two cattle needed more distance between him and them to not feel pressured, so he used adjacent land to reduce his power over the final pair of cattle he was moving.

"Used to be."

Jabbering got put away because Dragoon bellowed, filing a complaint about the other cattle being moved and worse, a dog being in his pasture.

Charley gave a little leap at the last two cows he was pushing and even though they were on the other side of the saggy barbed wire, they obeyed him, picked up speed, heading for the shed. I rode toward the breezeway with the eight.

From deep in the Buckeye's east field, the bull charged Charley.

All I could do was holler a warning to my great dog as I pointed the Quarter Horse at the gate and hunkered down to stay put and not slow him up. In that short sprint, my eyes teared from the wind and my heartbeats ran over each other. I heard Dragoon picking up speed, coming at us for sport. I didn't exactly feel like I was about to run out of horse, but then, I didn't want to find out either.

Cattle flowed with me, as we passed through the gate, then they passed me, joining the range horses.

Donna shot her horse through the gate behind us and sank back on a pull-rope, ready to snap the gate closed the second she cleared it.

Even after I heard the gate clack shut behind me, I put off feeling any safer. I expected Charley had gone back through the barbed wire onto the federal land. Now that Donna had closed the gate, the barbed wire snugged tighter.

"The bull respects a fence."

That didn't sound too likely to me. Bulls can walk through an awful lot of fences and the rest they can take down by scratching their heads and fannies on the posts.

Charley was circling wide. I thought how stupid I had been the other day to be afoot near the bull just to pick up that old horse-shoe, or twenty minutes earlier, to pick up that knife.

"Charley," I barked at the boy, "That'll do. Get out of there now." I waved my arm, telling him to go wide to get to me.

The bull snorted across the barbed wire at the dog once, twice, then pawed. His horns were wicked long, pointy enough to gore anything unlucky enough to be in his path.

Charley turned and faced the coming bull like he should have, but then got himself to the west pasture side by ducking under the barbed wire and coming on from the federal land rather than the bull's field. If that monster kept a coming and splintered the gate like his body was built to do, things would have got ugly.

But Dragoon stayed there and looked like we were forgotten. The deed was done and we set to ride in.

With her ranch stock shod for dispersal and her cattle now all in from the federal land, Donna said she felt a few things were getting organized. I suggested she get her tractor put away in the shed.

She grimaced and nodded, then shook her head. "One back tire's flat. Hadn't noticed that before. 'Course, I hadn't looked at it too close, been avoiding it."

When she let that hang, I couldn't help but say, "That's understandable."

"It's been hard, since he died."

"I'd imagine so."

"All on my own here. Past time for me to take care of that tractor though, you're right about that."

I hadn't noticed the flat tire either. The tractor was one of the old style tricycle built rigs, two skinny wheels up front, right close together, badly balanced. It wasn't going anywhere—least of all back up that hogback to the shed—without the tire being fixed. What was needed was to haul the tire into town for fixing.

We rode in silence. The sound of our saddles creaking and the horses' hooves thudding in dust and clinking on stones made good enough background noise for my tastes. As the barn drew near and my second day working at the Buckeye was about done, it seemed time to try to say something kind of nice. After all, the woman talked about her husband dying.

I thought about Loretta Pritchard's warning. I thought about Melinda Kellan watching everything and asking after things that were none of her business. I remembered Earl Delmont's wife's words. Then Sonny Weatherby's genuine sorrow when I'd mention the daughter.

"You know, you're not alone. You and Cam, um, been here a long time, got a lot of friends."

"Who?" Donna said this real pointed-like, near snapping. It fussed me into confusion but good.

I tried again.

"Cam," I said, frowning, catching on with my usual Molasses-at-the-North-Pole speed.

Donna swung her head away like I'd done her dirty. "You're being mighty familiar. His name was Cameron." She nudged her horse to a lope.

I followed like a puppy trying to say 'sorry for piddling on your slippers' but didn't get a chance to speak 'til we pulled up at the barn.

"Hey, I didn't mean any disrespect. I just thought . . ." I was going to dig myself a hole here if I didn't watch it.

Donna stood her horse silent, no eye contact for me.

Now that we'd reached her hitching rail, I was the only one swinging off a horse. Having something that was hers, I dug into my pocket and handed it over. I wished I hadn't forgotten about the knife earlier.

"This was behind the water trough up at the shed."

Donna stayed put, her hand around the knife I offered, though she pulled it out of the scabbard.

"Tell me something, Rainy, how long have you been here?" All friendliness had vanished from her tone. "About a year and a half?"

"Yeah, about that," I nodded, wrapping the lead rope over the rail and giving the slipknot more time than it deserved. I didn't know what else to do but deal with my mount, slip his bit out of his mouth, the usual stuff. I could hear the crunch of the over-dry dirt under my boots, but nothing more from this client of mine.

All we'd ridden through was yellowed grass and dried scrub branches. Fire problems are the plague of summer and, until the rains come, fall. Here was a blaze kindling I didn't see.

No amount of kicking myself later helped.

Donna undid two clips that let her shove her saddlebags off her horse's haunches. The part of my shoeing kit she was packing banged into the ground. Her horse flinched.

Then she tossed down the bone-handled knife, threw it right at my feet from her high horse. Not knowing what else to do and unable to stop my arm's curiosity, I reached down in the dust and picked it up, really looking at it for the first time.

There were marks in the handle. I puzzled on them but looked back up at her before I had time to get anything sorted out.

"You, too, Rainy?" Donna spat the words with venom.

"Ma'am?"

"You, too!" Donna glared at the ground, right where she'd thrown that knife at my feet, then wheeled her horse away. Like any good Quarter Horse, hers hit high speed in about twenty feet and left me looking at dust.

I unsnapped the dry leather knife scabbard as I wondered about her sudden anger. Then I looked in my hand at that knife again, holding it away, turning it in both palms. I brought it close and looked at neat carved figures in the handle.

A heart shape and then a big old capital R.

Dust settled.

Weird, it was all so weird, her throwing this knife down in the dirt, riding off, leaving me to pack myself out of there in the dying day. One thing suddenly made a little bit of sense though, even though it was way wrong. I thought again about those younger women, those rumors.

I hollered into the eerie evening, "Donna? It wasn't me." But she was way out of hearing range.

Chapter 9

GIVEN MY DAYS ARE SPENT WITH horses and horse people, it's a little unsettling for me to mix with townfolk who sometimes stare at the girl in dirty jeans, a handful of checks and a deposit slip in hand. A branch of our Savings and Loan is just across the way and up the road a piece from the Cascade Kitchen. As my work week wears on, I've earned hundreds of dollars, paid on the spot, and lots of it's in checks. Managing this side of the business—deposits and bounced checks and the like—is not why anyone becomes a shoer. I've heard of one stiffed cowboy shoer taking the iron off a horse when a client kept making excuses about not paying. I've been stiffed with a bad check a time or two. Mostly, I realize it's all in picking decent clients to work for. Folks who don't pay up can handle their horses' shoeing without me.

Was Donna ever going to pay me for the last six shoeings? I frowned.

Indoor air smells different than the real world, like the bank's recycled or purified air made me stand out worse. I looked away from a stranger who wouldn't quit eyeing me, and got back to puzzling on how on earth Donna could have thought that that knife

74

was mine—or worse, that it had been a gift to me or from me, which was the only assumption that could explain her reaction.

How long had she wondered if her husband had stepped out with me? Donna clearly despised me when she threw down that *Heart R* knife.

Wish I'd looked better at the knife before I handed it over.

Wish I hadn't casually referred to Cameron Chevigny as Cam.

Wish I'd talked to Donna about all this.

Too late now. Probably, I wouldn't be getting a call back from Donna Chevigny. I twisted my ponytail at the itchy idea of calling her myself. Seeing if she wanted to schedule any of her horses on down the road could wait a good while. The extra ranch stock might sell before they needed new shoes.

How could Donna even think that her husband and I had . . . well, we didn't. He was dead before I moved to town. Anyway, in the whole entire state of Oregon, Guy's the only fella I've ever dinked.

Guy had worked late at the Cascade and I'd fallen asleep before he got home, and I'd been out the door for an early shoeing today, so I didn't get to talk to my fellow about Donna and the knife thing. Should have warned him. I didn't want to be mixed up in anything, rumor-wise or whatnot. I didn't want anyone thinking ill of me. Didn't want other people's sorrow soiling me, getting me feeling bad.

But I was feeling bad. I looked around the bank.

The person in line behind me, the older fellow ahead of me, the tellers, and the customers transacting at the big counter all seemed normal enough. The other desks and offices where town folk came in and made arrangements to get in and out of debt were half-occupied, all doors open for the moment. Abby Langston's daddy, Keith, waved to me from his desk, looking over the top of reading glasses. I put a smile on my face and waved back.

The man in front of me turned and spoke. "Hollis Nunn."

"Right," I said, warming palms with him. "Rainy Dale."

I remembered him as the old guy who complimented my dog out at Weatherby's place. The man squared himself to me, not aggressive but plain that we'd be talking. "You're shoeing for Mrs. Chevigny, I hear."

"You heard right." Hollis Nunn rubbed his stubbly neck and studied the ceiling while he gave me free advice. "There's one bull out there at the Buckeye that I want you to . . ." He shook his head. "See to it that you give way to that bull. Don't even be in a pasture with him, hear?"

Sonny's warning came back to me. I hadn't gotten it then but now I did. Sonny Weatherby and this Hollis Nunn were trying to do me a favor.

I nodded.

"I mean it, girl, you keep a fence between you and him."

"I'll keep that in mind." I didn't want to say that I'd probably shod my last for Donna Chevigny and the Buckeye ranch.

A middle-aged teller called, "Next."

Hollis Nunn stepped aside, making way for me. "You go ahead."

"Thanks."

I walked up and asked the red-faced teller to put the checks in mine and Guy's new joint account. She kept her eyes down but handled the transaction just fine. I don't know what the old feller's problem with her was, but he winked at me as he strolled past to the next teller, a younger fellow. On my way out, I paused at Keith Langston's open office door.

"Did you ever hear anything about a land deal between Cameron Chevigny and his neighbor?" I asked.

"Stan Yates," Abby's daddy said, nodding. "Rainy, we don't really talk about things like that here, other customers' banking business."

"If we talked about people in general, Donna Chevigny would say her husband was the sort who'd do a handshake deal on something as big as a land purchase."

Keith Langston cast a quick look around but gave me a slight nod. "She probably would say that, and she'd be right."

"Would you think that Stan Yates fellow would buy land on a handshake?"

Langston exhaled, his lower lip pooched out and he considered his options, obviously interested and willing to entertain the question, plus its answer. Finally, he said, "Between you and me, I don't know of anyone but Cameron Chevigny who would have bought or sold real estate that way."

So Stan Yates could be telling Donna that Cameron made a handshake deal, and she was honoring it, but there never had been such a deal. Mulling this, I walked out of the bank right behind Hollis Nunn, thinking how weird it was that he'd avoided that first open teller for some reason that she seemed to blush about. Come to think of it, I'd about swear that my teller had pinked up even worse when she saw one of my checks was drawn on the Chevigny name. Small towns and their people harbor a special kind of weird.

* * *

Once again, I'd gone to town without getting ahold of the sheriff or Suit Fellow. Maybe I'd sort of forgotten but I was pretty well tuckered and bothered and wanted only to go home. If I'd gotten done with work sooner, I might have tried to go be a big sister or an aunty or something to little Abby Langston, see if her mood was sorting out and how she felt about getting shipped out for the best part of the fall. Once we bring Pinto Bean, the weanling, from the Langstons' place to ours, and my Red takes on overseeing the duty of turning little Bean into a proper horse, I expected to see more of Abby at our pasture. This wasn't my first rodeo of knowing that a little girl doesn't want to give up the first horse she's seen born. I was ten years old the day I saw Red birthed. When I was fourteen and my world was upside down, my daddy sold him. Finding and buying Red back was what brought me to Butte County.

Ol' Blue rumbled down Vine Maple road and I grimaced at my good old chestnut gelding, lonely in his pasture. The muffled thud of his hoofbeats, the nicker and blowing nostrils are good on my ears. Every girl deserves a good horse and vice versa. No, Abby's heartache was not my first rodeo with—wait. Rodeo.

Rodeo stock business.

Maybe the thread that pulled some things together around here was Hollis Nunn and Cameron Chevigny having gone in together in the rodeo stock business. Maybe there was bad blood there. I thought about the teller's anxious manner when Hollis Nunn sent me ahead in line, which meant she dealt with me instead of him. I'd paid not enough attention to what happened next—just gone and talked to Abby Langston's daddy. What else was I missing?

I shook my head, still bugged about Abby having to go away. Bugged about not knowing if I'd have to go to court. About a whole mess of things at the Buckeye ranch and let's see . . .

Delmont's colt. Maybe do something about that one.

That was making me twist my ponytail around my thumb pretty hard.

My Intended might be persuaded to help me work on the one thing that was bugging me that we might could fix. I got right to it as soon as I was in the door.

"Guy, did you ever want a Clydesdale?"

"How was your day?" His brow can wrinkle in the most interesting, topographical-map-like manner. Maybe it helps him come up with something more to say, since he finally added, "Did I want a Clydesdale to bring us beer?"

This from a guy who knows I don't partake.

"To be a horse," I said.

"Well, technically, no, I don't recall ever saying to myself that I want a Clydesdale." Guy grinned at me like I was amusing him.

Sighing over my own silliness, I squeaked, "Do you think you could manage it?"

"What?"

"Wanting a Clydesdale."

"Rainy, is there a shortcut you could take to tell me what's on your mind?"

So much for me finessing him to the idea of pasturing the Delmonts' shoulder-lame young horse. Guy does like his communication served without side dishes. Hitching my wagon to his will be interesting. And no, I have no blessed idea in this world why he picked me. As a means of testing him out—and because I've an ornery streak at least a couple feet wide—I've given him guff in large, daily portions, but he keeps asking me about my day and smiling and rubbing my shoulders and asking me about my day and handing me iced tea and asking me about my day and in general being a sweetie. I expounded.

Right then, he agreed to taking on a lame Clydesdale, like it was no big thing at all. That's being a sweetie, in any gal's book. I didn't even have to scare up some reasons why we should give The Kid a healing home.

Good thing, 'cause I didn't have any reasons.

Guy saw I wanted it and that was fine by him.

I could have gone on and on, made an evening of explaining Sweeney to Guy, but the phone rang and Guy started talking in a tone that surprised me.

"Yes." He listened hard, very quiet, brow a map again. And then after a bit, he said, "All right."

I listened to him saying nothing while he listened to someone on the phone and then he said, "Well, sure. That's fine."

Another half a minute watching him listen and then he said, "Okay. We've been living here together for about a year and a half."

I poked him in the ribs as soon as he hung up. "Just who were you telling about our sinning ways?" I said this as a joke, though it's true. "Who wants to know?"

As I don't even cuss anymore, I'm hardly a sinner worth noticing.

"Donna Chevigny."

"That was Donna? She didn't want to talk to me?"

"She," Guy rubbed his jaw and ducked his head a bit, working up some answers, "wanted to know how long you'd been here. In Cowdry. In Butte County."

I pursed my lips and knew we were both remembering when we met. We'd each thought we were looking at a lunatic.

"You saw me my first night in town," I said. We'd met at the 24-Fuel gas station, which is not how romances generally go.

Guy's forehead wrinkled up a good deal again. He had the makings of a confused and fussy man, but then he put away being confussed and just looked wry. "She sounded so sad—"

"Donna always seems sad to me, all wistful and worn out."

"She'd been crying." Guy's voice was so soft it was hard to hear. I don't know that I'd ever heard his throat catch like that. "I think so anyway. It sounded like she was trying not to. Trying not to let me know."

"Crying? Really?"

He nodded. "Pretty sure."

Ever since I left the Buckeye the day before, I'd been itching to tell Guy about a whole hayload of happy horse hockey, so I talked for about fifteen minutes straight while watching different expressions try themselves out on the territory between his hairline and jawbone.

"And you told her we'd been together a good long while," I said slowly, thinking this mess over. "That's good."

"It is good."

Oh, he didn't get me at all. But he would.

Took a breath, then I called Donna back.

The conversation went around how she'd jumped to a conclusion that was wrong and she was sorry and she liked my work and she was sorry and she sure appreciated my help and she was sure sorry.

I said I'd help her anytime.

There was a pause.

Maybe we were both thinking about how much she had on her plate and I said—I don't know where this came from, there's floor scrapings in my brain that surprise me whenever I set to mild thinking—maybe I could give her a hand sorting out her tractor. The thing of it was, getting the tractor dealt with was more of a chore than she'd been able to face in a year and a half.

"I just can't apologize enough, Rainy. I feel guilty, real bad." Donna's contrition wore her voice to a hoarse whisper. She berated herself some more, going into how frazzled she'd been and she just wasn't thinking right. While I listened to Donna, I watched Guy try his cell phone and get a fail notice on some text he'd tried to send. The end of Vine Maple road isn't a hollow, but you'd think it's the back of beyond, so bad is the cell service here.

"It's okay," I said." In letting her say her piece, we made peace. I almost asked about the neighbor, Yates, fixing to buy her land north of the ravine, didn't, then wished I had. There was something I was missing here. Something I should have noticed, or I had noticed, but didn't grab onto the significance with both hands.

Soon as I freed up the house phone, Guy tried to call someone. I heard him leave a voice mail for Biff.

"Maybe he's avoiding you," I joked. It was like joking about sinning with Guy. Sometimes, I'm not sure what I believe. Anyways, Guy's only a little bit right when he says we've been living together for over a year and I'm a lot more right when I say it's been a few months. The thing of it is, is I was his tenant, on account of me renting his garage as a bedroom the first night I was ever in Cowdry.

Both our faults that the renting thing slid into a sort of a boyfriend and girlfriend thing. Guy's asked me to not get stuck in a pickle about how we started. But then I went and got into a mongo pickle—made from the world's biggest cuke—back when I realized I'd fallen for him. Which was right after he'd fallen for me. Which was right before he asked me to marry him for the second or third time. Which was when I said okey dokey.

Or something like that.

Nights are nice here, in Guy's bedroom—our bedroom—even come mornings when he gets up way earlier than me, smooching me and telling me to sleep in, he'll toss hay to Red. Now that, that is a way-swell thing about a nice guy. Mornings he knows I don't have any early clients, I get tucked in right and proper for some extra loafing while he goes off to serve his breakfast crowd at the Cascade.

Guy's heartbreak and his joy is that diner, though we're not supposed to call it a diner for reasons that I don't understand or want to get into. Someday, he'll have his own restaurant—and he calls such a thing a resto or a bistro. But then, there's restaurant and diner people and then there's people like Guy.

Sitting on the front steps the next morning—thinking on my Intended and enjoying the thermos of coffee he'd left for me—would have set my day fine, but a strange dark car steering up with a driver in a Butte County Sheriff's Department uniform cracked it right away. Never mind the little tan sweater with a junior version of the Sheriff's patch, that meant the wearer was a clerk or some such, not a sworn officer. No, draped over the driver's seat was a jacket showing the *reserve deputy* patch through the window.

Chapter 10

"Fancy meeting you here," I told Melinda Kellan from my front step.

Having made a late morning of being in my socks, I wasn't exactly dressed for the front yard. The hazy sun felt awfully fine toasting my cotton-covered toes while I slow-sipped my second cup of black bitter coffee. I'd aimed to enjoy my drink. A little harder to do now that the little off-duty police clerk stood in my driveway.

"You a reserve deputy?" I asked.

Her chin came up a bit. "I will be. I'm in the reserve academy now."

Oh, goody. Those wannabes, they're something else. But I let my silence speak, wondering what she was doing at my home when she should probably get to work and answer phones or file something.

"I looked up your address in the computer—"

"Sounds like an abuse of your clerkly powers."

"Get over yourself." She checked her watch. "Donna Chevigny called the sheriff's office," she said, "to see if we could tell her exactly when you moved here."

83

Thump, thump. My heart did a jig for a minute as I tried to decide if I was being set up for a killing. Maybe Donna didn't believe me and Guy. Maybe she was going to loose the bull on me if I came back out to the Buckeye.

Real slow, I said, "Um, when?"

"Last night, late afternoon actually."

And then she'd called my house, but talked to Guy, confirming whatever the police might have told her.

"Who did she talk to at the sheriff's office?"

"Me." Melinda Kellan nodded a bit. "I'd like to see that horseshoe again."

Fetching isn't something I'd wish on a dog, except maybe a Labrador and them only because they'd sooner hit their block heads on concrete as not carry back whatever got heaved. But there I went, fetching up the shoe for this little police clerkette, in hopes that she'd say something quiet and knowing about Cameron Chevigny dying.

Fifteen seconds' study is what Melinda gave it.

"Pretty rusty nails."

Maybe she needed horseshoe basics explained. I obliged. "They're generally made of iron."

"No shit."

Well, someone missed the part in Young Lady Growing Up when we decide not to swear like a sailor.

Truth be told, I'd missed it myself until I turned over a New Leaf a couple three years back.

Moving across the yard to the side pasture to give Red a hey, I heard Melinda following me and left it friendly enough. Charley, grinning and touching both of us in the knees with his nose, was way-too friendly with her to suit me. Usually I trust his judgment, but he is an old dog. Everything's a possible herd to him. He helped me howdy Red and I automatically looked my horse over for any owies. Looking is just a good habit.

"Hey, you know that closed-down pizza place in town?" Melinda said this like we were old buddies or something.

"Huh?"

"My mom said the place is going to re-open. She's a realtor so she knows all the business stuff in town. Anyway, the grand opening's gonna have the lunch buffet half-off. Sweet deal."

Maybe she thought we could both use a lunch buddy but she didn't know all I knew. If the old pizza joint had changed hands, then Guy had missed his chance to get the location as a new restaurant, that's what I knew.

I knew someone I love was hurt and he hadn't told me. For crying out loud, people-wise, there's only one love for me in this town, this county, this state. I tried to scratch a note on a few of my little-used brain cells—it's like working with a child's magnetic letter board—to talk to Guy about losing his site. He'd hoped to set up his own place in that old pizza joint but the plan had been getting shaky for a few reasons. Yet he hadn't said a word to me about the deal being dead.

But then, I hadn't asked him. I looked at my horse and dog, who always understood me. These are the species to know. With cats and people, there's too little or too much to remember.

Melinda gave Red's legs and feet a good staring with me, then frowned. "Why don't shoes rust on a horse?"

"They do," I said. "I mean, steel shoes, they rust constantly."

She shook her head, still watching Red's feet. "When he moves, I see the bottom of his shoes. They're not rusty at all. They're shiny."

"That's because a horse's movement against the ground constantly buffs the rust off."

"Really?"

"You betcha."

She toed the mud, squinted this way and that, then got around to the start of a whole 'nother conversation I didn't think we ought to have. "Why do you think Donna Chevigny wanted the sheriff's department to say how long you'd been in Cowdry?"

"Look, keep me clear of this in your mind," I snapped. "I never knew Cameron Chevigny. I've heard rumors and I'd guess you have, too. But I—" Pondering on the knife and its carving, I tried to think if it was any of this girl's business. The same sick dread of accusation I'd felt when I realized Donna thought that knife with my initial on it meant something to me, about me, seeped over like fog.

But that Heart R knife wasn't mine or meant for me. Whose was it?

Melinda smirked and studied Red. "Like I said before, if you see anything, notice something that doesn't set right, you could just trot on over and let me know. Anything suspicious."

That's where we left it, me kind-of lying by not telling Melinda Kellan all the suspicious little nicks about the Buckeye.

My cheapie cell phone showed that Abby had tried to call me earlier. I had no time now to swing by her place. Shoes needing shaping were calling my name, as well as horse feet what were overdue. I pulled Ol' Blue around the back of my first client's house before the morning got too well set.

And I saw right away I should have been tending my tools the night before. My hoof knives were dulled, the regular one plus my loop knife. What's the matter with me, not minding my kit? I can't let other people's problems give me grief. It's just not my business if the sheriff's clerk is nosy or if Keith Langston and his daughter are unhappy or if Donna Chevigny and her dead husband had all kind of trouble or if some sweet young Clydesdale is dragging a leg through his pasture and going to become tiger chow.

I clamped the loop knife in my vise and worked the blade with my ceramic sharpener. I worked and worked it, squinting at its fineness. Made it surgery sharp and then got through two half-shoeings and four trims.

My last client of the day was at the boarding stable on the south end of town. I only have a couple horses there and it's not my favorite place to shoe. Places where more than one shoer works always leave the possibility that it'll be a day when more than one of us is on site at the moment. Could be fine but could be uncomfortable.

It left me thinking about other shoers and their work while I puzzled again about the shoe I'd found at the Buckeye ranch.

That small aluminum shoe, with a squirrelly toe and rusted nails and a mark on the outside branch, that shoe didn't belong on a ranch, the one Melinda Kellan had come to look at. Or had she really come to ask me why Donna Chevigny had asked her that question?

Marking the outside branch of a horseshoe is something shoers do when they bare a horse—pull all four old shoes at once—and then reshoe all four, instead of shoeing one hoof at a time. That baring a horse down, I don't work that way but I'm on my own and remote a lot of times. If I had a full-time helper, maybe I'd go ahead and pull all four shoes at one time and shape them all, then nail them all. It could be a scoach faster.

But I work one shoe at a time, so that in case I get hurt or something else bad happens, the horse is pretty well taken care of.

Like now, this last horse I pulled out of his stall and cross-tied in the barn aisle. Tiff, my client, had left a check for me tucked behind his water bucket. She's one of the few clients I allow to not arrange a horse-holder for me. Her job takes her out of town and her gelding Tommy is a decent horse except he can get bored and be a bit of a nipper. Tommy and I had discussed this ugly habit, me yanking his lead rope and growling and his eyes promising he'd try to be good, but I figured he could only try so long and then he'd be back to looking to taste me.

Bending over firms up the blue jeans over the cheeks, so it's sort of hard for a horse to properly sink his teeth into me then and there. All that's to the good, because just then I felt a quick bump of his muzzle—him testing the waters, so to speak—and I knew in less than a second his mouth would wander back with his horse lips scrunched up and teeth going for it.

I growled like a truly put-out demon and popped him with

my hand cupped against his shoulder—which makes a good loud clap—and we had no more of that nipping business. He sighed, fluttering his nostrils like his was a sad day, but we got through the shoeing with my rump and his manners intact.

A couple of boys who looked like they believed themselves to be cowboy-bred were holding up a fence, working on their loafing skills and watching me. Flies buzzed an out of tune, out of time symphony around a full wheelbarrow that wanted dumping, away from us. As I finished shoeing the gelding and was loading my tools, one of them came over and held down Ol' Blue's tailgate with one butt cheek, the better to ask me a question, I guess.

"How much do you charge for a straight shoeing, new shoes?"

When I told him, he frowned and went back to his buddies muttering that I charged as much as his regular shoer, Dixon Talbot, and maybe they'd check with the new guy.

New guy? What new guy, that's what I wanted to know. And was he any good or was he a Doc Quartercrack type of shoe slapper-onner? Some places, shoers can all get along and cover for each other and learn together a little bit, but that's not working out for me here. Oh, it could be worse, most of us don't steal clients or bad-mouth each other. I wondered if Dixon Talbot knew these clients of his were shopping shoers. We don't chat enough for me to let it slip anyways. It'd be nice if we got along better, but Talbot will hardly give me more than a growl.

The man himself drove in then, in his special-built shoeing rig. Drove in without giving me so much as a nod while the guy who'd asked me about my rates got a halter and lead rope off the rail and went into the barn. The other dude buddied up with Talbot. I was air to them. It should have made me put-out, but instead, I was studying on whether to call him Dixon or Mr. Talbot and it made me twist my ponytail, just chewing up the concern.

I'm a better shoer than old Talbot. He carved sole like he worked for the dogs. Even if he wasn't actually on the dogs' payroll, he left an awful lot of hoof as scraps in the dirt. When will people respect me as a shoer in these parts? When toadies like Talbot drop dead? Sometimes, it's a battle. And I know, I mean, I just bet I get judged on Ol' Blue and my wooden, homemade anvil stand and battered toolbox that doesn't have wheels and my canvas covers that I awl-stitched where fancy shoers have store-bought leather protectors for their rasps. I sighed over my lot as I fixed to head home, but gave myself a talking-to right away, because, all told, things are fine. No pity parties, that's my coming-adult rule. No circling the drain, hanging on to old hurts.

A little question was tickling though and I did a slow saunter to get my check. Stood there at one horse's stall door and made nice, chatted with some kid like a social critter about the weather and riding and her horse, mostly her horse. When I judged enough time had passed, when I could hear that Talbot had cut the clinches off and was pounding steel on a new shoe, I moseyed my sweet self back out to my truck and looked things over good and careful, studied the way he had his work laid out.

This was something I'd had opportunity to observe before, but I'd never bothered to note. Careful study was something that would tell me whether the shoe that Melinda Kellan came to see had been nailed on by Talbot. Not knowing was an itch what needed scratching.

Nope. Talbot shod one foot at a time, like me. The cowboy's horse stood with three old shoes and a bare front left while the new shoe being made was shaped.

So, Dixon Talbot didn't need to mark the outside branches of horseshoes as he made them. I needed to stop a minute and think here. The aluminum horseshoe I found on the Buckeye was put on by another shoer—not me or Talbot—or by someone who did their own shoeing. Given the specialty of the shoe, it most likely came from a pro.

And Keith Langston didn't see Stan Yates as someone who would buy land on a handshake deal, whether or not Cameron Chevigny would have done such a thing.

And Hollis Nunn had a rodeo stock business with Cameron Chevigny that went bad, maybe just because of Dragoon being a worse than usual bull, but maybe there was more to it.

And Earl Delmont's sister had had an affair with Cameron Chevigny.

I know me enough to know I don't study well on even one question when I'm moving. I needed to stop. And another brain would be handy. These were ticklish, these questions. There was only one person I wanted to talk to about this stuff.

Chapter 11

"RAINY, THEY'RE MAKING ME GO. WHAT am I going to do?" Abby wasn't really asking, though she didn't know that herself. She was just calling to tell me how miserable she was with the idea of being shipped off to her mama, away from her home, her daddy, her horse, her friends and school. Her life. Our cell connection cut in and out as Ol' Blue and I motored down the ranch road that would connect to the main two-laner leading into Cowdry.

"Aw, Ab, I'm sorry." I pulled over and shut Ol' Blue off, because it's so hard to hear over the diesel and I'd lose the connection as soon as I followed the winding, dropping section of highway. Maybe there's too much metal ore in the butte walls, but something sure drops a cell connection on this road.

Nothing came back.

"Did I lose you?" I asked. "Abby? Where are you right now?"

The voice that bleated back seemed much younger than Abby's pre-teen. She sounded like a seven-year-old. "I don't want to go."

"I know. I'm sorry." I was bear hungry, headed for the Cascade for some tuck when my stupid cheapie cell had beeped. Now I muttered something useless over static, but heard Abby say, "The judge said I'm supposed to go and visit the school she's near in

Portland. She's going to try to make me stay for the entire school year, or at least 'til Christmas!"

What could I say?

This is one put-out little girl to aunty right now.

Come to find out her daddy had fought this thing for a while. Abby was supposed to go for the summer but made all kind of excuses. I'd had her at my side, shoeing at horse shows and rodeos on the weekends much of the summer. Now I wondered if going to her mama's for the summer might have meant the kid could stay where she wanted, with her daddy, for the coming school year. Instead, all summer Abby had washed dishes and countertops for Guy, along with tagging along on my shoeing rounds every chance she could. She'd followed her daddy's suggestion that she not worry about it, not bad mouth her mama at all. And the kid felt like all her good behavior bought her nothing.

"Where are you?" I asked again. I could tell from her breathing she was on the move. "Abby?"

She was gone. Should I keep Ol' Blue pulled over while trying to get Abby back? Gun it and head for her house? Call her daddy? I tried every option, ready to go mama bear.

Voice mail and empty roads are poor consolation prizes.

Thirty minutes later, I was closing in on the Cascade Kitchen again when I saw the girl walking on the road. Just past her, I pulled Ol' Blue onto the shoulder and watched her come up my passenger side. She was all the while wiping tears away.

"I hate everything right now." Abby started crying again. "What's going to happen to Liberty while I'm gone? How could my mother do this to me?"

That parent, that's a woman my Abby-girl doesn't know or want to know.

"Doodlebug?" I sometimes called her that to annoy her, but this time she looked at me with big eyes.

"What?"

"Maybe you could ask her about wind farming. I have a client, Donna Chevigny—"

"She has the Buckeye ranch."

"Right. And her neighbor is some kind of wind farmer and he's maybe buying some of her land. I think there might be big dollars in that kind of business. If you get a chance, would you see what you could find out from your mama about that field?"

She agreed with sniffles, wide-eyed for a few seconds that the answers might mean the world for someone else, then sorry for herself again.

Well, at least my Doodlebug would have something safe to talk to her mama about. We were a couple minutes in the Cascade parking lot before I could whisper, "If it comes to it, I'll watch over Liberty for you."

Abby ran for the ladies'. I followed.

Something about hugging a sad kid breaks me.

* * *

Soon enough, really needing my best friend, I was ogling something all squishy green. It was like looking at something that'd arrived from under Bean's tail. Who picked this color anyways?

"Well?" Guy was about begging me for words.

Spinach appetizers are something that just sound like a bad idea. Why *wilted* is a word that anyone thinks would go with any kind of food, well, that's pretty far beyond my understanding.

And Guy looked so proud, leaning his lanky frame against one of the long steel sinks of the Cascade Kitchen's actual kitchen, arms sprawled out sideways. A lot better sight, he was, than the green stuff inside flaky pastry in front of me.

Popping into the Cascade for my Intended to hand over something to snack on—my plan from over an hour ago—wasn't working out so swell. I'd left Abby after she locked herself in the last bathroom stall. She still hadn't come out of the ladies'.

"Is she upset about weaning Bean?" Guy already loves his future horse—that's the way we think about Abby Langston's mare's baby, the one Guy named Pinto Bean the night the baby was born. He pushed the saucer of spinach-thingies toward me.

"In a week's time," I told Guy, "she's to go to the city and stay with her alleged mother. More than Bean may be coming to our place before winter if Abby gets packed off to her mama's long term. We might take Liberty."

He looked toward the Cascade's powder rooms.

Then Guy tried to be up about things, pointing out how me being packed off to Texas to live with my daddy after mama'd taken me to California for a year, well, that turned out fine for me.

"Eventually!" I snorted. Guy knows things got way worse before they got better for me.

"But Abby's older than you were then."

I nodded. "She's twelve going on either six or twenty, depending on her mood that particular—"

"Hey you!" Guy's voice was too bright.

Abby rolled her eyes away from him, went to his big sink and slopped dishwater onto her sneakers as she scrubbed one of Guy's super huge pots. She wouldn't look at us, only grunted when I said hey. Her scowl looked permanently attached.

And Guy put on an expression a little bit like Abby's when I leaned back from the saucer of spinach starters and allowed as to how I'd been thinking of something more rib sticking.

"But you said you wanted a snack."

"I meant a, you know, meal-type snack."

He spoke like he wasn't inhaling enough air. "A burger."

I looked right up. "Yeah, you bet," and went to my stool at the lunch counter.

It occurred to me that the last time I was at the Cascade getting fed was when those gals, Melinda Kellan and Loretta Pritchard, were behind me, one wanting me to report in, the other warning me to watch out at the Buckeye. So maybe I went to the Buckeye with the wrong attitude. Maybe I was too suspicious, thinking about things Donna told me, trying to latch onto the thing that didn't fit. My mind replayed all that had happened in two days' work at the Buckeye, everything, and one little notion tried to wiggle up like a puppy wanting attention that first morning. My brain couldn't grasp it though, as I itched about the end of my second day, Donna's sudden, hot-iron hatred.

And then she goes accusing me of something I hadn't done.

Yeah, she'd apologized, but don't guilty people sometimes accuse others?

I knew I hadn't done anything wrong. Donna shouldn't ought to have given me the stink eye, should never have suspected me of having been on her patch. I'd never known Cameron Chevigny. He died before I came to Oregon, or at least before I came to Cowdry.

Guy brought me some French fries, crispy-edged, fat, sizzling, and wanting more salt. "Well?"

That's when I knew what I had to do. I thought back to day one, finding stuff at the ranch, or her dang dog finding stuff just beyond the Buckeye. "That horseshoe."

Guy was on with both barrels. "The weird one you've got in the truck door pocket? That you showed Melinda outside of the Country Store?"

"I watched Dixon Talbot shoe. He does one hoof at a time, like me. I'm going to cozy up to Mac."

Guy gave me a look that is probably worn mostly by the institutionalized. Or Labradors. Kind of the I-Like-You-but-I-Don't-Understand-a-Thing-About-You look.

I took a cranium-clearing couple of breaths and explained.

"Dixon Talbot and me and one other dude are the main full-timers right here in Cowdry. There's supposed to be some new guy, and a few fellows from Gris Loup have a few clients who ride over here. And I could never check around with all the part-timers or folks who do their own, but Mac, over on the east side, does a pretty wide area. And you can figure how a horse could have been ridden onto that lease land from the national forest on the Gris Loup side, not the Cowdry side. There's a trail head not too far from the Country Store."

"I know it. That's where Biff and I park when we run the Keeper Lake trails."

"So maybe that aluminum shoe's from one of Mac's clients."

Still, Guy had the look of a dog that wants the stick thrown.

"The tarts," he said, and set the saucer of spinach thingies in front of me again.

"Huh? Look, if I watch him for a minute, I'll know if Mac marks his outside branches. Really, that's all I need to know."

And then we both said, "You're making me crazy," and stared at each other.

This saying-the-same-thing-to-each-other has been happening more and more and it kind of spooks me. Not the way a hot-blooded horse spooks, more the good solid, Quarter Horse version of spooking. Like Red. The way Red spooks is a good cold-blooded type of being scared. A quail can blow out from under some bushes in the startling way that sends a lot of ponies to pieces, wild-eyed in fear of a monster. Red, he'll just turn a casual head over, like he's slowly thinking, *huh, a monster*. Then, with any luck, he'll notice grass growing under his feet and he'll opt for chowing down instead of sprinting a quarter mile. Guy and I have talked about that kind of thing lately—horse behavior—since this little horse-to-be of his is an Arab-Quarter and is likely to be hotter than Red. A few years down the road, Guy'll be sitting more than his share of spooks. Until then, he can practice with his Intended, me, because he was still staring wide-eyed at my face.

"What?" I demanded.

"Well, see, I have no idea what you're talking about. All I wondered was if you liked the spinach tarts. What do you think of them as a starter?"

I grabbed the bridge of my nose because it's a break from twisting my ponytail and easier on my hair in general.

Not a *starter*. An *appetizer*. It's *an appetizer, it's an appetizer*, my brain hollered.

But not Rainy, not me. No. I was calm, took a bite, then lied like a dog. "Good appetizer. Interesting."

That seemed to please him, so clearly, worth all my good effort. But man, a lifetime of this will wear me out, I can see it coming.

Bless the boy, Guy did a little work. "Well, what were you talking about?"

So I explained to him about the habit some shoers have of marking the outside branches of the shoes as they're made, so the two fronts can be distinguished easily from each other and the two hinds can be distinguished at a glance.

Then I wondered if he forgot I'd found the shoe while working out on the Buckeye. So I added, "It didn't belong on the Buckeye."

"You just said you found it on the Buckeye."

Details like a double-aught, aluminum, slight squiggle in the shape, well that's all wasted on Guy, but I spent these specifics just 'cause I had 'em to spend. It was like Monopoly money, can't keep it, so might as well shell it out, bits of knowing like the peculiarities of the shoe. And Guy was trying to grab onto it all, gotta love him for it. By now, he can tell my hammers apart and identify all the other tools in my box, too.

With real proper thought, he furrowed up his skull over the horseshoe in the Buckeye's lease land and puzzled with me on the whys and whens of that shoe lying there. "Suppose the gate's locked? How would someone have gotten there on a horse?" he asked.

"I don't think it's ever locked. But maybe that horse wasn't ridden through Buckeye land anyways. Maybe it came across the federal lease land in the first place, from the other side, without riding through the ranch proper." My suggestion deserved some consideration, even though I'd given it none.

"And if not, if someone rode through the Buckeye to the land beyond the shed you say has the gate, well, someone could have broken through a wire fence anywhere."

We nodded together on his figuring. Laying down a fence is just about as old a way to get through a wire fence as the fences themselves. That is, if the fences were invented in the morning, pulling staples and standing on the strands as a means of moving stock over a wire fence was figured out by afternoon.

I had stuff to figure out, to nail down, this afternoon myself. The day had time enough left for me to woozle with another shoer or the sheriff, but probably not both. I was ready to prioritize in favor of the shoer. Maybe later, after I'd chased Mac down, I could get with the law then.

Guy brought me a burger with thick sliced onion and pickles on the side. "What's bugging you, Rainy?"

I dug in, shaking my head, liking that he had a sense of something scratching at me even though I couldn't name it. I could name plenty of things and did. Our wedding. Abby Langston's situation. Donna, and stuff at the Buckeye. But there was more. "I can't place it."

"Think we're going to have to testify?"

We. Sure, it'd be a *we*. And the boy doesn't evidence my trepidation at the prospect. He's steady and sure, as ready for the never-tried as he was the night he went into that battle with me. The night he asked me to marry him. Took me a week before I said yes. Couplehood is a notion that could take me. I'm still growing into it. Nowadays, I'm forever giving other couples a study and deciding how to go about this business of hitching up with Guy for the duration. I think each has to have a future to offer up. Someday, Guy would break from the Cascade, have some other eatery iron in the fire. He'd almost pulled it off once already but the deal hadn't yet panned out. I'll be fixing horse feet as long as I can, and I'll only get better at it. Maybe Guy and me won't be taking up space in the future's history books on shoeing and cooking but we'll have our crack at the trades.

And maybe someday soon, we'd pick a day and—no, let's think about one thing at a time, not consider a whole pie when a slice will do.

Going back to the comparison of couples of the world, I thought about the he-man wearing the reserve deputy uniform and his better half.

Turning on my twirly stool, I couldn't help but think that finding out who made that horseshoe would tell me who lost it. Anyone riding on the back of the Buckeye had to access the land either from the ranch itself, the federal land bordering the north and east sides, or from Stan Yates's property. I was going to check with every shoer until I placed that squiggly little aluminum horseshoe. Because Dixon Talbot is sticky enough with me that he likely wouldn't have given me a straight answer, I'd had to watch him work to know he didn't mark shoe branches as he worked. How many would I have to watch? I tried to think of east side shoers nearer to Gris Loup that I should check out.

Another thing bugged me—badly. Why did Cameron Chevigny roll his tractor, for crying out loud? Hadn't he driven that hogback a gajillion times? Didn't he know how to do it safe, up the long finger? Wasn't it daylight? It almost didn't make sense, him dying by rolling a tractor.

Then I remembered those relics on the shelf in the Buckeye barn—broken tools, a rusty old spur, a busted coffee mug, the pistol-sized shell casing. And I remembered Donna sliding the shotgun in the scabbard, saying it was the only artillery she and her husband ever had. If they had a pistol shell casing, then they had a pistol. Had Donna lied to me? Either that or someone else fired a pistol on her ranch.

Chapter 12

LYING'S GOT NO PLACE IN MY life. I'm a truth teller and truth's all I want to be told.

It was time to get some answers. There were a couple of shoers at the east end of Butte County, one name of MacGillary, another called Browne, who were going to get a visit. I don't get over that way much and they know I work hard on the west side, so we're not stepping on each other's toes any and we have a nodding kind of acquaintance.

MacGillary's always called Mac. I don't know if his parents didn't bother blessing him with a given name or if he didn't have parents or what. He doesn't work the same way I do or I don't do things just like him, but we do get to the same place when we're done. Plus, Mac would probably know if there was a new horse-shoer on the east side of the county.

Doc Quartercrack he's not. Mac's more than good enough, from what I've seen of his work, that is, his clients' horses' feet that I've gandered at a rodeo or two. But I hadn't ever watched him work enough to know what I wanted to know. I had to go to Gris Loup and jaw with the sheriff anyways. I know we've worked on each other's clients' horses when circumstances warrant it. Last rodeo I was at, I helped an owner who'd torn off a front shoe in the team roping in time for him to rope another round in the finals, and that was a Mac client. I've got a couple clients that ride with that Outfitters group, that go teepee and RV camping every equinox and solstice. Mac helped them out when they lost a shoe coming in from one of the big trail rides they do over on the east side.

At a recent rodeo, a client of Mac's had pulled off a shoe and couldn't find the missing shoe, sad to say. The fairgrounds are littered with them, no doubt. A thrown shoe is find-able after a show but right then when it's needed, they can be precious to spot. I'd made a new one for that owner and got a giggle out of the notion that one of Mac's horses was wearing my steel. It'd give me reason enough to rib him, a way to start a conversation without being too weird about what I really wanted.

Putting off the other errand for later, I found Mac working at a Gris Loup barn that's mostly the property owner's horses, though it's got a few stalls rented out. Hadn't taken much time at all to track him down there and now I sauntered up like it was all happenstance, watching him work on the dirt in front of wide barn doors. A black grade horse stood at a hitching rail, no owner in sight. Mac's forge was blowing good and his anvil strikes rang out.

He's one of those who doesn't cut his clinches when he goes to pull old shoes, which always makes me flinch when I see it, but that's just his way. Guess most of his clients squeeze all the metal they can off a set of shoes, have the very old fashioned, penny-pinching twelve-week schedule and those clinches are pretty scarce by that time. Anyways, Mac does that and a couple other weird things, like he pares the sole with one jaw of his nippers.

Old timey shoers like Mac do everything at once though, pull all four old shoes, trim all four feet, shape all four new shoes.

He gave me a nod and my name, "Rainy," then bent back under the horse.

That was supposed to be understood as "good morning."

"Morning," I said. That was our general howdy and then we did the usual ribbing, but his mind was where it ought to've been, at his anvil, banging a toe flatter. I did some waiting.

After a bit more time than good manners called for, Mac said, "Something I can do you for?"

"I was gonna ask if you remember this shoe." I pulled the funky aluminum horseshoe from my hip pocket. I'd knocked dirt off with my clinch cutter and taken the nails out after I studied their skew to understand from which way the horse had mis-stepped to pull it off. I hadn't straightened the twist from the shoe either. That twist and the nails' skew had told me the shoe was ripped from the outside.

Most horses yank off a front shoe by stepping on it with their hind toes, and sometimes when they run a hind leg between both fronts they step on the inside heel of a front shoe. A horse whose foot is fit full, or a klutz, or a tired animal does this a whole lot more often than a close fit horse whose feet are cared for more regular. Horses with enough experience to have some sense about where they step and horses that aren't ridden past the point of hard work keep their shoes better, too.

Casual-like, I showed Mac the shoe I'd picked up on the hog-back at the back of the Buckeye ranch.

He pursed his lips and looked up at the clouds like he was considering smooching the sky. The recollection came to him soon enough for shoer time, and he gave it a nod. "I got some clients with a couple of Pasos use these," he said, taking the shoe from me and considering it. He cockeyed the shoe and cast me a sideways look. "Oh, yeah. Has to be."

My grin let him know I'd noticed the slightly squirrelly shape. It was like the horse it was made for had a slightly deformed foot.

"Got a little low ringbone," he muttered.

I nodded. Nothing like a Paso for getting low ringbone. That trappy gait—nice from the saddle I hear, though I've never ridden a Paso—sure can't be the easiest way for a horse's joints to land. The ringbone explained wanting a lighter shoe, thus the aluminum.

For show purposes, Pasos have to have a light shoe anyways but a horse with ossifications would be more comfy in a light shoe.

Pasos move in a pretty inspired manner. They don't need weight to make their feet fly. Trail riders would like a light shoe too and aluminum could fit the bill except it doesn't wear well on rocks, so the average backcountry rider doesn't use aluminum.

"Shoe's seen some wear," I said. The breakover was well worn at the toe.

"Loretta gets the miles in," Mac said. "Not sure how much Vince gets around."

It jostled me, but I tried to act like a real unjostled kind of person. "Yeah? Loretta from the saddle shop? Um, Pritchley, or something like that?"

He nodded. "That's the one. Goes out on those rides with that group that plays mountain man, you know, the Outfitters group?"

"Um . . ." I was stuck on Mac's mention of how much Vince gets around, but my mind was getting none too far.

"Them people that have those gatherings a couple of times a year. Play cowboy and Indian. Have those big trail rides."

"Right." I nodded.

Mac shrugged. "I think there's more people on this side of the county into it. Darby over at that service station in Cowdry's the only one I can think of on your end that does the Outfitters."

"You're pretty sure this shoe's off that Paso?"

"Yeah, looks like."

"She covers a bit of ground, does she?"

Chuckled, he did. "She rides like she stole the horse."

Using an old rasp, he put a little bevel on the shoe he was working, then popped the shoe out of his vise and checked its width against a mark he'd made on his anvil. This left him back under the horse for nailing, finished with his anvil and vise. Nailing's a time for peace and quiet, so I stood still and studied on his kit while he worked.

Mac had one of those foot pedal-operated vises, so it was easy for him to pop the shoe out, bang a couple times back on the anvil—a monster huge anvil, I noticed—then pop it in the vise again and grind a bit more.

Someday, I'd have one of those vises.

The shoeing absorbed me like a dry sponge and a little spilled milk. Everything about it soaks me up. I noted the way Mac made every hammer swing count.

"Good catching up with you," I said, by way of parting.

But he wasn't done with me. "Are you a professional, Rainy?"

Not liking that Mac asked this in a tone that said I wasn't, I told him right away that I was, I am.

Well, I am. My kit looks better all the time and so do my clients. I'm consistent and I follow the rules, wrote up a price list and another paper with my terms and conditions for all my clients. I'm on time, which is more than can be said for half the shoers in the world, and I've got these business cards Guy makes for me.

Mac gave me an eyeball then banged his rounding hammer on a shoe branch, ringing it like a bell against the anvil. "You've been around a little bit now. Do you put in to the Injured Farriers Fund?"

After a while, I slammed my flapping jaw back up into the closed position.

Spare cash isn't something I have, not now, certainly not any other year I've been out on my own.

"I'll do it when I can," I said.

He nodded. "Good girl."

What am I, a puppy?

* * *

More anxious than I'd like to admit, I phoned Donna before I drove away from the better cell connections Gris Loup offers.

"It's Rainy." I spoke almost on top of her hello. The little plastic phone got sweat slick in my grip.

One or two quiet beats passed then Donna said, "I still feel like I owe you an apology."

"You've apologized."

"You're just a young thing."

I probably wasn't all that much younger than Arielle Blake, who clearly was into being with a guy who looked aged enough to be out to pasture. Now I felt I had to say again, "I'd never even met your husband."

Six or seven brain cells whirred with how to slip in something like, *hey, as long as we're accusing each other of stuff . . .* In my mind's eye, I could see the shell casing on the shelf in the Buckeye barn.

"It's maybe the worst thing about being cheated on," Donna said now, "that you lose your trust."

"Ma'am?"

"Rainy, I'm a straight shooter, as honest as your dog. I realize you give and expect integrity too. And I'm just so sorry I doubted you."

Charley is a pretty solid yardstick by which to measure a thing as grand as honesty. I try to measure up to him myself. A hard flush crept across my face. I had no business doubting Donna. If she said the shotgun was her only gun, then she didn't have any others. That simple. Relics on her barn shelf were just found objects. Stuff shows up on rangeland, like that squiggly aluminum horseshoe. Inspiration showed up—about dang time. "I'd like to help you, Donna, with that flat tractor tire. I could ride out there with a bunch of cans of fix-a-flat and pump it up. Will the tractor start?"

She chuckled. "The tire's got to be pulled off, hauled in and repaired or changed out at a tire shop."

"Why's that?"

"The tire's not just flat, it's punctured. I saw the puncture when I was up close, the day you shod the second half of my string."

Fixing a puncture sure enough meant the tire would have to be hauled in. The notion of fetching a humongous tire on a heavy rim made me finally realize how odd it was for the Chevignys to have had a tractor north of a ravine that a tractor could not cross.

"How on earth did you ever drive the tractor out there?"

"Years and years ago, we brought it in through Stan Yates's land, but he don't allow access no more."

"That's too bad." I wondered what it would take for Yates to reconsider. It would be a heck of a long tractor drive to bring her tractor through the federal land to the Country Store or some trailhead and then load it on a flat bed. The tractor driver would have to haul fuel as well.

A whole new idea on how to fix Donna's tractor tire started to hatch. Someone with a hauler was going to owe me a favor. I got on my CB and tried for the local loggers who hang on channel fourteen. Someone called Duke said the Delmonts had finished up and headed for home a couple hours back. I could put off my other east end errand, I decided. The Kid, with his Sweeney shoulder, and Donna's tractor were much more eager things to nail down than any notion of having to testify. I might not yet be so late in checking in with the sheriff that I'd be in actual trouble about it anyways. I left Gris Loup in my rear view and went back to my side of the county.

At the Delmonts' spread, approaching Earl with my Brilliant Idea turned out to be a whole lot easier than I'd reckoned. Maybe sometimes I build things up in my mind so's they seem a bigger deal in the meal making than in the actual eating. So to speak.

This plan I'd hatched, well, it was as full of holes as my last client's horse's last foot. I didn't know if the Delmonts' work-a-day Belgian, Buster, was broke to ride or just how fit he was or how spook-proof or cattle shy or if the Delmonts would go for the favor anyways. Maybe he harbored some ill will toward the Chevignys on account of his sister and all.

I tried to hint. It's not my big skill. Give me something to shoe, some lameness to find and fix. "What do you think about helping me with doing the widow Chevigny a favor? I mean, yeah maybe there was some partnering around before, I mean . . ." I didn't quite know what I meant, other than I thought that if he was pinchy over Cameron Chevigny womanizing his sister, he should realize it was none of Donna's doing and we could all lend her a hand if she'd stand for it.

Anyways, Earl said he'd loan me someone reliable to use a half-day at the Buckeye, said his big Belgian Buster would fit the bill. His wife nodded the notion up one side and down the other, some bit satisfied.

And halfway through thrashing it out, Earl had a brilliant addition to my brain squall, just to keep things good and complicated. But his quick agreement to handing The Kid over to Guy's pasture—a lame Clydesdale half-breed could be a good enough uncle, help Red oversee Pinto Bean's weaning—let me know that the Delmonts truly loved that horse.

That's how it came to pass that Guy and me got us a half-Clydesdale and a favor thrown in to boot. Earl felt he owed me, wanted to do something for me when I offered to give his shoulder-lame horse a home for six or twelve months.

"He handles fine," Becky added. It was like she was making some sort of peace offering to Donna Chevigny by extending the Delmont resources to the Buckeye, even if it was done through me. Women like Mrs. Earl Delmont, I don't have them figured, but I know this: they are much, much smarter than most folks realize. Becky Delmont's smarts made me smile and want to be her friend. I need friends.

She offered me a tea, the glass beaded with condensation. I took it with both hands.

Earl distracted me now with his improvement on my scheme. "So you want to ride my Buster to the back of the Buckeye and have him haul in a punctured tractor tire?"

Nodding, I allowed that was my best plan and I downed the sweet tea in three mega swallows.

Earl rubbed his overall's chest straps with both hands, like it warmed up his brain instead of his palms. "I might know someone who's hauling over there with an empty trailer, a super heavy one. He could take Buster."

The Missus beamed, having read her man's mind. She was liking this big exchange, too.

"Who's that?" I asked.

"Hollis Nunn. Just baled another cutting for her, gonna go pick up a few tons, carry them in to the co-op."

I nodded. The hayman, Hollis Nunn, who'd partnered with Cameron Chevigny on a rodeo stock business that never got farther after Dragoon showed himself to be a killer bull.

"It's kind of you all to help out Mrs. Chevigny in this way," I told the Delmonts, itching to know a little something.

"Between you, me, and the fence post," Becky said, "if Donna helped him to his death, she wasn't doing the devil a favor. That man got what he deserved."

I stared at her but she wasn't quite looking at me, just shaking her head in disgust at a dead guy. She fair spat out the words as she continued. "Running around on her like he did."

I edged away a step or two, so as to keep the heebie-jeebies from getting me. I swallowed it all down and turned back to the Mister. And The Kid.

There was still Donna to run my Master Plan by, but we had a nodding acquaintance with the idea already, so I figured it would fly with her. She had her hay cutting deal to work out with the Nunn Finer Hay operation, she'd probably work this tractor-fixing deal out with me.

An image of one thing I needed popped out. It's a strap hanging in the carport with Guy's backpacking stuff. I could see it there, dusty, a spider web on one loop of the blue nylon. He used it for tying stuff onto his backpack, like his sleeping bag or some such. Both ends have those quick-snap buckles on them and it's probably a good ten feet long. It would be perfect for the job I had in mind if I could remember to bring it along.

I wanted to clear it all with Donna Chevigny. I called Guy, happy to hear his voice, and told him my master plan. He said he loved me.

* * *

My last horse of the day was a jumper who got eight nailed and reshod every five weeks at that. And twice in the last cycle, he'd pulled his left front. A sieve for a foot, that's what he had. I had to be awful careful nailing him. He smelled like fly spray and his coat was slick with conditioner. I kept my mind off the stew that boiled in the back of my skull but as soon as I was loading up my tools, a booger of a thought presented itself for my consideration.

All this effort was to get the tractor tire fixed and it wasn't until then, trucking home in Ol' Blue that the whole point of my plan gave me pause. The actual reasoning, the problem all my solutions were aiming to fix. That tire and what Donna'd seen wrong with it.

That tire had a hole in it, which kept the tractor setting in the sun and storms for a year and a half.

One hole, a puncture, in one of the back tires.

A puncture hole.

A puncture.

What if someone had loosed that bull, Dragoon, on Cameron Chevigny and it had charged the tractor, punctured the tire, rolled the tractor, pinning the man for a slow crushing death . . .

But I reckon no one could have done that but the dead man's wife.

Chapter 13

WAY-TOO MUCH, THAT'S WHAT MELINDA KELLAN knew about my business.

Early that evening, she made herself handy when I stopped at the 24-Fuel to buy diesel. That Melinda digs at me like a chigger. I scratched my arm, tugged on my ponytail and had to pocket my hands to keep them off the bridge of my nose. It didn't help that I was already bugged beyond belief. I'd called in on the Langstons and heard words—"she's gone shopping"—that I've never before heard about little Abby.

The kiddo was gearing up for time with her surprise mama, okay, but did she have to act like a girl and go shopping? I had a lot of loafing planned for my evening and thought I'd hang with her, cheer her up, and give her a chance to talk. Sure, I had chores and such I should have been doing, but I wasn't in a good mood about Abby's situation or Donna's and I was edgy about the humongous chore I'd lined up with one of the Delmonts' draft horses. Lazying would have been the cherry on my moping sundae but now I'd never get there. Melinda pulling in for gas in her little piece of crap compact car then shinnying up to me did exactly nothing to settle my mood.

"Heard you're going back out to the Buckeye ranch," Melinda started as she stuck the gasoline nozzle in her car's gullet.

"Heard that, did you?" I was in no mood for Chat. The greasy feel of my boot toes sliding on the concrete's old petroleum product spills highlighted the environmental mess. I twisted my hair into a stiff stick one way then the other, knowing I'd have to loaf double hard at my next chance to make up for missing out on this evening.

"Guy mentioned it," she nodded.

"Did he?" At this rate, he wouldn't be finding a happy fiancée when he hauled himself through the front door.

"I ate at the Cascade tonight and we got to talking."

That's just ducky, I thought, wondering plenty of stuff. Like, why she was talking to Guy in the first place and how mad at him I should be for his blabbing. If I beat him home, my Guy, that silly boy, might come home to his very own agitated female.

Diesel pumps slow, foams up. And Ol' Blue has a ginormous tank, so I was stuck there at the fuel island with Melinda Kellan. I rinsed my lungs out with a couple three breaths and faced her.

"Why's where I go so interesting to you?" I asked.

"Why?"

"Yeah, why?" And, I thought, quit acting like I'm asking a dumb question.

A real good question is what it was.

"A woman's dead," Melinda said. "She went missing—

"Why did Guy get sent to look for her around Keeper Lake?"

"That's confidential." Melinda raised her chin. "Some investigatory details are not released because they could compromise a case. Now think about it. Arielle Blake went missing maybe a week before Cameron Chevigny's tractor rolled. And he's dead. And I bet you yourself have some doubts about whether or not that rolled tractor was a real accident."

I wasn't going to admit that. "You don't exactly have a dog in this fight."

"And your dog would be?"

"Well, at least I have a shoeing client who's been getting, um, you know, besmirched and I work where it happened—" Then I had to trot across the pump islands to catch up to her. "Where you going?" It was a question I asked the back of her waving hands.

Halfway to the 24-Fuel's convenience store, Melinda turned and glared at me, hands on her hips. "Did you say besmirched?"

I considered on that. "Think so." Had to nod.

"Jesus."

Well, besmirched *is* a word or maybe two or whatever.

Then Melinda gave me a pure challenge. "You think Donna Chevigny had something to do with getting herself widowed?"

"Nope. I surely don't." But I didn't know why I'd settled on the position. I'd been guilty of suspecting Donna myself, but back me into a corner and my gut told me that Donna had nothing to do with ending her husband's life.

"And how do you think Arielle Blake died?"

A breath shook me. I took a few more, and got it. "Oh. Oh! The sheriff's detective thought something was hinky between Cameron Chevigny and Arielle Blake?"

Melinda's voice dropped to something unhearable to anyone five feet away from us, though no one was there. "Her cell phone records showed intimate texts between them. And—"

"Between Arielle Blake and Cameron Chevigny?"

She nodded, barely. "And where they found her body, in that shallow grave—"

"What?"

Melinda shook her head. "I shouldn't be saying this to you."

Things were making sense. I nodded. "So, the sheriff's detective knew Arielle Blake and Cameron Chevigny were having an affair. Are you wondering if Donna killed Arielle?"

"I question everything," Melinda said.

"When did your detective know about the affair? Not before Arielle went missing?"

"Nah." Melinda shook her head. "After she went missing, they searched her cell phone records. It's standard in a missing persons case. And he saw the texts between Arielle and Cameron. The detective had to have a sit down with Stan Yates and say, you know, 'Hey, your missing girlfriend was having an affair with your neighbor.' Had to break the guy's heart."

I wondered what that conversation had been like. But, what if, I mean, suppose . . ? I took a breath. "When the detective told Stan Yates that Arielle was having an affair with the neighbor, was that before or after Cameron Chevigny rolled the tractor?"

"Around the same time."

"Before or after? It matters."

She pursed her lips. "Because you think that tractor rolling wasn't an accident? Isn't there a hill there, where the tractor rolled?"

I moved on. "And wouldn't your detective have considered that Stan killed his girlfriend because she was cheating on him? And hey, then maybe Yates went out back and opened a gate that turned Dragoon loose?"

"Dragoon?"

"That's a big dangerous bull on the Buckeye ranch," I explained, thinking not for the first time that the sheriff's people ought to be a little handier with the ranching life if they're going to police horse people. "Yates could have loosed the bull onto Cameron Chevigny out of spite. 'Cause here's the thing, that tractor has a punctured tire. Believe me, that bull could puncture a tractor tire."

Melinda pulled her head back as she shook it. "Our detective believed Stan Yates was innocent, had nothing to do with Arielle Blake's disappearance. Maybe he's a great actor but he said Yates was shocked about the affair. Yates just wanted to find Arielle."

"But then Cameron Chevigny rolls his tractor before your detective could—"

"He suspended the case after Chevigny's death."

And then I really got it. "Oh!"

Melinda gave a knowing nod.

"He really thought Arielle Blake's disappearance was suspicious? She could have just walked away. I mean, turns out she didn't but—"

"Disappearances are always potentially suspicious. We just don't say that to the family or to the newspapers."

"So if the sheriff's department always thought that she might have been murdered then they looked at her boyfriend—"

"And everyone else in her love life."

"Huh." Probably not many other people knew what the sheriff's department knew. "Oh, wow. So your detective, the guy in the suit, he thought . . . Cameron killed Arielle Blake?"

Melinda Kellan gave one more bare nod, like she was admitting something secret.

Double wow, I thought, my little brain spinning back in time, picturing how things had gone in old Suit Fellow's office: missing woman, realize missing woman was having an affair with the neighbor, neighbor dies in ranch accident before you get to confront him with what he knows about missing woman. Game over.

Melinda frowned and nodded. "He had a motive to shut her up, so she wouldn't tell Donna Chevigny about the affair. But the most likely person to kill a woman—"

"Is her own man."

We leveled looks at each other, and both of us got to wonder whether the woman in front of us had had the bad sense at some point in the past to choose to be with a man who hurt her. I had, and I hoped Melinda Kellan hadn't.

She sniffed. "You think I want to be a records clerk and an evidence tech forever?"

"I wouldn't know about that." How am I supposed to know what she wants to be if and when she ever grows up? I turned on my boot heel and gave her my back to study as I went into the store.

Left in the pickle of following me—and now I intended to

make an occasion of things, do some shopping in the convenience store—Melinda got to go away and leave me alone.

* * *

Spooky was taking a constitutional, running a few laps inside our little house at the end of Vine Maple road. I wished the cat would spare the sprinting. Or he could go with Guy to the high school track, which is where the boy tends to run a few times a week, plus extra when we argue. And I was half ready to schedule an argument.

I had a fresh box of Milk Duds warming inside my shirt. They're good anyways but better gooey. One of the best uses for a mouthful of coffee is to finish melting a Milk Dud in the mouth, that's my view.

Getting hugged melts them, too. Guy came in the door minutes after me and wrapped his arms around me. "Would you quit eating that crap?" He said when he realized what I had in my pocket, sighing like he's the most put upon man in captivity. Somehow, he was melting my mood off. I couldn't help smiling and feeling better.

"Okey-doke, as long as there's some of those chocolate ravioli around."

My comment put Guy's bashful face on, the aw-golly look that means he knows he done good. So to speak. When he comes home, I get all distracted and happy without knowing why.

"In the fridge," Guy said. He followed me into the kitchen and was soon frowning at his computer. I saw that he'd opened the website he uses to map his runs. The monitor showed a big green map and a yellow, wiggly track of one of his trails.

The chocolate ravioli were in a little Tupperware-type thingy inside the door by a brick of butter, and I popped a few in my mouth. The cheese inside was stiff, not melty.

Chocolate ravioli are a lot better warm.

"I'm almost sure something got deleted," Guy said. "I seem to remember another user map here. If it wasn't Biff, then maybe he remembers the other map."

Guy's running maps didn't interest me near as much as hunting up more dessert.

He answered the ringing phone like it was tough patooty for me that his ravioli were chilly. What a bad man. He made me take the phone, too.

Hollis Nunn's grizzly bear voice came through the phone. "You hate to butt in and you hate to stand by."

"Yes, sir."

"You're going to bring in that tractor tire from the back of the Buckeye?"

I gave him my I-was-raised-right answer again.

Hollis praised my fortitude and my plan for how to haul the giant tire through the ravine. "You'll have trouble getting that big old tire anywheres once you get it back to the barn."

Too true. It'd never fit in Ol' Blue's bed on top of all my tools. If I could winch it high enough using the barn, I could maybe tie it on top of the truck topper but that'd take some doing and I hadn't yet studied on the idea. I was handling one thing at a time. First the tire and rim had to be brought in from the back range.

Hollis cleared his throat. "You're doing a good thing here, lending Mrs. Chevigny a hand with squaring her tractor away. I think well on you for it."

That needed a waiting spell, not a comment from me. Once I'd waited on the quiet line another half a minute, he went on. "I'll leave my flat bed at the Buckeye barn. Got room enough for one little old tire at the end, I reckon. I can take it to Darby's for her."

Darby had the tool and tire shop in town. This was going to work. I relaxed a bit. "Okey doke."

"Yeah, Earl Delmont gave me a call. I'll do the hauling. We'll see how quick the tire gets fixed. Earl might just leave the draft horse at her place so it can haul the tire back out there again."

When I got off the phone, I made a wonderful discovery in the freezer. Some very dark brown stuff in a plastic container.

"Hey, ice cream!"

Guy shook his head while I grabbed a spoon. "That's gelato."

No, according to my spoon-and-mouth test, I was correct. "Ice cream," I told him. "Where'd it come from?" It was really Serve a Term in Hades-type dark chocolate and that's all that needs to be said about how good it was. I finished my spoonful and returned to the freezer. This stuff was dangerous. Size five jeans are going to my personal history book if I don't watch it.

I scolded my fiancé and fixed a couple stink eyes on his face. "Hope you don't leave that kind of stuff in the freezer too often."

Eventually, he came around to the path of peace. "Sorry."

Even if he didn't mean it, well, at least he said it.

And even if I didn't remember why he had all these fancy desserts going on—there was a contest he was entering and he claimed to have already told me about it twice—at least I was there to help try them out.

Oh, the man could go awhile on the subject. "I was going to do a brandy bombe with the gelato, you know, a non-dairy alternative."

You know? No, I don't know. A bowl of snoose noodles with floor scrapings would suit me most days of the week, but I cowgirled up and asked, "What did you settle on?"

"Chocolate waffles. Rainy, have you ever looked at a map of the land between the Buckeye and Keeper Lake?"

"Mmm," I said, at a loss for smarter words. I mean, hey, chocolate waffles. Who wouldn't get her ears pricked up over such a sound? "Maybe I should try those."

Giving me a look that could wither a Texas live oak, Guy must have been thinking about sharing our lives with each other. Wanting to know more about what I was hatching, he said, "This sounds like quite a production with this horse thing and tractor. I didn't get that entirely before."

So I had to explain about the Buckeye not using four-wheelers.

It wasn't just that the ranching techniques were old stuff, though it's a safe bet Chevigny doesn't mark cattle with a paint ball gun, nor cotton to the new pesticide use reporting rules. Their daughter had been killed on an ATV. I told him how worn out and sorrowful Donna looked and lived, more on her plate than she could handle.

"That's sad." Guy frowned. "How'd the Chevignys get their tractor on the far side of their ravine in the first place?"

"They used to go in through their neighbor's property." And then I explained about the old problem between Stan Yates and Cameron Chevigny.

Not having a four-wheeler might be seen as another problem but then again, it was a do-able thing to ride from the Chevigny barn all the way to the ranch's back pastures while dragging a heavy tractor tire on a horse-pulled sled.

Finally, Guy had something to say about this whole big mess I was fixing to jump into. "I'm setting coffee out for you in the morning."

Coffee? No, I'd need something stronger, like Guy. The last time I nearly ended up in a coffin, Guy showed up and lent a big hand so I got to not die. But something strong was going to be under me in the morning, stronger than anything I'd ever had under my rumpus.

Chapter 14

RIDING A DRAFT HORSE IS AN experience.

At first, he's brawny and beautiful and a body thinks, well, he's just a big horse, right? So put a ladder against his ribs, shinny up, and then kick the ladder away once up there. Or just hop on, bionic woman style, like me.

Or not.

Buster's not eighteen hands high, but plenty high enough to give a Quarter Horse-and-Arab rider an altitude nosebleed. I clipped one end of Guy's strap around his right front leg and threw the length across his back. On his left side, reaching the reins and his withers by standing on my tippy toes, I put my left foot into the other end of the loop. Once I'd used the loop for a stirrup, gotten astride, I freed my left foot and then leaned down to my right to unclip the end that was around Buster's right elbow.

And he stood like a prince while I gathered the reins, wiggled around on him for a sec and took a gander of the world from Belgian height.

Donna looked a little confused about why Hollis Nunn had hauled the big horse to her place for me to use. "You're doing a favor for Earl Delmont?"

"Well, we're swapping favors," I explained. "He's got a horse with Sweeney. I'm going to take the youngster in, give The Kid a home to see if he can recover in time, so Earl's letting me get an afternoon's use out of Buster."

Donna paused a minute. "I don't understand."

I re-explained my Grand Plan. "This is Buster. Earl Delmont's loaning me Buster here, and he or Mr. Nunn will haul him back home to boot."

Turning in her haze, Donna muttered something—"Nunn" or "none" I couldn't say which—then we saw the man himself.

"Rainy," Hollis said, "you want a rock sled to use for dragging that tire in?"

"The ravine's pretty rough. I figured I'd make a travois out there."

"Taking the fast route through the ravine then?"

"Yessir."

Donna sighed and nodded and said something about getting at some fences that wanted fixing.

Then Buster and me struck out on what I thought would be well over an hour's ride of his lumbering gait each way. He wore a collar with a light body harness that included breeching, so I expected he'd be able to handle dragging that tire into and back out of the ravine fine. If need be, I could always hop down and just lead him.

Anyways, straddle that broad back and in about a hundred yards the leg muscles mutiny. And it's not just the harness rubbing through the jeans that worries the flesh. One or two gajillion thigh fibers scream that they're being stretched and jostled and they don't care for it and how much longer is this going on?

When "more than an hour" is the answer, it's not an answer those twanging bits of my body want to hear.

There's a place to take the mind when the muscles have had more than they can enjoy and I went there, looking at the earth that passed below me.

Even though this was my third ride out to the back of the

Buckeye, it was my first north ride in this much daylight, the first on a horse with a lollygagging gait, and the first time I wasn't fixing to do a day's work shoeing once I got to the back of the ranch. My mind went to the hauling project in front of me and Buster. I had baling twine and a tiny folding saw and enough rope to tie together a travois. There was supposed to be a tire iron and jack in the shed and some scrap lumber I could use for cribbing the tractor, since there wasn't a jack stand of any sort out there. The flat edge of Buster's light freighter harness—the one that was rubbing at my knees—was going to give my hands the power of his chest.

His haunches would push if he needed to really haul, but I didn't think the excursion was going to be too much of a challenge for this prime puller. His big feet crunched the dry dirt like he was a horse on a mission and he was perfectly happy to hack out across the multi-section ranchland. When we climbed out of the ravine, the loose range horses stared at us from afar. I watched the Federal lease land loom closer and closer and I wondered about the crime scene where Donna's silly dog had found Arielle Blake's hand. Buster and I drew in on to that unknown area like a camera close-up until we finally got to the shed.

There, I told my thighs to spread a little wider and I'd reward them by getting down off the sweet beast. The thighs said they were mighty happy time had come for me to drop myself to the ground and I made it easy as I could on them, transferring my weight to his collar as I swung down, using my arms to lower myself 'til my toes touched earth. Still, I held onto the harness as I straightened out my legs and got the feeling back. And holding that scarred leather, I wondered how many logs and wagons it had borne for the Delmont family and if they'd maybe bought it used.

There's often a good story in old leather.

To hear my freshman history teacher tell it, the horse collar is the piece of technology that brought about civilization in cold country. Without the collar, we'd all still be hunting and gathering in cold lands or farming within throwing distance of the equator.

I don't remember anything else from high school, not from the classes anyways.

I tied Buster inside the breezeway of the shed for shade, using the gate's edge post. Finding the jack and tire iron for the lug bolts was easy enough and the cribbing was right where Donna said it'd be. How I'd not noticed it when I was there before, I don't know. It was just one of those things that belonged in a shed, so I didn't see it, I guess.

Down the steep little slope at the tractor, I got to work, shaking my head about tricycle gear design. It's real clear the plans for these things were drawn up by none other than Lucifer.

Tricycle tractors, with centered little wheels up front, are awful tippy. They're a bad idea that was copied by those three-wheeler builders, back when they were popular, before four-wheelers got built. Before the Chevignys lost their daughter.

Laying a piece of scrap lumber well under the tractor and one parallel just inside the flat tire, I stacked two more pieces across the ends of the first and then added more cribbing. It took a bit of doing, but I built a place for the tractor to wait some more. When it was solid, I scooped the earth away from the lame tire and found it was jacked well enough.

Turns out that cribbing up the tractor's frame wasn't the hard part. I had to get temperamental with some of the bolts in order to free the tire, but I got the job done and went to scare up a couple saplings from the land behind the shed.

From that hilly ground, a couple long alder poles volunteered so I didn't have to dawdle. Even though Dragoon was supposed to be in the east fields now, my mind stuck on the last time I'd seen him, charging parallel to the lease land. I made it snappy, wanting to get off the lease land back to the safe side of the electric fence, the west field, and its derelict demon of a tractor.

I was especially mindful of the bull, being as the least speedy and least agile horse I'd ever had cause to sit on was all I'd be able to get under my butt. I'd debated whether to leave Buster tied at the shed and just traipse around for my poles on foot or to ride him out onto the lease land where the bull might be if he'd gone through the barbed wire. Buster would make an awful big target if Dragoon happened across the hills and decided to run at the horse.

Back with my two poles on the safety of the west pasture, I laid 'em down side by side and fast tied them together near one end. Lashing the tire, heavy because of the farm-weight steel rim, to this end of the travois took quite a while and had me panting as I worked to get it secured and balanced. Then I eased the free ends of the poles, one at a time, up and fastened them to Buster's harness. That good horse stood like a stone while I weighted him. Handy thing was, I could use his end of the pole as a stirrup now, and it would be a sight easier remounting. The satisfaction coursing through my veins was real, earned. Too bad no one else stepped up to help Donna with the tractor long ago. Too bad Stan Yates wouldn't allow her access to the west pasture back here that abutted his land.

Then I remembered that the feds didn't allow motorized vehicles in that land, just boots, hooves, and bicycles. Given that the tractor couldn't cross the ravine and Yates wouldn't allow Donna to bring it through his land, she had no legal way to get this tractor back to her barn. By buying this Buckeye land north of the ravine, Stan Yates could be getting himself a free tractor. The notion made me pause as I stepped my left foot onto the travois rail at Buster's side and mounted. Was I fixing Stan Yates's tractor?

Buster and I took our sweet time riding back. I wasn't going to hand over a used-up horse to Earl Delmont and there was still the thing about needing to use Buster again to return the tire once it had been repaired.

Wasted worry though, 'cause I needn't have sweated about how much horsepower was under me. Back at the barn, Buster wasn't tired a whit. He really could pull all day, just like the Delmonts said. He hauled the tire all the way to Hollis Nunn's flatbed and that's where I left it. I untacked Buster in the round pen and left

him with hay and water, the harness hung on the pen's outside halter hooks. I was set to leave when Donna came out of her house,
wiping her hands through her gray hair that was showing its end-
of-the-day loose look. Surely my ponytail was looking a little used
and messy, too.

"Thank you, Rainy. That was a huge chore. It's good to get
things taken care of."

"Yes, ma'am."

She wandered toward the round pen, having another conversation about how swell people were, how helpful and kind some people were to her. Left me with the taste that some folk let her know
their ugly thoughts and I was glad I wasn't one of those. And I was
glad Hollis Nunn was in her corner, too. This woman needed some
kindness sprinkled on top of her life. When Donna got a little, her
gratitude was plain. It still seemed like she felt bad about having
suspected me of dallying with her husband and maybe it seemed
like I was still trying to prove I hadn't done it.

Then she pulled out the very thing that had had her hating me
at the end of our second shoeing day. We both looked at it and the
quiet was more than I could take.

"It's a nice knife," I said.

"That's as may be," Donna said. "But I don't know whose it is."

I swallowed and said it, that thing that hung in the air. "Someone
named 'R' is what I'd guess."

She nodded and frowned.

I asked, "Do you know who was meant to have it?"

Donna shook her head and moved her misty gaze away. It was a
sorrowful look I'd seen slipping from her too much.

"You keep that knife, Rainy." Donna pushed the bone handle at
me, the sheathed blade held light-like in her palm.

With its heart shape, neatly tooled in above the letter R, it
really was a nice knife. And I could sure see her not wanting it, not
wanting it on her place. I knew, just knew, we were both thinking
about the rumors of her cheating dead husband.

I just tried not to think of the other rumor, the one about her having a hand in his death. No, I looked back and knew we were thinking about that Other Gender and their Ways.

"You're engaged," Donna said. A wry smile twisted her mouth. Guy blabs sometimes.

She looked at the knife in my hand. The leather scabbard was rough weathered and dry. The knife wanted a cleaning but it could be saved, just like the Buckeye.

And this knife I'd found had been left out on her ranch, maybe by her husband or some little hottie he'd been with. Donna's eyes looked wet and I felt mine getting there.

For sure and for certain, we were both thinking about his habit of unfaithfulness.

"Maybe that's what we get," Donna said, "for being the way we are."

I shook my head near off, hers was such a bad idea. We don't deserve it, getting treated like trash, none of us. Not Donna, not me, and actually, come to think of it, not Guy.

Pretty soon, I'd better start being nicer to my Guy. I'm finding out they don't grow 'em on trees, not like him they don't, not around these parts anyways.

Donna Chevigny was still stuck. "I mean, that's what we get for not having our center of gravity at our hearts, for loving something that doesn't keep his center there either."

With that, Donna went into her round pen to love on Buster, sliding her hand across from his shoulder, stopping her palm a few inches just above and behind the point of his elbow. We thanked each other again and I called it a day.

On the long drive down the forest road from the Buckeye, there's just the one driveway to pass. It's Stan Yates's place. I was staring at it so hard, thinking, it took me a minute to notice the guy under an apple tree out front, pruners hanging still at his side. In my rear view, I saw Stan Yates lean, duck forward and gawk at me. He threw down the pruners. It sort of seemed like there were things to clear up, but like I'd said to Melinda Kellan, I didn't have a dog in this fight.

Would have been a decent ending if the next thing that happened was the last. Earl Delmont brought The Kid out to Red's pasture. Soon, I'd take The Kid's shoes off and that would be it for him for many months.

After we had our howdy, I fed the horses on a tablecloth of maple leaves—to keep the hay off the dirt—and put generous flakes of hay on the leaves, more piles than horses so they could all eat in peace. I poured a handful of oats on each pile and stepped back. The Kid got busy lipping his oats, pleased and blowing. Red circled and nicker-grunted, the horse boy sound of new acquaintance. And I assured Earl that the oats were just a welcome thing, I'd not be feeding The Kid rich. The young draft was going to be a pasture ornament and we'd see if he fixed himself to something like a sound horse in half a year or even a year, if that's what it took. Earl watched it all.

"Wilted maple leaves are bad for horses," he said, looking at the hay piles I'd left on fresh pulled leaves that would wilt in a day.

We had few maples in Texas and Southern California. New girl needs to learn this area better. "I didn't know that. Thank you." I pulled the leaves and figured I needed to buy some stall mats to feed on if I didn't want the horses eating hay off the dirt.

Guy said the sheriff's department had called earlier and asked for me.

When I phoned back, they put me through to that soon to be retired Suit Fellow who wanted to talk to me about an ugly manslaughter case and he griped at me for not getting myself into his office to check in on the matter. I grumbled some apology about being busy with work and whatnot and he told me to find some balance and make time to come see him at exactly soon. I agreed, just glad to be off the phone with the po-lice.

The detective wasn't so bad really. At least his words left me thinking without dwelling on the testifying thing. I thought about him having decided Cameron Chevigny might have had something to do with Arielle Blake's passing. Judging by looks, she had a thing for older guys. But maybe she also had a thing for younger guys. Just because Cameron had an affair with her, that didn't make him her killer. Maybe she'd been with other guys, too. I felt bad for everybody in the mess and thought about Donna's notion of loving someone who's not on the straight and narrow. What was it she'd said? Something about us loving things that don't keep their center of gravity at their hearts. I thought of our love of the species that does better.

My mind could see Donna's hand stroking Buster's side.

That's where horses keep their hearts.

Even carrying a rider, right near their hearts is where horses keep their center of gravity, their balance.

Chapter 15

THAT WEEKEND, THE BUTTE COUNTY FAIRGROUNDS had a reining competition, or, as the locals call it, a slide-in. I was mindful as I set my anvil on its stand that it might be the last weekend Abby and I would work together.

For two days, I kept my forge and tools at the ready in case I got a little piece of business. I wouldn't ever want to contemplate what hourly wage was earned by standing there from just after sunrise until four in the afternoon for the half shoeing and two quick fixes I was asked to do. In the idle time, I heated old shoes, cut them in half and twisted the metal, shaping it into hoof picks.

"You ready to give this a try?" I asked Abby on day two. She'd quit regular store-bought picks the first time I gave her one made from an old horseshoe. And the first time she made one herself, she was excited to act big by giving it away to one of her little 4-H buddies. Homemade hoof picks do make great give-aways and absolutely every one of my clients has one by now. Even Sheriff Magoutsen.

Abby nodded and I made her wear goggles when she pounded on the hot steel. I liked telling her she'd done well when she fashioned a couple hoof picks all by herself. Those, I let her keep.

After the Sunday slide-in, as riders were loading their horses into trailers, Abby and I wandered past the food carts offering the steam and smoke of barbecued corn cobs and fry bread and cinnamon churros. At the far end of the parking lot lay craft booths. An older couple had houseplants in homemade clay pots for sale. Another gal had soaps and candles. A whole gaggle of women sat knitting or crocheting or something like that, with their scarves and dyed yarns for sale. A gal with flowing print skirts twisted copper wire into earrings and the like.

Abby held a butterfly-shaped wire pendant up to her neck.

The gal behind the display said, "Every piece is one of a kind."

I found myself staring at the weird-shaped rings, similar to the one I'd seen on Arielle Blake's thumb in the photo from the old flyer at the Country Store.

Abby gave me a smile a set the pendant back down. The smile I returned was fake, distracted. I bet Arielle bought the ring from the gal who ran this booth. Where had I put that flyer?

Deputy Paulden had told Guy and me that they were waiting on DNA results, that the ring was the way they identified the body. Was I the first person to wonder if maybe the body Slowpoke unearthed on the federal land in back of the Buckeye ranch wasn't Arielle Blake after all? And if it wasn't her, where was she, and who was the dead person who'd been wearing a ring like Arielle's?

* * *

Contemplating from the couch at home Monday morning, it took me some time to realize Guy and I had fallen asleep there the night before. I stretched, checking for a muscle that didn't twang from overuse, but couldn't find one.

"We've got to stop working so many hours," Guy said, rubbing his eyes. "I'm doing the lunch and dinner crowds tonight."

That probably meant he was thinking we could have a nice slow-style breakfast at home together. I purposely schedule my

Monday mornings light so there's room in my schedule for emergencies. But I shook my head and finger-combed my hair for a good working ponytail.

"I reckon it's high time for me to gird up my loins and get myself into town for a sit down with Sheriff Magoo and his Suit Fellow about this trial thing we got subpoenas for." Still, the very idea made me grim. If I had to go to court and testify, it was going to do a lot of bad things. It'd make me get a case of the heebie-jeebies with the gut-knots to boot and it stood all sorts of chances of leaving a bad taste between me and one of my clients. Back when, Magoutsen and his investigator, Suit Fellow, had promised to keep me up to speed on whether or not this thing that was hanging over my head was actually going to have to happen.

Now my Guy set one hand over mine. "Want me to go into town with you? The drive will be our only time together today."

That was all it took. Charley and Guy and me piled into Ol' Blue for a run into Cowdry's sheriff's office.

In the parking lot, I was of half a mind to leave the engine running—shutting on and off isn't what diesels were meant for—just to be for sure and for certain I was in and out like a half flash.

"You know," I said, "I'll just be a minute."

"Well, fine." Guy's forever writing up menu ideas and he was happy now, scribbling notes and drawing on a pad of paper with one hand while the other ruffled Charley's coat. But I was still muttering something from the back of my brain.

"I hope it's not her at the front counter."

"Hmm? Who?" Guy looked up, pen wavering mid-sketch.

"That um, Melinda Kellan, the clerk there who was at the counter that time." I looked at the steering wheel while he looked at me. Charley looked straight ahead through the windshield like he could wish up some sheep or cattle to gather.

"She's not your cup of tea?"

Shrugging, I said, "Got quite an attitude on her."

Guy howled, which caused me and Charley to look around for

coyotes. Finally, I about had to ask Guy to pick himself up off the truck floor and give a reason for his mirth.

"Oh, nothing," he said, wiping his eyes and working his mouth corners hard to wrench off a grin that didn't belong there.

Could there be a sillier man in all of Cowdry?

Well, apparently so.

The west end office of the Butte County Sheriff's Department is in a strip mall, and not too awful impressive as a place where state of the art policing might occur. I do like the big map in the little public area that shows all of the county, but didn't get a chance to study on it as Vince Pritchard swaggered up to the front counter.

"I'm here to see the sheriff or Suit Fellow about a testifying thing," I said.

Remembering my manners, I pulled out one of my homemade hoof picks and offered it to Pritchard, who was decked out today in his reserve police uniform, brown and badge-y.

"Suit Fellow?" Pritchard took the hoof pick, distracted.

These picks Abby and I'd made out of old horse shoes really are nice, great for getting the hoof's commissures a quick cleaning, easy in the hand with the gentle curve of half a shoe forming the backbone.

"Thanks." Pritchard tossed it in the air and grinned as he caught it. "That's mighty white of you."

I wanted to snatch my hoof pick back, and I kept up a good scowling while Pritchard said the detective wasn't in, got called out on something, and they didn't have a firm court date, but he'd left an appointment open for a conference meeting with the prosecutor. More, he said the case might *plead out*, which sounded like a good thing, and he handed me a Butte County Sheriff's Department pen, a black ballpoint with the name and logo in gold letters on the side, to write it all down.

"You can keep that," he said.

"Thanks. That's mighty beige of you."

Pritchard looked to be trying to fire up both brain cells, deciding if I was as big a jerk as him. I needed to move his mind in another direction.

"Hey," I said, "I was chewing the fat with Melinda about some things. And I've got to wondering about how well that body on the lease land was identified as Arielle Blake because I've seen rings similar to that thumb ring she's wearing in the flyer that her boyfriend put up around town and—"

"Melinda Kellan's been talking to you?" There went Vince Pritchard's meaty arms, first squared across his chest, then on his hips as he dipped his jaw down hard at me. "She's not a sworn officer, you know. I am. Reserve deputies are duly sworn. If you've got anything police-related to say about Arielle Blake or any other case, you can say it to me. Now."

"She was just, we were just talking, I guess." It was a weird place to be, feeling guarded about Melinda. And I bet Charley wouldn't have cottoned to Pritchard at all.

He gave the nod that said he knew all about everything, which maybe is a thing these reservist cops do. Then he snorted and rolled his eyes and I just knew we were still on the subject of the other deputy-wannabe.

"Little girl," he said, "lives with her parents." His scorn was burning.

I wondered if Magoutsen knew about the little tiff between his assorted wannabees, the reserve and the almost-a-reserve.

Probably. The sheriff didn't miss much. At a team roping benefit put on by the 4-H a couple months ago, the two cowboys just ahead of Magoutsen had riled all the waiting steers by shouting and swinging their ropes and spinning their horses. Magoutsen's roping horse is one of the better heelers in the area and took it all in, blowing his disagreement at the roughnecks. I think only the sheriff and I noticed the little drama. He doesn't know that I watched him raise one hand to take a few minute's pause, while he stroked his gelding's strong brown neck with the other. Then he turned around with a quiet nod to indicate the gate-keeper should release the next steer. His header was hot, got the steer roped and turned. They'd barely cleared the chute when the sheriff snagged its heels and they won the pot. Then he donated the cash to the 4-H kids on the spot.

Guy doesn't miss much either. When I'd told him what I witnessed at the roping, he'd called the rough cowboys' behavior passive-aggressive. I just thought it was aggressive. But Guy also notices stuff that might not want to be noticed. Like me, now, lost in thought. Wanted to know all about my trip in to the sheriff's office, Guy did, but I was curt as I drove us home.

"And?" he asked, as I pulled Ol' Blue onto the highway. "Who was at the counter?"

"Not her," I said, my mouth twisting. "Had that going for me at least."

"Well, why? What's your heartburn with her?"

"She's a little bit of a witch."

Guy knows that that's how I pronounce the word 'witch' without the B in the beginning since my language makeover. It's pretty tough talk for me. And he knows better than to give me a little ol' lecture about my opinion even when we both know I'm being crusty. Instead, he just looked at me out the corners of his eyeballs, his lips rolled in like he was suppressing all kinds of words. It didn't soften me much but I did allow, "Anyways, that reserve guy, Pritchard, he was there."

Guy shook his head. "I don't know him."

I shrugged. "Lives in Gris Loup. Runs the saddle shop with his wife. I think he's going to be the next full-time deputy they hire. Maybe the Pritchards would move to Cowdry. Loretta had mentioned going riding with me. And she's got a good trailer."

"Well, fine. So, you saw him on your way to see the detective and you got the court date and the case might not even go to trial?"

I frowned and gave half a nod. "I didn't get any of that dealt with, but he's a jerk."

"Who?"

"That guy. Pritchard. He's a real piece of work."

"For crying out loud, Rainy, are you mad at everybody?"

That needed less than a few seconds' thought but I gave it miles before I kissed my dog and gave Guy an honest answer. "No, Charley's okay."

Guy rolled his lips in and this time let out a sigh like a tire losing air fast. All over that, I shut the truck off at home and asked, "What are you so grumpy about?"

"Me? Nothing. I'm pleased as punch."

Which is a comment that makes me think of the time I poured a bunch of Jell-O in the punch bowl at the PTA meeting, the only time mama and daddy both went. I'd been itching to see what would happen to the meeting when their drinking bowl congealed but my hopes were crushed, crushed, I say, when mama and daddy got into a spat about me and we got asked to leave early so I never did know for sure what happens to peoples' punch with four boxes of Jell-O poured in, but I bet they weren't too pleased.

And I was none too pleased with the sheriff's apparent replacement prospect of new deputy when he promoted one of his old ones up to be the investigator after Suit Fellow's retirement. Vince Pritchard was so puffed up and edgy, I thought. Why? It bugged me.

"Pritchard was like . . ." Even back on Vine Maple road, where I do my best thinking, it was hard to put a finger on the problem.

"Like what?" Guy asked.

"Like he'd been chained to the wrong end of a huge hog."

After I shut Ol' Blue off in front of the house, I reached for the glove box for my new, old knife and reminded myself to fetch my honing stone from my shoeing tool box in Ol' Blue's bed so I could give the knife a good cleaning.

Guy gawked when I showed it to him.

Heart R.

Well.

Well, it was a decent knife and Donna didn't need or want it on her place. "Donna Chevigny gave it to me."

Guy looked at it none too close, just glanced and grimaced at me. "She gave this to you?"

Nodding as we headed inside, I took the knife back from him, palming that bone handle that would have been so smooth, was so smooth, except for the heart and the R carved into the upper reach.

Guy had some bug up his backside, it seemed. He turned this way and that, then made some more faces before gesturing with both hands. "You said she seemed pretty much, kind of . . . oh, what did you say?"

"Worn out."

"Right. Sad. Like she was depressed."

"Well, sure, who wouldn't be? She's struggling to make ends meet, she's got more work than she can say grace over, she's alone and widowed and—"

"And she's giving away property," Guy said. "This knife."

Now Guy, hands on my shoulders, gave me a little shake, then slid his hands down my arms, squeezing me just above my elbows. He cocked his head and leaned in, then back as he muttered. "She was crying, I thought, the other day when she called."

Swallowing, I waited for him to come clear.

He didn't, he stood in our little dining area and festered.

"*Guy.*" It means so much when I say his name as a one-word sentence, with my eyebrows just so. It means: Make Yourself Clear If You're Able. Plenty of days, it works like a dream on Guy, but today he just fidgeted, looking concerned and uncomfortable.

"Can't you tell me what it is that's on your mind?" I asked.

"Well, fine. What I'm wondering about is if Donna Chevigny is thinking of, er, well, of hurting herself."

"Hurting herself." I thought about those two words. People hurt themselves, I reckon. I've done it, for sure and for certain. But there was a rank darkness in Guy's voice, a strain that meant more than plain bad choices that we all make now and again and again. "Now, when you say, *hurting herself* . . ."

He winced and turned his head away and studied his sneakers. I watched them with him and only learned that my Intended was getting himself mighty worked up. And that his shoes are worn nice and even. A level stride, Guy has. No wonder he's fast.

"It's supposed to be a classic sign," Guy said. "Suicidal people give away possessions before they do themselves in."

Guy's mama is a psychologist, and he's taken way too many college classes about why people do the things they do.

"Suicidal!" I said it like a dirty word, scared Spooky as I spat it out.

"Well, yes. And now as I think back on how she sounded when she called here the other day, she seemed bleak."

Bleak was the word. Donna had been lonely and overwhelmed and I've been there myself and what if she saw her situation the way I did?

Worse, suppose she saw it the way Guy did? What if he was right?

I hated the thought in so many ways, I turned on him. "Suicidal?"

"Well, yes."

"I can't believe you said that. You shouldn't have said that. What a thing to say."

"It's just a word, Rainy."

"Yes and no are just words but it does matter all day long which you say, doesn't it?"

The notion was still stuck like a turd on a hot day. "Suicidal?"

Guy nodded looking more than a little bleak himself. I was not liking the flavor of this conversation. It was about too much to wrap my mind around, but suddenly it slid and felt like it fit. It fit way too well and I was sick cold with the fear that he was absolutely, completely a hundred and seven percent dead right. I went for the house phone, Guy on my heels.

"It just rings. What do I do? Go to her house and ask her if she's killing herself?"

"Isn't there someone who can check on her?"

"Stan Yates is her only neighbor, and he's a long ways from the ranch house."

I didn't know what to do. Most of my brain figured I was over-reacting, running with this awful maybe of an idea Guy'd come up with—maybe Donna was thinking of ending her life. But another part of me knew that if Guy was right—and it sure felt like he *could* be right—then I had to find Donna, stop her before it was too late.

Chapter 16

HERE'S THE THING WITH LETTING THE mind run with the worst possibility, imagining Donna had gone and done herself in, what-if-ing myself stupid: it's hard to stop.

Storm clouds forming on the horizon didn't help my mood at all. The air smelled like lightning was coming. The static made my ponytail fly and arm hairs stand up. An anvil-shaped thunderhead lifted off the far mountains to the south. Gray skies can make for a murky mind. If Guy was right about my client being depressed, I hoped it wasn't catching.

I blazed the many miles back up the long forest road toward the Buckeye ranch. If I dawdled there at all, I'd be late for my noon shoeing appointment, first time ever late for a job.

Stan Yates—I assume it was him, it was some dude with a short gray beard—was out front of his house, weed-whacking around the edge of the driveway. As I drove by, he raised a hand in what could have been either a hail or a howdy. But the thing with thinking that a sweet old lady might be considering doing herself in is that once you start such rumination and you get busy with going to check on her, every second feels like a life might be draining away. I powered Ol' Blue right past Yates's wave. Soon

Charley and me pulled up between the Buckeye barn and the house. Time for action.

Her house is a sprawling rambler with a gaping, wooden porch, but no answer at the door. No problem, I headed for the barn. In the round pen just beyond, Buster rested, bulky and full of power, content with hay and water.

"Donna? It's Rainy. Rainy Dale." I stood at the hitching rail and water trough at the edge of the barn's dark aisle and listened. Charley placed one front paw on the trough's lip to pull himself up for a quick sip. I tried not to think about Slowpoke packing the gloved hand of a dead woman in from the back of the ranch and dropping it at my feet in this very spot. Creeped out, I stepped into the barn's darkness.

Horses blew that wonderful breathy, understated greeting.

"It's just me," I told them, making myself walk the length, in total darkness to the end where I found myself wondering about the sheriff's Suit Fellow theorizing that Cameron Chevigny might have killed Arielle Blake, then accidentally killed himself. But if Donna was unhappy with her husband, why not get shed of him?

What if Suit Fellow was wrong twice?

Charley followed me into the darkness with the merely half-interested way he has when there's not enough else going on and that's when I realized for sure that Donna wasn't around the barn. The Buckeye barn held good Quarter Horses, but no over-worked old woman, no silly young dog. I went back to the house and knocked again, harder. The front door gave enough to show it wasn't locked and I stood debating whether to turn the knob. A long gun hung over the fireplace mantle. I shaded my eyes to the door's glass pane and peered. Large bore, a shotgun. I thought about the other weapon or tool, the knife.

If Guy was right about suicidal people giving possessions away—well he would know, he'd half-followed his mom's head-doctor footsteps in college where he'd learned stuff about how people make their choices. Donna had given me that fancy knife. She was widowed and sad and worked near to death. Lost her daughter too, and how bad an ache would that be?

So, if she was a danger to herself, I should walk right into her house to make sure she wasn't in there, half-dead, having swallowed a bottle of pills or something, shouldn't I?

I turned back for the barn. Charley chuffed.

"I know you said she's not there," I told my good dog, "but what if?"

This whole check-on-Donna thing was *what if*. I stopped at Ol' Blue and checked my cheapie little cell phone.

No service. No surprise.

The heebie-jeebies I'd arrived with turned into a case of the screaming meemies. I walked around the house. Good as abandoned. I made to do the same at the barn, ending at that rough wooden shelf that packed a few dusty relics. The shell casing was still there, next to a rusty spur. The shell was silvery, smooth in my fingertips.

The shotgun's the only artillery we ever had. That's what Donna told me. Donna didn't have any reason to lie to me, did she? Or if she did, what was it?

This was too much dawdling. I barely had enough time left to make it to my noon shoeing appointment.

The crunch of gravel, the rumble of a rugged diesel drawing closer, called me back to the front of the barn, by the water trough.

Donna. It was Donna Chevigny driving that approaching truck and I was so glad to see her breathing, I could hardly move my boots.

"Rainy," she said by way of greeting. She peered at the hand I waved. "What have you got there?"

The shell casing was between my thumb and index finger.

"An empty," I said.

"Oh, that." Donna shrugged while turning for her pickup. She dropped the tailgate and tugged on one of many sacks of feed in the truck bed. "I found that on the lease land, back when I turned the cattle out there. Summer before last. Thought it was a shoe at first. You know, one that a horse had pulled off, just the end of one heel showing in the sun? I remember dismounting to pick it up." Her last words came in a breathy grunt as she lifted the first sack of feed.

I stepped up and took her load, hefted fifty pounds of oats to my shoulder.

"Thanks, Rainy." She gave a nod toward the back of the barn as she began to tug on the next sack. "No, they asked about reloading, but we never did any."

"Huh?" I'd already headed deep into the barn aisle with the oats, liking the scent but not the plastic feel of the feed bag. The scratchy burlap bags of my childhood are gone—grain is sold in slick synthetic bags nowadays. Slowpoke scampered after us in between trying to hassle Charley into playing. I hollered back, "Reloading?"

As my eyes adjusted to the dim, I noticed the empty, beater pallets by metal trash cans Donna used as feed bins in the far corner. Then I stood there like a special kind of idiot 'til she struggled up hugging a heavy sack to her chest. Her burden sunk as she neared, slipping to her belly, her hips, then slid off her thighs as she barely made it to the bins.

"Whew! Just put it down," Donna said.

I did and went for another bag, then another and another, setting them wherever she pointed.

"The sheriff's team found lead shot way out there, on the back pasture or nearby on the federal land," Donna said. "Asked if we did reloading."

"Shot?" The word has a bad sound. I sweated at the idea. "Shot, did you say?"

"Yeah, there was a bit of lead shot out there, spilled somewhere. It was strange, and they were looking at everything that was unusual. But I didn't know why shot was out there, so . . ." She spread her hands and gave a slight shrug.

"Lead shot?" I set a forty-pound sack of beet pulp pellets down, trying to catch up. Failing.

Donna was nodding again, sounding like she was talking to herself. "The sheriff's men found a little spill of loose lead shot, back when Cameron had his accident, and they were asking if we did any reloading, but no, we never did."

Puzzling on spilled lead shot just left me puzzled. Anyways, she'd found the shell long afterward.

And I'd found the shoe even more recently.

And then Slowpoke found a hand, presumably Arielle Blake's.

"I don't understand," I said, a little meek.

She shrugged again. "I don't either, but some things are never going to be understood, I suppose."

Twisting my ponytail did not help me understand, but it's what I did until I could come up with a maybe. "Do people ride through your land? Maybe getting to the national forest land on long rides or pack trips? Maybe coming from the Yates place?"

She shook her head like a woman who doesn't waste motion, two short swings, one each to the left and right. "No, you can't get to anywhere but the Buckeye—"

"You could cut from Yates place to the federal land through the Buckeye."

"Yates isn't horse folk. He was never a backcountry kind of fellow."

Her answer frowned me because it would have quieted down my itchy brain parts right away if I could have just chalked up the shoe to some unknown rider that passed through like others do.

But there were no others passing through, if Donna was to be believed.

And why shouldn't I believe her? Say the shotgun was the only firearm she owned. I wondered if Yates had a pistol.

Donna got one more sack of feed, I did the other eight. Her breath came out in little puffs as though she was beat shy of a summit. Her thanks came with shaking her head, telling me how she used to be stronger.

"Rainy, what are you doing here?" She seemed in a strange state, staring glassy-eyed around the barn like she didn't quite know how we'd walked ourselves in there.

"I came to check on you."

She froze. Her eyes misted. She looked away, then strode off to the open barn doors where strong noon light split gray clouds. The sun's strokes cast a light that made Donna look as aged as the relics on the shelf at her back. So as not to look too long at her, I set my eyeballs on the rusty old coffee can, the glass insulator, the spur, and all those other things.

Donna started crying. "I know guilt. Do you know the feeling? Really know it?"

Fact is, I have a real close acquaintance with that yuck but our private shames usually ought to stay private. I wasn't about to tell her about my unmentionables and I wasn't sure I wanted her telling me hers. I was fresh out of ideas on how to ask a woman if she was thinking about quitting life, but I was going to have to stick until I felt okay that she'd not be giving it all up today.

She said, "I feel so guilty about Cameron."

"Ma'am," I began, straining with why she felt guilty, passing it by, and the difficulty of forming my question. I hoped she wouldn't put me on the spot like I was about to put her. *Oh, please, don't ask why I'm asking.* "Do you have some friends you could stay with or who could stay here with you? So you're not alone?"

"I am alone. I've outlived all my family. Lost my best friend, my best girlfriend three years ago. She went and died."

We met eyes and I was sure she was making it plain that she wasn't putting her husband on that short list of best friends.

Hey, that ground was dry. Not at all like my eyeballs that studied that dirt.

"She had a stroke. And she was two years younger than me."

Well, hey, these people eat steak and eggs two or three times a day. Even I know better than that.

"I'm sorry you're alone," I blurted. "I feel bad."

"I feel bad, too."

I nodded and said I was sorry again.

"It's because I didn't check on him," Donna said suddenly, speaking with so much hot pain, I half expected her to hiss with steam as the sprinkling started. There'd been no watering down of Donna's pain.

"You didn't check on your husband the day he died?"

"End of winter," she said, with a wry smile. "Didn't know it was starting the winter of my life."

She wiped her eyes and looked at me like comfort lost. "Every farming and ranching wife knows to check her man regular when he's on a machine. Doctor said he had a lot of weight on his chest, but it wasn't enough to do him in right away. No, it was the time he was there, just too long with all that dead weight on him. A slow and horrible death. Cameron deserved better." She shook her head. "Hardly a mark on him, open casket, but it was a bad way to die."

I'd fancied the tractor must have squished Cameron Chevigny or a whack on the head had done him in, but no, it was worse than a rancher's quick death.

"Maybe . . ." I started, "I mean, do you want to come on out there with me? I'll be there, be there with you. You and I can take care of the tractor together."

Nothing. That's how much response Donna gave. That's what I know—nothing about nothing. Just who in Hades did I think I was to be making such suggestions anyways? When her widow's eyes went wet, I felt several kinds of awful.

"Hey," I said, "I'll go. I don't need help and I said I'd do it. I will. I just wondered if you might have wanted to and you don't have to, of course." What other words could I say? I hadn't meant to be shirking what I'd promised to do, just thought it might help her to face the fear of the place where her husband died.

Donna shook her head with a grimace at last. "I wouldn't want to exorcise my demons. I take 'em out for a spin now and again.

That's good for them and me. Pain and the past makes us breathe today. When I lay flowers for him, I do it at the tombstone where it says Cameron Bickford Chevigny, husband and father, and the days he was born and died."

* * *

Mulling Donna Chevigny's words as I drove off, I was startled, braked up a cloud of dust when, a piece down from the Buckeye main entrance, Stan Yates ran out of his driveway into the center of the road, flagging me down.

Chapter 17

O L' BLUE SEEMED TO PULL OVER real natural and next thing, I was face to face with Stan Yates himself.

He eyed my truck doors. "You're the one who found her."

At first, I was thinking of Donna, since I'd come all the way out here to check on the Widow Chevigny.

Yates wiped the corner of one eye. "You found Arielle."

Ol' Blue is, after all, a rolling advertisement for Dale's Horseshoeing, with the house phone number to boot. My breath taken away, I needed a few seconds. I didn't want to say something like 'no, it was Donna's dog Slowpoke what found her' or 'no, really, only found her hand.' I was not going to blow it. Not.

"We searched out there. Because she used to take these really long walks. We never found her."

I told the truth. "I'm sorry. I really don't know what to say." But I thought things like: Are you trying to stiff a sad widow, making up a handshake land deal with her dead husband just so you can steal her land? Are you stealing her tractor that I'm fixing? Did you kill Arielle? And Cameron?

A closed mouth is a good thing for me to wear.

He rubbed his mouth. "Ah, Ri—" Then Yates cut himself off to clear his throat.

Sounded like he said 'Ree' and I was a step behind, distracted. "Pardon?" I said.

"Rielle liked to explore."

"She went by Rielle?"

Yates gave a sad smile. "Arielle. Rielle. Ree. ReeRee. She used to call herself Elle when she was younger, before we were together."

I had a pretty good idea of whose knife was in Ol' Blue. Not exactly a case-cracker that I could establish hanky panky between Arielle and Cameron though. I felt bad for this stranger in front of me whose girlfriend had played around on him, who'd learned of her cheating after she disappeared and the deputies searched her cell phone records.

But what if he was a pretty good actor?

"Um, Mr. Yates, I'm going to be late for my next appointment and there's no good cell—"

"No cell service out here. Yeah, I know. You can use my phone. We still have a landline."

"We?" I grabbed my appointment book and followed him toward the house. I should have thought to ask Donna for the use of her landline.

"Me. Just me now. Me and her cat. Our cat."

Sounded lonely.

We edged around his electric car and its tattered Sanders promotional material over the car's right hip. Centered, where a trailer hitch would never be, peeled the remains of an even more faded sticker. I didn't expect to see a rifle over the mantle.

There wasn't.

Inside, the house was cleaner than mine. A better-mannered cat than Spooky prowled up, purring, but not pushing.

"The phone's in here."

I followed him into a den. The paneled walls smelled of cedar and were covered with Thespian awards.

"Nice." I reached for the phone, flipping through my appointment book to tell my client Leigh Ann that I'd be late, first time ever.

Yates waved at the wall. "Those are from my Ashland days. We used to create magic on the stage. Now I want to create energy."

"Wind farming," I said, distracted. I have clients, the Quistlands. Green as trees. They're good folk, real good. Horses are barefoot and well-cared for, ridden bitless and treeless. I left a message for Leigh Ann, picturing her standing in a barn aisle, holding a horse that needed to be reshod. I closed my appointment book and stared at the broad table under the phone. There was a map of the lease land. The flyer that had been posted around town. The article in *The Western*. A Sheriff's card with a case number on it. A sheet of paper with notes about "find my phone" and "Biff C" and "expand search grid?"

"Biff C?" The room was warm enough, but a cool draft wanted to give me the chills. Maybe I'd worked up enough of a sweat lugging feed for Donna that my clothes were moist against my skin and now I wasn't moving enough to stay warm.

"I don't want to tell you what that means." Yates folded his arms and looked at the floor. Nice floor, like bamboo or something special.

"I know a guy named Biff." Truth is, I can hardly tell the three guys that Guy plays poker with apart, but I know Biff is one of them. Maybe the little one.

Yates rubbed his watery eyes. "I looked all through Rielle's stuff in the days after she didn't come back. And we searched her phone. It was tough."

"We?"

"The sheriff's department and me. They had some good ideas on finding her, I thought. Her phone pinged to the trail around Keeper Lake, which is an awfully long walk, even for Arielle—"

"TrailTime," I snapped my fingers with the thought. What was it Guy had said about that app he uses to track runs? And Keeper Lake. And Biff.

"What's that?" Yates looked mystified.

"TrailTime? Did Arielle use a tracking thingy called TrailTime? Like, from an app on her phone?"

He started to speak, started to lose it, cleared his throat and tried again. "I tried to find her by doing the Find My Phone thing. The other stuff I mentioned about her phone, well, I'd rather . . . it's personal."

"I'm truly sorry for your loss. I never knew her, but I sure am sorry." I shoved my hands in my front pockets.

"Thanks."

There was something metal, weird, small in my right pocket. I wiggled my fingers and remembered having that shell casing in my hand when I started helping Donna move feed. I must have pocketed it without thinking. I turned to go and saw the wall by the door for the first time. Covered in pistols, blackpowder guns, more modern-looking shooters, too. I faced Yates again, pulling my fingers free, leaving that shell casing where it was. "You shoot with the Outfitter group?"

"What's that?"

But halfway through my explanation about the Outfitters, Yates shook his head. "I don't shoot at all. Those are all replicas. Non-firing. I just like old guns. They're a clever invention, mechanically. Like locks or clocks or, I suppose, bicycles. Things with levers or gears, these old inventions, they've always impressed me."

There's such a thing as too much speculation. I thanked Yates and drove away thinking in too many directions.

Soon as I got close enough to town for cell reception, I reached my client and rescheduled, squeezing her into a slot later in the day at her best convenience, not liking the hole I now had in my time. Gave me spare hours to wonder.

* * *

Would Stan Yates go out to the shallow grave where his girlfriend's body had been recovered on the federal land and grieve? Donna wouldn't, said she wouldn't be exercising her demons. But there, at the high school track was Melinda Kellan exercising. With my apparent demon, my husband-to-be. My god—my flipping—supposed soon-to-be spouse. Mine.

I pulled Ol' Blue up on that high school parking lot like a woman ready to chase some sniffing witch off my patch. I'm pretty sure that's not what I'm all about though, so I don't know where that came from. I mean, if Guy doesn't want me or if he wants to be the dallying kind then he can just take his bad self and—

The voice of a fellow behind me sounded off. "Hey, Brainy!"

In as bad a mood as I'd been in for six months, I was more than ready to take someone's head off. I whirled and paused, saw the lime green El Camino and the skinny little guy in running clothes.

"Biff." I studied him, choosing where to begin. He's built like a ten-year-old boy, but not as tall. Pretty sure he's shorter than me. Guy says he's speedy as heck. The shaved head probably makes him aerodynamic. And I can't tell what he means by that stupid nickname he's tried to hang on me.

"So, Biff . . ."

"Brainy?"

"Arielle Blake."

"She's dead."

"Yeah. Guy wanted you to check—"

Biff unzipped his sweatshirt pocket and pulled out his big, important-looking phone—definitely not a pay-as-you-go model from Walmart, like mine. "What was that all about?" He started swiping away at the screen. "That was, like, a year and a half ago? I don't use TrailTime as much as Guy."

"Did you delete a map on TrailTime from when you and Guy searched for Arielle Blake?"

Biff shook his head, still staring at his phone. "Didn't make one to delete. Still got my pics from that day. See?"

His screen showed the glorified pond called Keeper Lake, and the typical sage scrub beyond that mixed with the pines. We're right on the edge here in Butte County, with the land half wanting to be like the wetter hemlock, fir, spruce, and cedars of the moist low lands and half high desert, with a few pines and a lot of scraggly brush. A person can ride over a ridge and be in a new climate.

"Hey, what's that on the water?" I squinted at the phone's picture.

Biff set two fingers together on the screen and moved them apart, zooming in on the image.

I can't do that on my phone. I don't even use it as a camera.

Anyways, it was trash floating on the lake, black plastic something. Why in heck do people litter? With Keeper Lake being close enough to the Country Store, it's sometimes one of those areas where dumpers drop their unwanted sofas and fridges and cars and scrap material.

"Why in heck," I asked, "did you and Guy get asked to search around Keeper Lake?"

He shrugged.

"You sure you didn't know her?"

He shook his head, stamping his feet, stretching, then sprinting off, his sneakers slapping the track in a crunch of the red cinders. The same sound played out toward me as Guy and Melinda Kellan finished their lap.

"Hey, sweetie!" Guy hustled his darned self up, grinning like a fool, arms spread in a hug or surrender or something.

Huh.

"I saw you driving by and I thought, 'ooh, I wish she'd pull in and let me smooch her,' and here now, you've made my day." He kissed me like he meant it.

With his slick arms still around me, I couldn't see Melinda as this was going on, but I wondered if she was now green from envy or from nausea at how sweet he was or what. She'd started out red and sweaty, like Guy, I'd marked that much.

He still had his arms and perspiring pits on me as he asked what I was up to.

I wiggled free. "Thought I'd stop in at Darby's, you know?"

He shook his head, not knowing much about my mind.

I swallowed a sigh. "Getting that tractor tire of Donna's fixed at Darby's."

"Ah," he allowed, his gaze wandering back to the red gravel track that circled the football field.

"And you?" I brought back a little of my earlier bristle—a shame to waste it—and gave him a good stern looking-at. "What were you up to?"

"Well," Guy stammered a little, like this question was too easy or too hard but not just right, "sprints. Of course."

Of course. Several times a week, Guy runs around the high school track to make himself beet-faced and sweaty and whatnot. Studying him as he studied the lanes was like watching a colt eyeball a big, beckoning pasture from the confines of a box stall in a barn. Guy loves to run. My everything relaxed. Maybe it was the high school itself what brought out in me a petty and jealous little teenybopper. If anything, Melinda was looking a little shy and embarrassed, standing before me and my man.

"It's my first time," she said.

First time, what? Acting pleasant? I gave her my grim grin and waited for words.

"I've got to get faster," Melinda said, like a wistful kid wanting the Easter Bunny and chocolate eggs. "I can jog two hours straight, but I'm not as quick a sprinter as I should be. I've got a schedule for track workouts I downloaded off the 'net, but the idea of going and running around a track, ugh. It was easier with someone else here."

Guy nodded at her and I could tell there'd been a short talk on this notion before I chanced upon them. They talked now like they were finishing a conversation about 10k trail races. Guy warned, "They'll dairy-queen you for course-cutting."

"What?" Melinda asked.

"DQ," Guy said. "They'll disqualify you.

To me, DQ means a *dressage queen*, a hifalutin rider who makes it all about herself.

Guy went on. "We'll burn our legs again in a couple of days. Biff will probably join us. Maybe sixteen reps of quarters with a recovery interval after each sprint?"

Melinda gave the up half of a nod, her chin staying high like someone who was in over her head, but trying not to let on. "That's what it takes."

"Yeah, just keep running sprints." Guy watched Biff fly around the track.

For sure and for certain, Guy had no interest in Melinda, even if she was taking a shine to my own personal fella. I had no worries, right? Guy had himself a fine woman, one not living with her folks at this age, one who could take care of herself and had a handle on life. That would be me. Maybe Biff would be a good match for Melinda. He had a job in computers or construction or something and I'd no idea his living situation.

Struck, I asked Guy, "You'd already asked Biff about the deleted TrailTime map?"

"Yeah, it wasn't him."

Chapter 18

GUY NODDED AND SHOOK HIS HEAD. "Yeah, it wasn't his entry in the database. He'd carried his cell that day and shot some pictures around the lake, but he wasn't using the TrailTime app when we were out."

"But you're sure you remember another TrailTime track in that area?"

Biff could be lying to me and Guy. Guy would never suspect a thing.

"I'm sure. TrailTime sends little alerts to your account. Teasers about how another trail user beat your PR—"

"Your PR?" I asked.

"Personal Record. I remember Biff and I were both carrying our phones that day—I remember I had activated TrailTime to track what we did that day we were looking for Arielle Blake. Next time I logged onto TrailTime, it had a notice that someone else had the record for a segment on the trail along the west side of the lake. But later, I checked, and there was no other trail user segment."

Biff came puffing up, shaking out his legs from another sprint lap. Guy explained it all to him again.

Biff said, "Bet they have it on their server. If it's that important to you, Brainy." He touched his watch and took off in another all-out effort around the track.

I don't know anything about computer servers. Just knew I was missing something. Again. "I'm going to Darby's, tend to Donna's tractor tire."

Melinda dawdled instead of clearing the track, hanging around Guy and me like part of her thinks she's our buddy or something. Guy got his water bottle from the ground. Its white plastic blended with the chalk line in a middle lane so I hadn't noticed it, but I think I caught most everything else. Melinda's toes crunched gravel as she spun to jabber at me.

"Darby, that dude with the tool and tire shop is in the Outfitters group, isn't he," she said. She had quite a habit of saying her questions, not asking, then acting like she knew the answer but she was letting you take a quiz for extra credit. She started looking impatient with me, a lot in a Guy-kind of way. "The Outfitters group. That guy Darby's in it with the Pritchards, yeah?"

I nodded. The Outfitters group. Those people have been happening in Butte County since I don't know when. They shoot arrows at targets, cook in Dutch ovens and consider their time well spent. The Outfitters are the sort that find a lot to love in the past and go pretending they're living like a bunch of prairie peasants. Except, some of them get to the so-called camp site in motor homes with TVs, fridges, hot showers, and microwave ovens.

The old days don't appeal to me at all. Back then, Melinda and me would both be birthing babies and hoeing corn 'til our hands bled, while we wore long skirts just to prove ourselves women. I wanted no part of the past. Figures that some guys think olden times were all wonderful.

"I'd kind of like to tag along to Darby's," Melinda said. Still shooting for Busybody Award, as she got into her car and fired up.

What the heck? I made a face that only Guy caught. He grabbed me in a goodbye hug and smooch, whispering in my ear. "She's trying to befriend you."

I pushed away, aghast. "Why?"

He laughed and looked right into my eyes, palms on my shoulders. "She thinks you're cool. And she's right."

Melinda didn't quite tailgate me, but we did pull into Darby's Tool 'n' Tire like we were together. I'd ditch her as soon as I went on my shoeing calls.

* * *

Darby Ernst has a catch-all corner in the back of his service station. He'll special order anything for anyone and a lot of folks use him as a bulletin board besides. Somehow, he always knows who's got what for sale. Looking for a bumper-pull two-horse trailer? Drop in on Darby and he'll tell you the Sennets are thinking of upgrading to a three-horse slant, might part with theirs, which has been kept under a roof the five years the Sennets had it. Want to buy something you saw online, but freak at putting a credit card across the Internet? Tell Darby what it is you're after and he'll have it here in a week. And tools? Oh, Darby can do tools, antique, super specialty, shoeing tools. That's how Darby and me got to be chums. He got me an old Heller Brothers hammer that I since took to using as my primary driving hammer. It feels right in my hand and I like the idea that someone drove nails in a century ago with it. This hammer will always have more experience than me.

But Darby, Darby's a different duck. He looks like he gets his hair cut during Machete Night at a drunken barbers' hootenanny.

"Rainy," he said with a nod sent my way. He gave Melinda Kellan a plain nod and I liked a lot that he knew me best. She'd likely not bought any tools from him and maybe committed the sacrilege of getting her car serviced at the chain gas station on the south end of town. Well, okay, I tend to service Ol' Blue my own self, but I did buy the fuel filter from Darby last winter when mine iced up. Besides, he was getting to Donna Chevigny's tractor tire then and there, had it on a steel worktable next to the semi-automatic tire changer, working a plug into the hole. I nodded. It made a cheaper fix than busting the tire off the rim and replacing it.

Feeling like I had something on the offer, I whistled up words without thinking too hard. Melinda folded her arms across her middlin' chest and kept quiet, hung back. She didn't even know where I was headed. Well, neither did he, so I moved along.

"Hey," I said to Darby, "some of you Outfitters folks take pretty long rides out into the federal land, that part back of the forest where the grazing lease is, right?"

"Could be. Why?"

"Just wondered. Someone said Loretta Pritchard rides out there. She invited me to go ride sometime." I could almost feel that aluminum shoe's shape in my hand, the shoe I had in my glove box. I could see Mac telling me it was probably Loretta Pritchard's Paso's shoe.

He nodded. "Yeah, Loretta. I remember her gone a good long while from the Outfitters camp one time. We worried for her 'cause there was talk of cougars 'round some of that country."

"Cougars?" I shot a look to Melinda but her expression wasn't exactly of the readable variety. "Which time?"

Darby nodded. "Spring campout. Year before last. Word was, cougars in the area."

"Cougars, huh?" Big cats aren't too awful common around here, but I guess they scream deep in the national forest a bit.

"Yeah, cougars," he said, looking up suddenly at Melinda waving at us.

"There's a reason that tire was flat," she said.

"Sure," Darby allowed.

"So," she went on, "maybe you could check, you know, inside it."

Like he maybe could improve on just plugging the puncture? I stared at her bad manners, but Darby shrugged and went for it, heaving the rim and tire onto the changer. That ear-splitting sound of the tire coming off the rim made me and Melinda wince. I don't know how Darby can handle the noises of an indoor shop. At least my hammer strikes steel out in the open, where sound can walk away. In his shop, every slang of steel and creak of rubber echoed in a way that made me think my eyeballs would bleed. Charley would have skedaddled for sure with that racket.

Somehow, we adapt. We could all hear something—sounded like a little rock—rattling around inside the tractor tire as he lifted it clear of the changer. Melinda and I heard it before Darby, we've still got all our ears' ability. We leaned in as Darby kept warning me to watch for mountain lions near the Buckeye lease land.

"So you be careful out there, Rainy."

"I'll be careful," I said, thinking a whole lot of things to be careful about as I stared with Melinda at what was in Darby's hand—a little chunk of mushroomed copper—after he reached inside the tire to get the little thing banging around in the rubber walls.

Melinda turned to use the phone without even asking for permission. Darby pursed his mouth up and no one said enough.

"The thing is . . ." Darby rubbed half his jaw but didn't rub up the rest of his thought clear enough to speak.

"The thing is?" I asked.

"I guess I'd like to call her up, let her know what I've found."

"Her, Donna Chevigny?"

Darby nodded. Me, too. This was, after all, her tractor tire.

"No matter what folks say about . . ." Darby's jaw took another rubbing, both sides this time. He shook his head and shook the little copper chunk. ". . . this."

"What's this, exactly?" I asked.

"Exactly, I'd not be the one to say. But I'm sure someone at

Sheriff Magoutsen's office could put a finger on it." He jerked his head at Melinda, talking low on the phone.

"Well, less exactly then." I wanted the answer and I didn't want to be the one to say it. I nodded to give him the prodding he seemed to need. "That's a . . ?"

"Why, don't you know? That's a bullet."

Chapter 19

T HE UNIFORMED DEPUTY WAS ONE I'D seen before. It hadn't exactly been a speeding thing. I don't think it counts when you get a warning. But he showed up at Darby's like he'd been set on us by dogs. Or Melinda. And his big news was that Suit Fellow would want a short statement from me and Darby about seeing the bullet come out of the tire. He called it establishing the evidence's chain of custody, then said we could bring our own selves down to the sheriff's office. I'd be seeing Suit Fellow again. I thought about what was shoved way down in my right front jeans pocket. I could hand it over to the deputy right now, but then Darby and Melinda would see and I'd have to explain it in front of them.

"Got a horse to shoe," I said. It was true, though I could have put it off. It's one of the few accounts I have where the horse is so smooth, I'll shoe when the owner's absent. I was supposed to get this old pet done any afternoon this week and I'd penciled it in for myself this afternoon. And I had another one-horse account hard scheduled in for late afternoon, plus Leigh Ann to make up for. There. That ought to get me clear of Suit Fellow. The deputy turned back from his phone, took in Darby's agreement to head to the sheriff's Cowdry office right away, then nodded at me. "Four thirty's fine. The investigator will see you then."

"Okey doke," I promised. When I saw the investigator might be a good time for me to unload my right front jeans pocket, too. I moseyed on out of Darby's shop, followed by Melinda.

"Hey, can I talk to you?" She tailed me to my truck.

There wasn't much for me to say but, "Donna Chevigny doesn't have a pistol."

"Mmm." Melinda cocked her head.

I kept my eyeballs looking straight ahead. "Do the police think someone shot that tire to roll the tractor on purpose?"

"It's a possibility. You don't have to be a rocket scientist, don't even have to be very awake to figure that one."

A possibility it is now. Not something she thinks, it's just a possibility.

But she didn't know the lay of the land, the way the barbed wire separated the lease land from the Buckeye proper, the way the electric fencing separated the hay fields from the rougher west land. The shed. I frowned. "Or maybe someone on the lease land did some sloppy hunting or target shooting."

"Could be," Melinda said.

Never, never, I thought, will she go with the likely answer. How can she get anything done? Melinda was one of those who watches a lot and grunts and asks a few questions but her commentary, when it comes, doesn't always sit right with me. And that's where I left it and her. If Melinda was trying to befriend me, she was none too skilled at the job. When I pulled out of Darby's lot, I saw her in my side mirror, standing by her little car, watching me, like she was sizing me up.

Ol' Blue rumbled me to the three-acre place where Bill Ruddington's silly two-year-old sorrel colt lost his sense when I called his old bay grade mare over to rotate her tires, so to speak.

Ruddington's mare's a sweetie and that's all I've ever heard him call her. He still rides her on Saturdays but mostly, she keeps his pasture looking good. Land looks much better with a nice horse or three ornamenting it, that's my view. I shod Sweetie and got to my next client, where I did three trims, then on to a larger barn, just a mile down the road.

Turns out, that horse wasn't out and ready for me there. Some guy in cowboy dress-up was, waiting like he thought he was Mr. Business, one spanking clean boot on the bumper of a shiny blue short-bed pickup.

"You the girl come to work on the horse?"

"Sure am. You the flunky that's gonna go fetch it?"

Now that we were better acquainted, he got his boots moving in the right direction, away from me. I knew he was no horse-fetcher. At this barn, my only client was Leigh Ann, a real nice gal with good taste in horses and bad taste in men. I apologized up and down for not making the earlier appointment and felt my face go red as she brushed it off.

Down the barn aisle, I got my toolbox out. Leigh Ann had just brushed off her Palomino gelding in the stall. Her man cluttered around like a skunk who was probably afraid of the twelve-hundred-pound golden muscle mass at the end of Leigh Ann's rope.

Mighty pretty like her gelding, Leigh Ann's nice too, but she sure seems to attract a stupid brand of male. This cowboy wannabe had too much bluster for me to give him another glance. She was ignoring him now, frowning at the gelding's dirt-packed foot when I bent over at the horse's right front and it lifted automatically.

"I picked him out this morning."

I believed her, too. "S'okay," I said. Her gelding's tender soled, so the dirt packed in his hoof helped pad the sole when I reefed with my shoe pullers to get the old iron off his feet. As I leveraged the pullers, the scent of old earth mixed with manure releasing off the sole chased the hoof pack that followed the shoe. I gave the shoe the wear-inspection warranted and racked it on my toolbox.

Makes for a quiet piece of work, a couple of extra people with nothing to contribute there, no one sure what to think of anyone else.

Almost an hour later, I was glad to finish that fourth foot, load my gear and get my check. The guy playing dress-up watched Leigh Ann put her horse in the paddock and never had two more words for me.

* * *

In the little lobby at the sheriff's station, I wondered exactly who knew exactly what about that bullet in the tire, about that spent shell casing Donna found that was, oh yeah, still in my jeans pocket.

Suppose someone had been at the Buckeye shed, gone to ground and waited and watched while Cameron Chevigny drove up the hogback? It had occurred to me that someone could have turned Dragoon loose and the bull had been the one to puncture the tire.

But, no.

Still, it got me to thinking about that bull because I was trying to come up with a reason for wanting Cameron Chevigny dead. Someone has to want something, some satisfaction, to go after someone else.

A top rodeo bull who breeds well could be worth north of five figures. People don't go to a rodeo to see a horse dead. A cowboy tossed around, sure, that's a whole 'nother deal, but no one wants to watch a bull charge and crush a horse. Dragoon hadn't rodeoed well, but maybe his value was in breeding.

The Cowdry sheriff's office's *Authorized Personnel* door swung open and my brain—such as it is—came back to the here and now, expecting Suit Fellow, but it was Vince Pritchard in his reserve deputy uniform. He shouldered into a jacket, rolling his arms around like he was almost too much man to fit in clothes.

"Hey," I said, "I need to—"

"I'm pretty busy," he said. "Got a lot going on."

Maybe while he was busy writing himself valentines he could fit in showing me the way to Suit Fellow?

"A deputy said for me to come in and give a statement 'bout seeing that bullet come out of the tire—"

"Bullet?"

"Yeah, Darby and me saw it. And Melinda," I said, "I was at Darby's when, well, see Melinda suggested—"

He shook his head and snorted, "Melinda," like it was a cuss word and I thought he was going to tell me again about how she lived with her parents. "She doesn't know what she's doing."

Then he had another story and somehow the time to tell it. I'd heard about the fire last winter but not about the sheriff's reserve deputies being there. Not the detail Vince Pritchard blabbered.

There was a house fire in town and Melinda had been the one told to sit with the old lady that got burned out. I remembered reading in *The Western* that it was an old house, insulated in its attic with ancient newspapers. After it burned to dust, there was a follow-up article urging people not to heat their houses with the stove and oven, listing the government people who'd help out, listing the bank that donations could be made to help out the old lady.

"All she had to do was keep the complainant—" Vince Pritchard swirled his eyeballs a lap in their sockets and explained to me "complainant means the owner in this case." Oh, he loved his police-talk.

I grunted. It was all the encouragement he needed.

"At any rate, all little Melinda got tasked with was keeping the lady company while the crews worked. I handled the traffic detail."

Nodding, I could see it. Melinda the wanna-be reservist made to babysit, the full-fledged reserve playing the big man, telling people where to go. When I didn't comment on his heroism, Pritchard went on, getting so scornful of Melinda Kellan it made me straighten up and lean back from the man as he got down to his complaint on her actions.

"She's a crier." His voice boomed in the tiled lobby—lo, I hadn't realized before what an echo chamber is made of tiling the floor and walls of a mini-office. Pritchard folded his arms across his chest.

When he wouldn't say more, I asked, "What? She cried?"

He nodded and snorted in disgust, rolling his eyes and shaking his head like he was embarrassed to have to say it all. "Yeah, she cried. Tried to act like she didn't, but I caught her. Tears coming out both corners." He pointed his pointer fingers to the outside of his own eyeballs to make it all clear.

It was easy to picture, except I imagined me instead of Melinda. Me sitting with an old lady who'd lost all her sweaters and pictures and dishes and maybe a little dog whose job it was to warm her lap when she's reading a magazine in the evenings. An old lady lost her belongings, her all. I could see Melinda there as though I'd witnessed the sad scene, I could see me doing in her boots the same thing, if I'd been made to hold hands with an old lady in that fix. I pictured Donna Chevigny there, sitting on the bumper of a fire truck, while crews made work of trying to mend a problem that couldn't be mended.

I'd have leaked a few, I know I would have. And I'd like to think by now, maybe since last week or so, I'm a big enough girl to not be ashamed of having just a little bit of heart, enough to spare some kindness and sad feelings over someone else's bad luck. What a nightmare, and in the daytime.

Once this day-mare was done having its way with me, I looked up again, wrinkling my brow because it was all so sad to think on. Pritchard pulled the right spot up in the computer and gave me the dates and times and phone number I needed and then he got right back to chewing on Melinda.

"She cried," Pritchard said, "like a girl."

Chapter 20

Maybe Melinda Kellan was supposed to have cried like a boy when she commiserated with a burned-out-of-her-house little old lady? I almost mentioned Pritchard's crummy attitude to Suit Fellow, but come the moment, I was glad to just make my two-minute statement that I was there at Darby's and saw the bullet come out of the tractor tire.

"Just documenting," the investigator, Suit Fellow, said. Under fluorescent lights, he looked more than tired and needed a fresh suit.

Maybe a bullet cropping up on a case you'd ruled an accident a year and a half ago made for a bad day at work.

I stood up, the better to get into my pocket and pulled out the shell casing, handed it over and explained where it came from. He set his head in his hands, elbows on the table, like he had no manners at all, then snapped to.

"I'll talk to Donna Chevigny about it," he said. "Miss Dale, you seem to be putting your fingers on things that might be evidence."

It didn't sound like a good thing, the way he said it.

"About the subpoenas Guy and I got," I said. "You said before that if it went to trial, we almost for sure wouldn't be needed on

166

the first day, and you'd have a better idea from the prosecutor as the trial date got closer. You said there's sometimes last minute negotiations and a plea, so it might not go to trial at all. Well, we're getting closer. Do I have to go to court?"

"I'll let you know."

I went for the door, pretty sure I was free, looked back to see him poke the shell casing with the tip of his pen.

"Ten millimeter," he said.

* * *

My last stop was at the Langstons' where I found my little buddy crying like a girl. Abby was going away in a week and she'd decided her mare Liberty was going to wean Bean while she was gone. The girl wasn't quite hostile but she wasn't her usual fun self, wouldn't smile.

I nudged one of her tanned arms with one of mine. "You're getting pretty brown, girl. Been out riding a lot?"

"No, I've been going to the salon in town."

"The tanning salon?" I snorted. "Why go pay for skin cancer when it's free under the sun?"

"Girls in the city don't have man tans," she said.

We scowled at each other.

Then Abby frowned her mare up and down. "Liberty won't get any exercise. She'll just be hanging out here in the pasture."

"Maybe you could get a friend to come and give her some riding time," I said.

"I don't want anyone else riding her." The girl's face showed all sour-like. "I did ask my mom about wind farming for you. She said you're right, there's big federal money in it right now. Some program for Oregon. She said she was going to do a presentation on it at what she called *my* school. What if they make me move in with her and go to school there in Portland? I won't have any friends."

I gave her response the minute it needed. "Ride along with me for shoeing tomorrow, 'kay?"

Sniffle. "'Kay."

* * *

I picked Abby up early and we had a pretty good day, my mind all in the present work under my nose. Shoed the heck out of a bunch of horses, no time to clean up and restock or sharpen, so I'd be having to work on my kit in the evening and Abby would be good and tuckered. One client the next day had some special shoeing needs that I could get a jump on with some forge work at home, so I'd be tuckered, too. A good tuckering fixes many a 'tude, I think.

Not until I dropped Abby off at home and she said, "My mother said there are no federal contracts for wind energy in Butte County," did I recollect the very notion of murky messes hereabouts. But as I drove off, watching Abby head inside to her sad daddy, I thought about seeing a wind turbine way off to the west when I'd been astride north of the ravine at the Buckeye. And thinking about being on the chunk of land made me remember Dragoon, too. The bull that should have brought Cameron Chevigny and Hollis Nunn a nice side business in the rodeo world, but instead tried to kill horses. This was not my world.

Guy was working late at the Cascade, so it was just Spooky and Charley and me at home. Rain came. Shoes needed making. I'd a good idea about the shape of those horses' feet waiting for me at my first job of the morning, could get a jump on the bar stock work. I backed Ol' Blue into the carport. With the rig turned around, I had a dry place to fire up my forge to a good roar. It was a better idea for me to be heating steel and shaping it, rather than stewing on failed businesses of wind farming and rodeo stock contracts.

* * *

In the morning, I left the house before Guy was out of bed, didn't leave him a doodle, and went out for a full day's shoeing at the one big training barn a bit of a drive north of Cowdry. The clients use several different shoers, but the barn owner uses me for four show horses. Their last horse came to them with a lot of foot problems and we've tried a few different things to get him comfortable and moving well. His frogs are growing better now after several shoeing cycles, and it's an interesting but hard day when I work there.

A day of pounding something as strong and malleable as hot steel can set a girl to rights. I worked for those horses, is who I worked for. I worked hard for them. Finer feet were never presented as when I finished those horses. I was about beat by the time I leaned against Ol' Blue's tailgate to quit sweating before I washed up in my cooling bucket.

The kid who'd been fetching and holding horses for me all day wasn't done working though. He pulled his hat down hard and licked his lips as a big hay delivery came in. Bucking hay'll make a man out of any lad. I didn't even want to think about hauling two hundred bales of sweet-scented mixed grass into that loft for restacking.

The hay truck driver had the same thought, left her cab with a Pepsi in one hand and came to the shade by me, social as a dog. An older lady, she wore a work shirt, straw cowboy hat, and jeans, looked just like a female Hollis Nunn. I saw him and a couple other young fellas dripping sweat, moving the hay.

"Glad that's not me," I said.

"That's a job for youngsters," she snickered, inclining her head toward the guys working at the unloading. I looked over at Hollis again then back at his . . . wife?

They had the same set to their jaws, the same broad pale foreheads over tanned faces that show they're outside aplenty but wearing hats while they're there. Both had the thick iron gray hair thing going, too, and were built the same wiry way, in medium.

Scary, the way a couple starts looking like each other.

I scheduled my client's next shoeing and heard a "Thanks, Rainy," as I got my check. Those are all good to get.

"Oh," the woman from the hay truck said, looking up from the paperwork Hollis brought her. "You're Rainy Dale? I'm Holly Nunn."

What are the odds? They look alike and their names . . . it's too much.

Guy and I don't look alike. I'll never be blonde. He'll always have his angular face and Thoroughbred legs. Me, I'm a good old ranch type, some softness and more hardness to me.

Holly Nunn about scared me then, raising her voice like she had to, like I was just so deep into some crevice in my mind.

"I said, nice to meet you."

I nodded. "Likewise."

"I didn't know you worked this far up the county," Holly added.

Did she think I was too far from home?

"Really," I said too loud, "it's not all that much longer to drive out here than it takes me to get to, say, the Buckeye." Those were my two longest drives. I'm fortunate to have most of my clients within ten or fifteen miles. This barn and Donna's place, at better than thirty miles, take driving time.

"Ah, the Chevigny place. Yep, Hollis said you were working there."

"I've done some shoeing for Donna," I said immediately, "I never knew Cameron Chevigny."

"You didn't know him?" She asked like there was more than one meaning.

"No, he died before I moved here. He shod his own. She did too, for a while." I was talking horseshoeing only.

Holly's voice stayed friendly. "Hard workers, the both of them."

"Yes, ma'am."

Then she nodded toward Hollis and raised her voice enough to say, "Would have been fine if it had worked out."

He turned back toward us—nothing wrong with his hearing— and shook his finger at the world. "Well, it didn't."

"The rodeo stock business?" I ventured.

She nodded. "Hollis was going to handle the trucking. Cameron's end was going to be keeping the broncs and bulls."

"Interesting work," I said, not sure what else to say for it.

Hollis snorted. "That man worked beyond his ranch, if you get my meaning."

"Now, now," Holly chided. "He's dead and gone."

This made me wonder how far along in their business Cameron Chevigny and Hollis Nunn got. If one owed the other money, if there'd been bad feelings when their partnership died short. If, if.

Hollis ducked his gray bristles away from Holly's scolding and my scowl. I knew I looked puzzled.

Holly Nunn put it plain for me, shaking her old head and whispering when Hollis couldn't hear. "Well, it is true that Cameron Chevigny was a man with a married wife."

I cocked my head like Charley looking at Guy's blender whirring away. Holly nodded like she'd said something real and gave a little tip of her head to go with the little truth she mentioned. "There are plenty of men like that, men whose wives are married. With some fellows, it's just the nature of the beast."

Chapter 21

MEN WITH MARRIED WIVES.

That's a heck of a thing to think on. Grabbing feed was my last errand in town, and I studied the notion of Holly Nunn's words without rest as I pulled Ol' Blue into the Co-op parking lot, went in for fifty pounds of alfalfa pellets—horses need their lysine and the local grass hay doesn't have enough—paid and bulled on out of the store, my body spent by the time I hurfed the load onto my truck's passenger seat.

"You're the little girl who shoes horses, aren't you?"

I turned to see a couple of middle-aged ladies, one beaming at the other, then both gawking at me.

"Isn't that right?" the one in a blue pantsuit asked, looking from me to the other busy bee. "You're the girl who shoes horses?"

Breathe. "Yes, ma'am. I shoe." I closed the truck door and stepped aside enough so the door decal with *Dale's Horseshoeing* in an arc over the house phone number showed plain.

The little girl who shoes horses. What am I, five years old?

The two women wearing polyester looked at me all expectant. They'd come from some office next to the co-op and clearly, one was introducing me to the other.

172

I sort of nodded.

The other woman said, "Well, they'll need a horseshoer when they move over here. And a veterinarian."

"Everything's convenient here," the first lady nodded, like she was selling the second one on the town of Cowdry, metropolis that it isn't. "I'm sure we can find suitable properties for you and for your son."

"My daughter-in-law does love her horses," Other Woman said, waving at the woman buzzing around her and then at me, with a smirk that said we'd all grow out of it someday.

Little does she know, some of us horse-crazy girls never grow out of it.

In the way a mammal likes air, yeah, I like horses.

The hive mate said her own daughter was spared that pining. She smiled at me like she was a friend, like she knew me.

Then I placed her. She's a realtor at the one podunk office in Cowdry. Her and an old coot partner. I don't know how they stay busy. Maybe by dragging out a property showing by introducing the prospective buyer to everything in sight. There's the grocery store. There's a vet's office. See that church? Looky, there's a horseshoer. Having just chucked fifty pounds of feed into my truck, feeling like a real woman in jeans, with no polyester in eye-watering colors, I was ready to be clear of these gals prattling about one of the properties being a bit of a fixer-upper.

Other Woman sighed happy with her wad of papers the first lady gave her. "Vince can fix anything. He takes things apart just to see why they don't go."

She got in her sedan as I went around to the driver's side of Ol' Blue's cab. Queen Bee realtor stood near me like we were going to have a word when alone with our consciences.

"That was Mrs.—"

The name this realtor lady mentioned didn't even make it far enough to enter my ear.

"Mmm," I said, looking around for a way to excuse myself. Made no sense for her to be jabbering to me.

"Oh, my daughter'll hate it if that woman moves in from Gris Loup, you know."

"I *don't* know," I said.

"Well, my Melinda said she's friends with you. Anyway, that other woman's son would move here if he gets the deputy job out here in Cowdry. Which means Melinda will stay a clerk. Not that we'd mind that. Maybe she'd go back to college and do something more white collar. More regular."

I'd just learned more about Melinda Kellan than I'd ever wanted to. At least I now knew who the other woman's horse crazy daughter-in-law was.

"But maybe a move would be good for her son and his wife," she went on, holding up my end of the conversation real well. "They had some trouble. The wife, you know. It doesn't do to talk."

I suppressed a snort. Can't be good for the sinuses, that kind of pressure.

"They were getting it on like bunnies," the realty woman said, tittering and pinking just enough as she whispered, "Her son's wife and that gentleman who died in the farming accident year before last."

"Ma'am, farming accident?" I began.

"Mr. Chevigny, at that place way back behind the forest land." Her voice grew stern.

I thought about Vince Pritchard's wife having an affair with Cameron Chevigny, that older rancher whose appetite seemed to have known no bounds. I chanced to ask, "Ma'am, who else knew about that affair?"

"Besides me and you?"

"Yeah."

"All of Butte County, honey." She had more to say, but I only half listened, busy thinking.

Loretta Pritchard was less than married but was a woman with a married husband. Cameron Chevigny took up with his neighbor Arielle Blake, as well as Earl Delmont's sister over at the bank as well as Loretta Pritchard over at the Saddle Up tack store in Gris Loup. Poor Donna. I didn't mean to, didn't want to, but I thought about Guy talking up Melinda, running sprints with her. I thought about Donna saying it's what we get for loving someone who's not centered on the heart, and Holly Nunn telling me about the stupid beasts' stupid nature.

I needed a shower in the worst way. A person oughtn't be able to smell herself standing out in the breeze. I thought about Melinda sizing me up like I was the competition.

And I got madder by the minute.

* * *

When I got home, Guy saw the angry all over me, dripping off. He backed up when I bailed out of Ol' Blue.

Trading off between shaking a couple fingers at him and gripping my hips, I railed about his stinking gender—I called 'em rat bastards and didn't excuse myself for breaking my oath against foul language—for a while, then got down to having him explain his own self to me.

That pure perplexion look of Guy's? That gets old.

"What?" he asked again.

"You tell me what's it gonna be."

"Well, fine. I will." And he waited, looking all expectant even though I was the one truly waiting on words. We trundled inside and plopped down at the dinette.

"Well?" I prompted him.

"Well," he began, "Rainy, I don't know what we're talking about."

What is he, begging me to kill him?

"Figure it out," I said.

"You're being pretty disagreeable," Guy said. "It's a little hard to take. I feel like you're upset with me for no reason."

"Poor you."

"Yes."

"You want me to feel sorry for you?"

"Well, sure. That would be fine. I would welcome your sympathy."

"If you run around on me," I told Guy, drawing a finger up from my fist in a way I know I'd hate to be pointed at, but it felt right natural all the same. Then I didn't know what more to say or do.

"First of all," Guy said. "I won't. It's just not my nature. Second, if I do, well then, what? And third, what in the world brought this on?"

"Go back to second of all. You want to find out what I'd do if you run around?"

He shook his head. "No—"

"You said you did, just one second ago."

"I've changed my mind, thought better of it. Don't need to know."

"Then why'd you ask?"

"Because my sweetheart was being a bit cantankerous and I bit back."

My dander and my red face rose, as well as my butt, right out of the chair, even as Guy waved me down with both palms, fingers spread, asking for another minute.

I took one good breath, gave him nothing other than, "What's the matter with you?"

Guy shrugged like he was fixing to give up. He stepped to the kitchen counter, pulled out one of his kitchen gizmos, and started pulling the green rind off a lime. I watched the pile of curly strands build, felt our tension grow as he reached for a couple more limes. "Scurvy."

It'd been so long, I was a little lost in the conversation now and was obliged to do some fast thinking to place the comment. I tried again with, "What are you doing?"

"It's a margarita key lime cheesecake."

Well, this needed no response. He knows that I don't partake of the demon medicine known as alcohol.

"We could take marriage classes," Guy said, like he'd just been dropped into the room from Outer Space. "There's a session starting in Gris Loup. It meets once a week for eight weeks."

Pfft, I lost that breath I'd taken. "Do what?" My mouth fell open again in pure appalledness at the words that escaped his mouth.

"Marriage classes." Guy said it like he was trying to muster a little dignity for the idea.

Please. It didn't merit looking into, this come-from-a-ditch idea. It didn't deserve a response or repeating but, oh no, try and tell Guy that.

He said again, "We could take marriage classes."

"We could pull our toes off with rusty pliers, too."

He rubbed his jaw. "Well, technically, yes, we could."

"So?"

"So. You're not big on the idea?"

My breath channeled out for half a minute. "Donna Chevigny's husband was bedding half of Butte County."

"And you thought I'd do the same?" His wrist whisked away, beating lime rind into creamy something in a bowl.

My head dropped. Calming down, I could smell the tang of the citrus. "I'd no reason to think that of you. I'm going to feed the horses and come back in a decent mood."

Guy kissed me. Charley followed me out to Red and The Kid. I told them that soon we'd have Bean to creep feed. I told them I'd picked a fight with Guy. They nickered their blessings. I told them about Cameron and Loretta playing post office or house or whatever they played last year, while Donna Chevigny and Vince Pritchard were knowing and hating.

Like Arielle, Loretta was young enough to be Cameron's daughter.

Running my hands over Red, feeling the warmth and muscle tone, the thickening of his chestnut coat brought on by our days getting shorter, I recalled more of what the realtor had said.

"*Yes, it would be good for the Pritchard family to get a change of* pace, have a move, but my Melinda will sure be sorry if they move here. She is in a mood about me showing them property."

Right, I had to remind myself, this realtor was Melinda Kellan's mother.

And Melinda Kellan's mama left me thinking on Vince Pritchard, his wants and his ways. He was with the Outfitters.

Vince's wife wasn't the only one who might have been riding that Paso with the funky footy.

The big reserve deputy's mama said he took things apart.

Maybe Vince should have tried that with Cameron Chevigny.

Maybe, come to think of it, he did.

Chapter 22

I N THE MORNING, I WOKE UP alone.

It's happened before. The Cascade's breakfast crowd is a hungry bunch. Guy goes in mighty early to prep stuff, lots of baking. But he usually smooches me howdy before he leaves. A good enough smooch to remember. I'd wear Guy out if I kept my bad attitude up. Six kinds of stupid is what I am.

Someone should do something nice for Guy, cook for him. I am that someone and if I pried myself out of bed now, buying and making a quick-cook dessert could be accomplished before I went to shoe for the day. He'd come home to a treat.

The little grocery store in the strip mall coughed up marshmallows, peanut butter and a box of cereal. My mama used to melt the first two, add the third and that's how treats happened.

In the parking lot, I saw her, Melinda Kellan, getting out of her little car. Surely her mama had shared with her what she thought everybody knew, Vince Pritchard's wife knowing Cameron Chevigny in the biblical sense. If Vince Pritchard went sling blade on anyone, his likely pick last year would have been Donna's husband. Given that Melinda was aiming to edge Vince out on the deputy job he wanted, and Melinda's mama is the county's biggest gossip, maybe the police clerk would be Vince's current choice to take apart.

I expected Melinda was maybe thinking about dallying with my man, even if Guy wouldn't behave like Cameron Chevigny. Ol' Blue seemed to idle in the parking lot, like my truck wanted me to defend my home front. My fiancé's track-running partner and who-knows-what-else looked flat startled to see me.

Her face softened.

Not at all the way a face ought to go if she was angling for my man.

"Hey." She smiled.

"Hey, yourself." That's exactly how my daddy spoke and it's a fine way for not getting to the heart of any matter, what was running through my head. *Are you even thinking of dinking with my supposed Intended?*

"Are you going shoeing? I'd still like to watch that sometime, if you don't mind. But I'm going to work now. Off at three."

Diesels are so loud, they're hard to talk over. I killed Ol' Blue's ignition and the comparative silence let my words mean more. "I met your mama."

Her eyeballs took a few laps around their sockets. "Oh, Jesus."

My master plan that developed a second earlier was working. Melinda was unsettled by her momma chatting with me, which made it a fine time to put a fine point on the real question at hand.

"So, you got a boyfriend?" *And stay clear of my patch, I thought. And get your mama to shut her trap. And—*

Her mouth fell open and she pinked up. "You *did* meet my mom. Jesus."

She looked embarrassed and it all made me recollect the way Vince Pritchard sneered at her for still living with her folks. Now I felt like I was as big a jerk as he was, looking down at her. Because there was nothing in her, really nothing, to think she'd sneak into my bed while I was gone.

She swung up from her car and came to lean on Ol' Blue's open window. "It was a ten mil round." Her lowered voice seemed to indicate we were talking some top secret shit. Oops, I mean, top secret stuff.

"How about that," I said.

"Do you know anything about ballistic profiling?"

"Nope." I shook my head, not having had to spend any time on her question.

"Well, that was a ten millimeter round inside the tire and it's in pretty good shape. If we had the pistol that fired it, we might be able to match it to the gun, provided the gun still has the same extractor and firing pin, which it probably does. After all, who changes that kind of thing?"

Who indeed? I had a better question. "Who's going to check every ten millimeter pistol in the world?" I wondered if old Suit Fellow had shared with her that he now had a ten millimeter shell casing that came from the Buckeye.

"When you hear hoof beats in Oregon don't look for zebras," Melinda said.

First of all, let's not be having a gal so new to horses she probably doesn't know which end to bridle go around mouthing off big horse analogies, like she's born to it. It's unbecoming. And B, what the heckfire did she mean? Just lately though, Melinda Kellan was getting as good as Guy at figuring out when I was going to hold up her end of the Clearness Quota and when she ought to get busy and do it herself, 'cause she explained her meaning.

"I bet that someone shooting at Chevigny or at the tractor or whatever, well, it was someone from around here, not some hobo in the night, you know?"

Borrowing from Guy isn't something I do too much of, but now was a time to start. I said, "Well, fine." After all, if she had a point, maybe she'd get to it someday.

Melinda thrust her lower jaw forward, looking smug. She knew a bit about rifles and was ready to let me know, I figured. What I hadn't known was that she knew who had this special shooter.

"Ten millimeters aren't all that common. They're not rare, but they're not super super common either. Everything unusual has to be reconsidered."

I spread my hands wide, since my mind doesn't go that way. Not that I'm narrow-minded, it's just sort of a two-lane dirt road-type brain in my skull, and it peters out into a single-track trail. Definitely not a multi-lane interstate.

"Okay," I said, "how would you ever figure out who's got a ten mil pistol and who doesn't? Even if you checked with stores, I mean, people can buy them privately and could have had them for a long time. You wouldn't be able to trace it down."

She looked at Ol' Blue's door, warming up in the sun. My truck needed a washing.

"Vince Pritchard has one."

Looking this way and that, then doing some squinting and boot scuffing didn't get my question any closer to asked, so finally my mouth moved. "How do you know he has a ten millimeter pistol?"

"Because he's a jackass," she explained.

Sure, I thought. If a guy's a donkey's dooby, it follows he'd have a ten millimeter pistol, particularly one that spit a shell out behind the Buckeye ranch. Absolutely. Makes sense.

To let her know she actually made no sense at all or at least a lot less sense than a shod hog, I said, "Huh?"

"Vince thought the Sheriff's Department should get away from forty-fives and go to carrying ten mils." She sniffed as she said this piece of wisdom, like it was just so silly or hoity-toity or something. We'd need to talk horse feet if she planned on making herself understandable to me.

"What's the big deal?" I asked. "After all, it's just a bullet-thrower and who cares what caliber the thing is?"

"Oh, there's more to it. Pritchard says that the Department should carry tens because they have better penetration. Says you can't shoot effectively through cars at bad guys with forty-fives."

That needed several seconds of thinking from me before I found the obvious reply. "Deputies around here do a lot of shooting people through cars, do they?"

Melinda sniffed again and turned away like I was talking down at her, headed into the strip mall office to file papers or something.

Funny, she and I could basically agree on a thing—that Magoutsen had his deputies outfitted just fine—but we could still scrap about it. Melinda's just cantankerous, I reckon. She can be however she wants to be.

I hurried my tail home for redemption. I can be the way I want to be, I'd decided, but I had to want to be better.

In the kitchen, I spread out my special groceries, wishing I'd made good on an effort for Guy days, weeks, and months ago.

Pretty soon, I had lots of things bubbling away, pretty well convinced that this cooking thing, in addition to smelling better than shoeing, was a pretty loose way to work. All good. The peanut butter was melting and the marshmallows were real interesting in their saucepot, but not melty enough. I sped things along into the microwave, so I wouldn't be late to shoe.

Big hero, that's what I was going to be.

The thing with melting a bunch of stuff, it actually takes time. And I'm not one for staring at a saucepot when I can be standing in the front door, sending Charley to gather the geese, calling to Red and The Kid, and thinking about the horses I'd be shoeing for my nice client, Jean Thurman.

* * *

How best to tell the betrothed that I blew up the kitchen, that became the question before me.

That whole deal about metal in the microwave, well, apparently it's a for-sure, no-joking kind of thing. And yeah, stuff that you wouldn't even think can catch fire, well, it can. But I know enough about fire to know that you don't give air to one you don't want. So I left the microwave's plastic door closed even as it started to melt.

Plastic fires reek, too. I resolved to never again put something with foil in one of those magic boxes called a microwave.

And I'd do whatever I had to do to get this stench out of my poor put-upon fiancé's kitchen.

Guy had been a lot more patient with me than I deserved.

I'd marry that man.

If he'd still have me.

Chapter 23

WHEN I WAS YOUNG, NOT LIKE I am now, but real young, I thought about how life would be, when I'm old, near half through my twenties, like now.

I was way off.

Not wanting to crud up Guy's kitchen towels wiping up the sweet, sticky black mess that will happen in anybody's kitchen when flaming marshmallows make the range-hood microwave door melt enough to fall off and knock the pan of burnt peanut butter off the stove, I went out to Ol' Blue for salvation.

Stuff I don't use too often in my daily work calls is stored way up at the front of the truck bed. It takes some undignified crawling over my bar stock, shoe inventory, pads, hoof packing, and extra tools to reach that beat-up cardboard box of super-absorbable disposable diapers. The didies are for wrapping hooves, but it's got to be said, when sopping up a microwave situation that includes a melted and blown off door, diapers are the tool of choice.

The chore let my mind work up a brilliant notion. The clock said I barely had enough time to buy *The Western* on my way to the shoeing appointment.

"Charley, let's go." Lots of times, he seems happy to stay home when I'm driving from one appointment to another, but right now, I needed his moral support.

I got the paper then drove one-handed, paging to the ads and calling the Cascade with the other. The Gris Loup appliance and furniture store's advertisement was right above the gun store's ad. No ten-millimeter pistols on sale, but some nines and a couple rifles.

I wondered if Stan Yates had a ten millimeter, a working one, amongst his replicas. Wondered where he bought all those guns.

Charley looked concerned with the paper spread over the front seat, rattling, and he didn't care for my lane swerving either. I told my good dog, "Sorry," and straightened out.

Smooth, is what I was when Guy answered.

"Hey," I said, "if you scoop up the newspaper you'll see an appliance ad on the back page. I'm buying a new microwave."

He sighed, didn't even summon the question of why we needed a new microwave. He didn't summon any words at all.

"I like the one on the upper left of the ad," I told him. It was on sale and had the right features.

Guy sounded mighty unimpressed but maybe that's just the way he is with me on anything having anything to do with a kitchen.

Makes my ponytail need a twisting and I got busy with it.

He finally asked, "Why?"

It sounded like The Big Why, like the man was having more thoughts than merited chewing. I needed to get him on point.

"It's got a button for potato and another for popcorn." That about covered things for me.

He still wasn't talking. He wasn't Guy. Brilliant idea number two had showed up.

We wouldn't be buying a microwave at all.

It'd make a lovely wedding present from someone.

"See you tonight," I told Guy. "And, I love you."

* * *

The usual mess of critters and kids cluttered my client's place. Those Thurman kids are a wonder, from the snot-nosed hair-puller up to the biggest one, a near teenager with a jaw set at the world like his daddy's. Mr. Thurman's scary to look at, but a nice man. Anyways, I always deal with Jean.

She had more on her plate than many moms. The Thurman kids, for sure and for certain the boys anyways, are Shetland ponies, prone to orneriness and straight hocks. If Jean Thurman doesn't boil that youngest boy-child of hers in oil before he makes ten, it'll be news.

"Hey, Rainy." Jean was a little breathless. "Glad you're here. The pony chipped a front a couple of days ago. Dunbar needs new shoes all the way around."

I'd already checked my notes. The whole Thurman family rides, filling up their six horse trailer. "Dunny's were new last time, right? Not re-sets?"

She nodded. "Yeah and I've put some good miles on him in the last few weeks. Been getting in some riding yourself?"

"Not enough," I admitted. Red's shoes are needing some wear.

"Darby said you were asking about the Winter Outfitters. Shame you just missed our summer event. We had all-day trail rides from the camp every day."

I gave that a face wiggle of no commitment or comment, and looked out to where there should have been a horse tied up and waiting for me. Really, really, clients ought to have their horses ready for me. I'm pretty good about being on time and it's hard to be that way if I have to spend extra minutes at an appointment while either the client or—curse them—*I* catch their horses for shoeing. Jean's usually got it together though, so I just looked serious instead of scowling like a badger.

She muttered something about the kids trying her pretty hard today and she'd grab the horse quick as she could, sorry.

As Jean trotted off, her youngest boy got a set of orders from Bad Kid Planet, which I reckon is in the same solar system as Horse

Planet. The kid went after one of the barn cats, managing just one quick grab at a tail. Hard on cats, that boy. Barn kitty needs to get a lot harder on little boys, if anyone's asking my opinion. All the tabby did was scoot for a high beam in the overhang of the barn and blink down at the boy.

The kid was not without a plan. Straight to a fresh pile of green horse apples he went, digging in with both hands, packing enough ammo in his fists to have several tries at hitting the cat.

Zing. Thwack on the wall, high and near the beam. Then with his other hand. Zing. Thwack. For a tyke, he had a couple of pretty good arms on him. Zing, thwack on the bottom of the beam. Getting closer. The kid's tongue was out in concentration and he wiped the back of one manure-crusted hand across his forehead and grunted on his next heave.

"Stop that," I said. "Why you throwing horse pucky at the cat?" I wasn't asking just to make conversation.

"I ain't s'posed to throw rocks," he said, like that explained it.

Morning wore into afternoon as I squared away the Thurman herd. I love feeling a slight flare in the toe wall, reducing it with my rasp, then stroking that smooth, straight alignment I've returned to the hoof.

Jean was putting away the second to last horse when the little thrower got back at it.

"Your mom's gonna see," I warned while hoping he'd get what he had coming.

We both heard Jean picking up speed, gravel scattering as she hustled down the barn driveway. The kid and I both knew a talking-to was coming on but only one of us was looking forward to it.

"Joby!"

It was like one of those commands some people can give their dogs to drop the ball or bone or whatever. With priceless speed, the boy's hands opened and the last of the manure dropped like he was standing over a pocket of Super Gravity. Then his feet woke up, and he seemed to remember a pile of pucky elsewhere that needed his urgent attention.

Interrupted by needing to give her boy a killing, Jean'd stormed back from her pasture still packing an empty halter and lead rope.

"So," I said, "not supposed to throw rocks, is he?" I couldn't help grinning. Most times, this youngest boy of the Thurmans pesters the daylights out of his sister who gets tasked with keeping him in check while his mama writes me a check.

His mama looked like thunder now. "I saw him throwing something. Did he throw a rock? I will skin that child alive and feed him the hide."

I waved my hands to stop her. Bet that child of hers never knew I saved his life. "No, no, he was chucking pucky at the cat. He sort of explained why. No rock throwing."

She rolled her eyes and checked the rafters for the barn cat, set her eyeballs on green smudges where the throws had caught timber and scowled. Then she gave a holler for the boy that there was no way he could later say he just hadn't heard. Charley, waiting for me in Ol' Blue, heard that bellow. I could see Jean was of a mind to chase the boy down, but she saw me standing there, antsy to be getting my work done.

"New rule, no rock throwing," she nodded, her glare finally rewarded with seeing the boy coming up to turn himself in. "Well, not that new. It came up during one of the Winter Outfitter camps. His buddies hatched a little plan to prove themselves tough by throwing rocks at the Buckeye bull, of all things. Mercy me." She shook her head, admitting she'd birthed the most trying child the world's ever known. Joby was kicking the ground all the way back to us, his lower lip sucked in.

"The Buckeye bull," I said, slowly.

"Oh, I could have strung him up by his toes when he got back. And it was after dark, too. He'd been all over camp, and Jim thought he was with me, while I thought he was with Jim and all the boys told their folks something different but it turns out Joby was the only one who kept this stupid dare to hit the bull's eye—"

"Do what?"

"They wanted to hit the Buckeye bull in the eye. Can you believe it? They thought they were hilarious. Being mean to an animal, provoking a dangerous animal, sneaking off, lying, out after dark." Jean Thurman ran out of fingers listing her boy's crimes on the incident.

It was worth saying twice, and I did, eyebrows up. "They wanted to sneak from your Outfitters camp over to the back of the Buckeye ranch and throw rocks at Dragoon, the Buckeye bull."

Jean rubbed her head. "I know, right? I could have killed him. Joby went in on this dare and snuck out there. His friends didn't even get there. He says he did, but then he came up with a story."

"A story?" I asked.

"Something about seeing someone out at some shed, stuffing something by a water trough or something like that." Jean sighed and shook her head again like she was both surprised and grateful to my stepping forward with interest. Maybe we both knew I'd usually be looking stiff on account of Jean still not having her horse front and center for my attention. Maybe I'd best lighten up a scoach.

"It was last year?" I asked.

"It was the year before," Joby said, looking from his mama to me and back again with hope. He seemed awful ready to have something to talk about other than his pucky-throwing crime of the last three minutes.

With the fall equinox only weeks away, Spring Outfitters was not much more than six months ago, so maybe Joby wasn't talking about the Outfitters that happened around the time Cameron Chevigny died under that tractor.

"So, this was two years ago?" I said, just to make sure. Pretty good memory for a little kid.

Jean shook and nodded her head. "He meant the spring before

last, so a year and a half ago." Meeting eyeballs, we understood each other. Little kids think the year begins with school, in the fall. I know, 'cause I still think of it that way my own self.

Which meant that Joby Thurman had a story about seeing something strange around the time Cameron Chevigny died.

Anything unusual's got to be looked at, that's what Donna said the Suit Fellow told her. That's what Melinda told me, too.

The sheriff's investigator hadn't looked far enough.

He hadn't looked at who-all wasn't staying in their own beds and leaving calling cards and maybe leaving a man to die under the slow crush of a farm tractor.

If Jean Thurman's little tail-pulling, sister-bothering, horse-apple-throwing, two-legged beast had seen something, maybe Melinda could shine with finding it out. Maybe it was high time for the law to pay attention to my being able to put the Pritchards' Paso throwing a shoe at some point on the Buckeye ranch, about Donna having found that shell casing there, too. It wasn't too tough to believe that the shell and that bullet found inside the tractor tire were from the same pistol.

Most likely, the shell casing and bullet came from the exact same pull of the trigger.

I checked my little phone and sighed. A Guy-quality sigh, it was. No cell service out at the Thurmans. "Can I make a call 'fore I set to shoeing?"

"In the kitchen," she said, jerking her thumb thataways as she moved off to the pasture. "I'll catch Dunny."

Chapter 24

THE THURMANS' OTHER HORSES ALL STOOD well, Dunbar was the only dancer. By the time I got the fronts off of Jean's last horse, her boy was set on a turned-over bucket to be my official horse fetcher and holder. The little guy could hang onto a horse's lead rope as well as his mama, plus have time to sit in a chair and think about what a stinker he is.

Melinda got there just as Jean was fixing to go in the house anyways. When Melinda asked if she could talk to the young man about what he saw at the shed, Jean looked a little mystified, but said sure as she headed for a ringing phone in her kitchen. I bet the woman never gets to sit down.

"What did you see, son?" Melinda asked.

I found myself stepping back as she used that too familiar term to this boy. Little Joby was no relation of hers and to my way of thinking, she shouldn't ought to have talked to him like he was. Watching and listening to this slowed my work down considerably. The boy already knew he was in some measure of hurt with his mama and now this strange woman was at his place, quizzing him about something that happened forever ago.

The kid wrinkled up his face when Melinda got on her knees in front of him.

"Do you know the difference between telling the truth and telling a lie?"

Joby nodded and looked like he thought he might be about to catch a spanking. I decided I'd wade on in and stop her, if that was what she was a-mind to do.

Melinda was on a roll, pointing at her jeans. "And if I said my pants were red, would that be the truth or a lie?"

Joby's voice was hoarse and he looked ready to crack with the pressure but he managed to whisper, "A lie."

She gave him a severe nod. "Good. Now if I said my jacket was brown, would that be the truth or a lie?"

"The, um . . ." The kid went to gulping like a guppy pulled out of his fishbowl. "That would be the truth. Your jacket's brown. Ma'am."

"Good. We'll only tell each other the truth, agreed?"

His eyes were too full for words now and he just nodded.

"So, tell me what you saw. Will you do that for me?"

The little guy nodded and looked a bit less likely to wet his pants as he got down to telling his story. He'd ridden from the Outfitters campsite through one buck fence on the forest land. He'd tied his pony and was sneaking up to a shed that had a barbed wire fence that extended off both ends of one side of the shed. On the other side, the shed had an electric fence over a water trough. He'd wanted to win the dare by hitting the bull with a rock, "Either in its bottom or its eye."

Properly distracted by that memory, Joby sniggered as he told the rest of his tale. His face lit up as he relived his moment of near glory, his hands flapped around helping him talk and his tongue went over his lips when he got to the juicy parts.

Melinda wore a wood plank face that left me wondering if she realized that we'd heard a pure description of the shed at the back of the Buckeye ranch. When the kid described the water trough at the back of the shed, I could see plain that what I thought of as the front of the shed would seem like the back to the kid when he was standing on the lease land. And the kid hadn't known the difference between the forest land and the lease land. He'd just known he wanted to hit a bull with a rock.

Joby bent everything, hips, knees, ankles, shoulders, even his green-stained fingers as he told about sneaking up to the shed. He went still as stone, telling how he'd seen someone else was there. At first he thought it was one of his buddies that he'd bet with, that another boy would beat him, be the first to hit the bull's eye. Then he realized it was a grown-up riding to the shed, so he hid and watched.

"Was it Mr. Chevigny?" Melinda asked.

Joby shook his head. "Nah, I 'member him. It was someone else."

"What did the person look like?" Melinda asked.

"It was kind of dark, you know." Joby shrugged.

"About how old?"

Shrug. "He was just a grown-up."

This little dude didn't know his momma's age, I bet. Jean was probably ten years older than me and he probably had us both pegged as the same, just grown-ups.

"What was he wearing?"

"Couldn't see. So he rode up and tied his horse and walked over and leaned across the water tank and put something down." The kid talked with his body, reaching toward a pocket on his T-shirt that didn't exist. Pretending to hold something in his hand, he leaned far out in a stiff-bodied way, bent at ninety degrees in the hips, knees locked, chest parallel to an imaginary water trough's surface as he reached straight out with his arm.

Body-talking was good for Joby Thurman. His eyes dried up as he automatically acted out what he'd seen. He was busy and lost in the moment of memory, showing how the person he'd watched lifted something off the ground behind the trough, put an item down with the other hand, then put back whatever the first hand had lifted. Melinda had him go over it a couple different ways and they went on past my interest in the hows of it all. I was left squinting away, looking at the Thurmans' stock tank as I thought about the one at Donna's shed. Hypnotized, I was, watching the way the sun danced off the ripples worked up by the wind at the water's surface. The reflection danced on the barn wall like a disco show.

What I really needed to be doing was finishing this Quarter Horse's shoes. I got busy, only catching part of Melinda taking in Joby's Big Serious story.

"He leaned over and reached for the ground." True to the little kid style of speaking, the boy moved as he talked.

Someone might lean in that weird way to avoid a hot fence, especially near the water trough. Especially in steel shank shoes and clothes that are sweaty from a hard ride. All of which would be all the better to conduct elec-juicity.

Hot, hot, Donna's wire was. Electric fences needed a lot of power to hold cattle. People who know that, well, they wouldn't like the gut-kicking jolt that comes from accidentally touching a bull-hot fence.

But everyone knew about Dragoon, right? I shook my head, more and more thinking I was dead wrong to have sic'd Melinda on this little boy, to have wasted one of my very precious brain cells even thinking on something I didn't understand and wasn't my concern.

While Melinda Kellan was making important breakthroughs in the proper interviewing and scaring of small children, I finished Dunbar and started loading up my tools.

A hot wind coughed across the little prairie land beyond the Thurmans' fields by the time Melinda was about done working Joby over and I went up to the house to get my check from Jean.

Joby and Melinda were paused by Ol' Blue when I got back. He hadn't quite got himself free of her.

"Has everything you told me been the truth?"

With his thinking wrinkles strapped across his forehead and nose again, the boy came up with, "Yes, ma'am." He laced his fingers together and rested the works on the top of his skull, smashing his overgrown crew cut with green fingers that left bits of pucky everywhere. I thought he was trying to keep his head from exploding since she'd made him think much harder than any little boy ought to have to try and do.

"All right, buddy," Melinda told the boy.

Joby Thurman wiped his face with the backs of his fists and puckered up a good sour face for her. No little fellow likes a woman who about makes him bawl. They both seemed like they were glad to be rid of each other as he trundled off to the house and Melinda and I hung at Ol' Blue. And I got to feel six kinds of smart, explaining the hot fence thing to Melinda as we left. I mean, she makes Guy look like horse people.

"So, what was all that about?" I asked her.

"All what?"

"Look," I said, "if you wanted to freak the kid out, why didn't you pull a gun or smack him in the face or something?"

She looked miffed, but I'd quick gotten used to that look from her.

"There are procedures to go through," she said. "In the interview of a child, it has to be established that the kid can differentiate between truth and lying and the kid has to commit to telling the truth."

Understanding that whoever the boy had seen visiting the Buckeye shed from the federal land was the last person to see Chevigny alive and probably the one who made him quit being alive, we were both sharp. But then Melinda extended herself to me.

"Let's get some dinner. Maybe the Dairy Queen?"

I nodded, thinking that's what people do. Friends, like maybe girlfriends, they have lunch. Then I said something about how mean she was to the kid and she said something about how ignorant

I was about police procedure. So, we had our second fight of the day. Maybe this having a girlfriend thing wasn't for me.

The girlfriend prospect muttered as she got in her little two-door, something about a ten millimeter round and about the Pritchards being in that Outfitters group and about a few folks knowing about Cameron and Loretta having an affair. I had a half notion that she was going to run to Magoutsen and tattle her big suspicions about Vince Pritchard. She wanted to make herself look good with her boss, get clerk of the year or something.

In Ol' Blue with Charley, I could think better about things Melinda mentioned that made Vince Pritchard look bad in this deal, and I tried to consider the situation from a couple different directions. I had no bone to pick with Pritchard, even though he wasn't on my Christmas card list. If two men were scratching on the earth and peeing on trees to mark territory, either could be wanting to do the other in, though Cameron Chevigny's reason to be after Vince Pritchard wasn't as good as Vince's reason to have gone after Cameron.

And Stan Yates. Just because the investigator thought Yates was surprised to learn his girlfriend was having a horizontal rodeo with the neighbor, well, the investigator could be wrong. Old Suit Fellow had been wrong when he called Cameron Chevigny's tractor rolling an accident. Maybe Stan had killed Arielle and Cameron.

But if the sheriff's detective was right about Yates being innocent, I could think of exactly one person in the world who made no bones about not liking Vince Pritchard.

And now I had a dinner date with her.

My gut said Melinda Kellan was wrong about Vince Pritchard. I'd an idea or two that he wasn't tough enough stuff to handle a hard ride and hike from the Outfitter camp to the back of the Buckeye. He was one of those that seems to think he's a big man and when push comes to shove, he'll push and shove but he's not an actual worker bee.

But Melinda Kellan could run for hours. And what better way to disqualify a guy aiming for a job with the law than to accuse him of murder?

Chapter 25

Some thinking needed to be done, preferably by someone with more smarts than me, but hey, work with what's there. Okay, Melinda'd been maybe too insistent that Darby pull the tire off the rim. She'd been ready to see what was there. She'd pointed out that Vince Pritchard's gun fired the same caliber bullet that Darby found inside the tractor tire. She probably knew Pritchard's wife was dallying with Cameron Chevigny. Could she have swiped Pritchard's pistol long enough to get out to the tractor from Keeper Lake and shoot the tire?

The next thing I knew, I'd reached the Dairy Queen parking lot and there was Melinda Kellan, waving big. I pulled in and parked right under the big red plastic ice cream cone.

It could well have been Melinda who shot at Chevigny's overturned tractor in order to pin the killing on Vince. Had I ever explained to her that the horseshoe was from the Pritchards' Paso?

Or that Stan Yates called Arielle 'Rielle' and maybe Cameron did, too? I smacked Ol' Blue's glovebox, pulled out the knife Donna had gifted me, undid my belt and strapped on the scabbard.

Melinda Kellan came up to me like we were friends, just gal pals having dinner. If she kept acting like that, it was going to be hard to hang onto my number one theory.

"So," she said, "Darby and the Pritchards are in that Outfitters group with your clients the Thurmans and a whole bunch of other people."

I turned my hip to show her my weapon. "I can put the Pritchards' horse on the Buckeye, near the shed Joby Thurman was talking about. That shoe I showed you came from the Buckeye, but it's off their Paso. And I reckon this knife is what got put under the cinder block behind the water trough."

Melinda frowned. "It wasn't Vince that the kid saw put that knife behind the water trough and—"

"Why do you think it couldn't have been him?" I gave her a look, my You're Not as Smart as You Think You Are look, but she wasn't as good as Guy at understanding my stares. "He's the one with the best reason to go after Cameron—"

She waved her hand. "Easier to show you than explain. Anyway, I checked the date. That kid saw someone at that shed the day Mr. Cameron Chevigny died. That was the Saturday night of the Outfitters campout. Same night. It was remote—"

"The kid was definitely talking about the Buckeye shed. His description matches that shed exactly."

"Yeah? Sweet. I'd like to see that. Most likely, that someone was the person who shot the tire. Which means the kid, Joby Thurman, saw the killer."

"I reckon that's right. You going to go after the kid some more?" I snorted. "You were pretty hard on him."

Her jaw flapped up then down and then around for another lap at not knowing what to say. "Was I?" She furrowed up her brow and pinked all at once.

"Yeah, you were."

She shook her head and I got set to hammer in my point since she seemed to be arguing. But she said, "Crap. I didn't mean to be. If I was, I screwed up."

Well, hey. She reminded me of someone. Except she admitted when she'd made a mistake.

For the first time, it occurred to me that if I let myself, I could like Melinda. I could even learn from her.

"Got to think outside the box," she said. "Come up with stuff that hasn't been considered, maybe some far out stuff, just every kind of possibility there is."

"Like?"

"Like the person who fired that round might not have been the only person involved in this mess." She ticked off one finger, several spares at the ready.

"Or?"

"Or who else possibly had something to gain by Chevigny's death."

Giving this the brow-scrunching-think it deserved, I pursed my lips and offered up, "Maybe some other stock contractors? Someone who wanted Dragoon?"

She nodded, getting into this. "Or had a grudge against him?"

"Cameron Chevigny or the bull?"

"Either or both. Maybe someone lost money in a bet or a ride or got hurt."

"And that someone bumped off Cameron by rolling his tractor?" I snorted 'cause it was too far out. And it was getting hungry out. I headed for Dairy Queen's glass door. "Let's eat."

In the lobby, an older couple with what looked to be a passel of grandkids stared when I asked Melinda, "So that someone bumping a man off by shooting his tire out would be who, the cowboy mafia?"

"In a manner of speaking."

"Well, there isn't one."

"Says you."

"Yeah, says me. Look, I'm saying this as a cowboy."

"So now you're a cowboy?" Melinda tried for a real superior look, her tone full of all kinds of the knowing of someone who doesn't believe a thing.

She didn't know who she was messing with. My eyebrows can arch up like that, too. I proved it then and there.

Nothing like a Dairy Queen kid in a paper hat to break a mood. "Can I take your order?"

No skinflint, that Melinda. It'd be a safe bet that I had more pocket money than she did, but she stepped up first when the kid totaled our order.

"On me, next time," I said. She grinned and I think it struck us both that there'd be a next time. We spent an hour, jabbering over sandwiches and sundaes. She punched my phone numbers into her cell and I scribbled hers on a paper napkin to put into my address book and little phone later.

I said, "You tell that Suit Fellow about Jean's kid seeing someone out there on the Buckeye? He's gotta be impressed, what and all with you basically finding that bullet, too. No wonder you're an evidence tech."

Melinda's head was nodding and shaking all at once. "Yeah, well, checking into that tire, was, um, I went about it wrong."

I wasn't with her at all on this one. "You solved the deal," I said. "You're the one who thought to check inside the tire, the only reason we know the tractor rolling was no accident. And today, you've got it pegged that someone was out there fiddling with something behind the water trough on the day Cameron Chevigny died." I patted my hip, pulled out the knife. "This, most likely, 'cause that's exactly where I found it, behind a concrete block that they have as a spacer back of the water trough."

She studied the bone-handled beauty again. "Heart R. Think this was meant as a gift?"

"Yep. And Arielle Blake went by Ree and Rielle and things like that, too."

Melinda gaped. "How do you know?"

"Yates told me." I ate the hot fudge first, because it's at its best right away.

"Well, she was having a fling with Chevigny. Poor Stan Yates."

Melinda took the knife, then stared at me as she returned it. "I didn't solve anything."

I holstered the knife. "But you, I mean, you figured out something happened. The guy who investigated Chevigny's death said it was an accident. Someone shot out the tire and rolled the tractor."

"Someone could have shot the tire any time after it rolled." Cheeseburger grease rolled down her elbow and she used the last napkin.

"True, but what's more likely? That someone shot the tire to roll the tractor—and maybe they were really aiming at him but settled for rolling the tractor—or that sometime after the tractor rolled, someone came by and shot the low tire? Think about Stan Yates. Your investigator thought he was innocent, but he also thought Cameron Chevigny died in an accident. You nailed that part."

"No," she said, shaking her head. "I didn't figure out anything. And what I did do, I messed up, did it wrong."

"How's that?"

"What I did, asking that guy Darby to check inside the tire, it was bad police procedure. It didn't impress anyone." Melinda was turning into a kid now. She sounded mighty glum, like she was moping.

Made me think of Abby. I missed that girl, the one I'd aunty'd and been a big sister to. Abby was just starting to grow up in the promise of a good way, not the sullen, unhappy girl she'd turned into in the last week or so. Now that Abby was going away, things were different. People change when life happens to them and it would happen to my sort-of niece this year. People change for better and worse, their minds and pasts and futures all lock up.

Melinda did some a-hemming and said, "The *mens rea* isn't necessarily all that hard to point to here, you know, if the Chevigny death was a homicide, but the evidence, I mean, crap."

Knowing a bunch of Greek or Latin doesn't mean it's got to be said with every breath, am I right?

"I envy you," Melinda said. "You know what you want to do and you're already doing it. You're on your own. I'm still waiting for the starting gun to go off in my life."

In my whole entire two-and-a-half decades, I'd never heard something so silly. "What's there to wait for?" I asked. "Be independent. Go after what you want."

"Well, in the job I want, what I really want to do, well, I'm dependent on others to get it. I can't just go out and be what I want, I have to get picked, get hired."

"What do you want?"

"I want to move up in the sheriff's department."

I set my burger down pronto, wondering on her words. "I figured. But, why?"

"Why?"

"Looky, those uniforms."

"What about them?" She was starting to give me an undeserved stink eye.

"Well, they look so hot. Overwarm, I mean." I can never tell if she's laughing at me or with me. But I sobered her up right quick with the observation that word had it there was a hiring coming up at the sheriff's department. "The sheriff's probably going to hire a reserve to become a full-time paid deputy, huh?"

"Other than me, Pritchard's the only one with the department who put in for the job. And he's been a reserve way longer than I've been a clerk, so, yeah." She frowned.

"So that's why you're trying to make him look bad," I beamed. "Seriously, what is it with you and Vince Pritchard?" I cocked an eyebrow.

She looked a little scolded and said, "I'd be a better cop than him."

How could she know something like that? I offered another stern scowl. Good thing my supply's large.

Then Melinda opened her heart wide. "I want to be a cop."

It was like looking at me, just a few years ago, wanting to be a horseshoer. I could fall in like with Melinda, surely I could.

I did.

"Well," I said in my most helpful way, "you've certainly got the mouth for being a cop."

"What's that supposed to mean, the mouth?"

"The vocabulary," I explained. "You cuss."

My friend, the potty-talking cop wannabe, gave me a withering look that only increased when I spoke.

"It doesn't look good, you making Vince look bad by pointing a finger at him."

She howled. "Oh, it couldn't have been him who fired that round."

"Why not?"

"The person that kid Joby Thurman saw leaning over the water trough? It absolutely could not have been Vince Pritchard."

Chapter 26

"THE THING IS, I'M ACTUALLY KIND of full."

"You ate out," Guy accused. He was sitting at the dinette whisking something that had the makings of a fancy-pants happening going on in the kitchen. Ingredients I don't know and utensils I can't work were all over the counters. Trying to ignore the burnt plastic smell of the passed-on microwave was a little piece tough. I felt as bad as things smelled to have forgotten about dealing with the ruined microwave.

"Uh . . ." I made an effort to not burp.

He was on his feet now, pacing a little. "Fast food, I'll bet."

"You'd win," I admitted, sure he'd understand when he found out dinner only set a body back two dollars. "The cheeseburgers were ninety-nine cents."

Guy looked like he was hurting somewhere deep, maybe under his liver. He spread his hands wide after taking them off his guts. "Why?"

I shrugged. "There's a special going on. Why do I have to explain how Dairy Queen sets their prices?"

Guy groaned. "I mean, why would you eat that crap?"

Okay, now first of all, he's just got to get over the food thing, right?

But then, he's not going to, is he? And spoiling for a fight isn't like Guy. He wants to cook and hang out in the evenings. When we're getting along, our evenings together puttering like we do, it's my favorite thing. I ran a few more breaths in and out of my lung pipes while I was thinking. Guy stayed tetchy. Getting along isn't enough, I realized. Where I'd let us down before was in not showing myself to Guy. And I'd kept letting us down by not considering him in the way he does me. Guy puts me first.

"Look," I said, "cheeseburgers aside, I've been being a jerk to you and I shouldn't have been and I'm sorry." Whew. Give the Melinda thing a whirl, I thought. Own up to my turdiness right away and show some regret.

A smile tugged at one corner of Guy's mouth, then the other. "You mean you're ready to—"

"Please, not the marriage class thing?"

He countered like we were negotiating a sale. "Do the marriage thing?"

"That, yeah. Guy, I'm sorry." I took a knee, I really did. Reached for his closest hand with both of mine. "Marry me, please?"

He laughed and turned red. He's hard to resist like that. "Marry you," he repeated the words, drew them out for savoring as I stayed in my begging position. "Well, fine."

"I'm not joking. I mean married like marriage. Like, with a wedding."

"You're ready to plan?"

"Heck yeah." I would have apologized for cussing, but my mouth was busy being kissed. We grinned at each other. "I'll marry you this minute, tonight, tomorrow, next week, any day you say."

"Well," Guy said, "I'm going to cook everything we have. We have to pick a date, a location, an invitation list."

"Watch this." I dialed on the house phone.

His brow furrowed and he raised his hands in a question. "What are you doing?"

The right voice came on the line and I asked one thing. "Want to be my maid of honor?"

It was quiet. Throat-clearing came as my friend made the right guesses, got herself caught up, and then I heard, "Yeah, I do."

"Come on over. We'll gab and Guy'll feed us."

"We just ate."

"I know. And we're in trouble over that. But if we hang out long enough, we'll be hungry again."

Guy stood there, relaxing a bit but still a little wary-looking when I told him plain who I'd called. Then he had to go and say, "Melinda Kellan? You said she's a bit of a witch."

I nodded, but now I had an amendment to the observation. "But she's a good witch. And now she's going to be the maid of honor in our wedding. Who else should we invite? Can I ask Donna? I just really like her. I'm hauling that tire back out to the tractor for her tomorrow and I can ask her then."

"Invite anyone and everyone. That reminds me, I saw the Nunns in the Cascade today. The hay guy has the hots for Donna Chevigny." He looked happy-naughty with knowing. Grinning, hands folded across mine on his chest, Guy told me about Hollis Nunn coming into the Cascade. "He said she puts lead in his pencil."

"He's out of luck 'cause Donna would never take up with a married man."

"He's not married."

"He's so married that he and his old lady, Holly, look like each other."

"Holly? That's his sister. They stopped in to eat and he called me over. Hollis mentioned you in a very nice way. And he said you should be careful on the Buckeye because of a particular bull."

I sat up.

"I thought Holly was his wife."

He smiled. "Not so much. She's his twin. But listen, I don't want you to come a cropper out there dealing with the tractor around Donna Chevigny's bull—"

"You sound like Hollis now."

"His words," Guy nodded. "Rainy, I want you to be careful. You know what? Just wait. Wait 'til I get off work tomorrow. I'll go with you on that tire favor errand deal of yours."

"His sister. Not his wife. Huh." I shook my head. I thought about how mysteriously certain Melinda Kellan had been that Vince Pritchard was not the person little Joby Thurman saw skulking around the Buckeye shed way back when. Melinda knew something, like the police tended to, that she wasn't sharing.

If it couldn't have been Vince Pritchard, it sure could have been Hollis Nunn. I hadn't known Hollis was interested in Donna. Hollis and Cameron Chevigny had a falling out of some kind in their rodeo stock business. Suppose Hollis Nunn had made the tractor roll, killed Cameron on purpose?

Guy kissed me. "Since you picked a maid of honor and called her over, I'm calling Biff—"

"Biff." I snapped my fingers, recalling my time with Stan Yates, Arielle's note.

"Anyway, Biff will stand up for me. Hey, Abby could be your flower girl. By the way, Bean is here, in the pasture with Red and The Kid. Keith Langston got his neighbor to do the hauling. He said Abby wanted him to bring Liberty, too."

The horses had been off in the back of the field, out of sight when I first got home. I went out now to take a look and a think.

The pasture situation was going to take some figuring out. Bean was hollering his little head off, put-out with being de-mama'd. The Kid came dragging himself up for a nuzzle. I was staring at the field for cross-fencing ideas, when my friend Melinda showed up.

Red gave Melinda his mean face, definitely getting some order from Horse Planet about putting off the newby. It didn't strike too well for Melinda's points, this bit about Red not taking a shine to her.

"You've got to get on his good side," I said.

"Which side would that be?" Melinda asked.

"The outside."

She smiled so friendly, I couldn't help smiling back. That is, until she said, "I think I'd like a mule."

That was a little bit of a horrifying idea, to be honest. Some mules will wait a decade to step on your foot over an old resentment. If they're not handled right early on—and most aren't—they can be a bear to deal with for eternity. The old boys on the ranch where daddy worked said that mules'll haunt a ranch, break stuff even after they're buried. They have a thing about their ears, and their braying scares some horses.

But they are tough and they have tough feet, even if they are shaped weird.

"I did some reading," Melinda said. "A Quarter Horse to race a quarter mile, a Thoroughbred to race a mile or three, an Arabian to race fifty or a hundred, right?"

I nodded.

"And to race a thousand miles, get a mule. I read that."

Not much for me to say. She was right, but no one goes hard a thousand miles. That's life.

She about squared off in front of me for an answer, badgering me with, "Mules stay, right?"

I nodded. They do have amazing strength. Like Melinda.

"They're stayers," I admitted.

More nodding. "Raise 'em right, they can be a world of miles. They're strong and smart."

Oh, she'd been reading up.

"They never forget and they can hold a real grudge." Then I thought, well, hey, of course she'd like something born of a horse and a donkey, they're just like her, and me.

"You're a mule," I said.

"Yeah, I am."

"I always try to figure what kind of horse someone would be. Like Magoutsen? He's a grade horse, but a good solid reliable one. That other deputy? He's an Appendix Quarter Horse, got a little Thoroughbred in him." I tried to think of others at her work place. "That other reserve, Pritchard—"

"You can't compare him to a horse. He's a gutless fuckwit," she said.

"Halfwit," I suggested.

"Sorry."

I considered what she'd said. "You really think he's gutless?"

"It's his defining characteristic."

Being a coward is a heck of a thing for one person to say about another. Having eaten a few chicken chances myself, I'm not about to point any fingers. But if she'd caught him being less than brave, it'd be a story worth hearing.

"Are you guessing? About Vince?"

She gave a bare nod that set me to shifting about like Red when he's been asked to stay put for longer than his mind can stand it.

"I think you're right about the horseshoe, about it coming from one of the Pritchards' horses," Melinda said, "you've got to be."

"But there's no way of telling what day that shoe got thrown out there."

"It still proves their horse was ridden out there, and if they say it wasn't, someone's lying. I'll bet the horse was out there, the knife was put behind the water trough and the shot was fired by the same person the same night. And I'll bet it was Vince's pistol that put that round in the tractor tire."

A sigh escaped me. "You and Vince are gunning for the same job. It doesn't look great for you to go back to making a case against him, though I do see that he's the one with the motive to hate Cameron Chevigny over dallying with Loretta."

She snorted. "I'm not making a case against Vince. I told you, it wasn't him the kid saw skulking around that night."

"How do you know?"

Melinda grinned and nodded like, yeah, she did know. "There's a thing I heard, long time ago."

I gave that notion some thinking, trying to imagine what she thought she knew or what she might actually know. Finally, I asked, "Something 'bout Vince?"

She shook her head. "About men."

"The rat bastard thing?"

Rolled her eyes at me. "Rainy, they are not all rats."

"You know for a fact they're not all rats? You checked all of them?"

I was feeling a smidgin proud of my arguing abilities.

"You're about to marry a prince, Rainy."

She had me there. "Yeah, I am."

"You got me off track—"

"I do that—"

"The thing is, a guy can't pick heavy stuff up when he's bent over the way that kid showed us."

She went over to Ol' Blue and bent at her waist bent in a perfect ninety-degree angle, her back parallel to the ground, arms hanging straight down from her shoulder sockets.

"Try this," she told me. Then she waved for me to wait a minute and pointed to my toolbox. "Try it leaning over like I just did, like the kid showed us and see if you can pick it up."

"I can pick it up," I assured her. "I can lift real weight. Shoeing builds a back."

She just looked at me, a tiny grin trying to creep out the right corner of her mouth.

Sliding my toolbox into position near the wall, I leaned over in the same Army Girl posture she'd done. With my hands dangling, I grabbed my toolbox up from down low and pulled it to my chest without a peep.

"Okay, call Guy out here and get him to do it." She was out-and-out smirking now.

"What are you up to?" I asked.

"Humor me, please? I bet you Guy can't pick up your toolbox if he's bent in that position. And if Guy can't, then Vince Pritchard couldn't."

Chapter 27

TAKEN ABACK, I BIT AND EXPLAINED to Melinda that Guy wasn't a bulky muscle man type, but he was a plenty strong guy, just not a flaunter. He can hold a plank position, even a side plank, for five minutes. But even as I promised Melinda that Guy could lift my toolbox, she annoyed me shaking her head and daring me to call him out.

Then she double dog dared me.

"Hey, Guy," I bellowed at the house.

Oh, if only he hadn't been wearing that apron when he stuck his head out.

"Hmmm?" He was stirring something in a teeny tiny saucepan, using a little Barbie-doll-sized whisk.

"Would you come here a sec?"

He looked a little hesitant to give his future bride, like, two seconds of his valuable time. And then he saw her looking fit to skin him.

"I don't want the sauce to curdle," he explained.

Oh.

My.

He was trying to antagonize me, surely. I was put to whisking while he was put to the lifting task. Doing exactly what Melinda told him to do, exactly how she told him to do it—oh, he'd make a fine husband—Guy set to pick up my toolbox with his back and legs straight, hips at a perfect ninety-degree angle.

He fell over. My Guy couldn't lift my tool box from that position.

Such a spectacle would have knocked me on my butt for a good giggle if I hadn't been stirring—hey, what was this sauce? It smelled like caramel.

"Mmm, will this stuff be ready soon?"

Guy took his little saucepot back from me. "Come inside, both of you."

Biff drove up in his eyesore of a lime green El Camino.

"My best man," Guy said, switching the saucepot to his left hand so he could shake hands with Biff.

"Congratulations, bro." Biff grinned all around, eyeing Melinda with interest.

Her face was poker straight, watching Biff as she told Guy and me, "I bet Biff can do the lift."

Biff went along, his faced perplexed, cooperating with a silly, put-upon grin. And he lifted my toolbox while in that ninety-degree bend, no problem.

"Enough," Guy said, stirring. "I need to add the cream. Inside, everyone."

"What's this all about?" Biff asked. "I thought we were celebrating."

"We are celebrating," Guy said. "And that was mysterious women stuff. I don't ask, and recommend you don't either. Inside, everyone. Please."

Melinda lit up like she'd been invited to a swell party. A part of me flinched with the feeling of having missed something, not getting what Melinda's deal with Biff was, 'cause she wasn't wary of him, just pleased that Guy couldn't lift the weight. I'd wait to ask her why she knew Biff could and what it meant, but a niggling thought—

Guy said, "I'm going to feed my fiancée, maid-of-honor-to-be and best-man-to-be." He smooched me, his gaze full of meaning, and I felt a blush seep across my face. Guy's known I needed a friend here in Cowdry. Making a life, a family of friends in a new place can be tough. We all crowded the kitchen, my nice guy offering beers, pouring me iced tea. I wanted to think and I could see Melinda wasn't done thinking and glowing with whatever she'd figured out.

The caramel cream sauce wasn't curdled, as far as I could tell anyways, it was poured over thin sliced pork roast and just as good mopped up with the crusty bread Guy kept coming.

After dinner, Guy turned to ask Melinda, "Do you ride?"

"I'd like to."

"She wants to be a cop," I said.

Melinda pointed to an open catalog on the coffee table. "Why are those horses wearing thongs?"

The ad showed photos of horses outfitted for backcountry hill climbing.

"That's a crupper," I said. "And you're embarrassing me."

"Is that a Western or English saddle?"

Oh, so she knew a tiny bit. "In between," I said. "It's for trail riding."

"What kind do you have?" Melinda addressed Guy, acting like she was a little suspicious of any answer I'd give. So I gave it.

"He doesn't have one. Rides bareback. So do I, just 'cause I can't afford a saddle yet."

"Well, technically," Guy explained, "those slick leather saddles don't offer much purchase. Nothing to pucker up on, if you get my meaning."

Laughing, Melinda and I kicked back in the kitchen chairs. Rocking on the back legs, I balanced with my core, like riding a horse. I could all around have a fine time, enjoying my friend's company. If I were a drinker, me and Melinda, we'd be drinking buddies. Sure I could do it, have a friend, a real girlfriend. Guy had been in Cowdry just a couple years ahead of me, already friended up with poker and rugby and running buddies like Biff and some others with similar names. A Chip? An Eddie or Teddy or something like that. Biff leaned against the kitchen counter, watching us, beer in hand as I talked about my post-shoeing plans for the next afternoon, hauling the repaired tractor tire to the back of the Buckeye.

Melinda was one who couldn't leave a thing alone. "I want to take a look at that area where the tractor is. I'm supposed to work, but maybe I could get off a little early. I'd really like to go."

Okey doke, if she wants to go, no harm in her tagging along. I'd bet Donna'd give me the loan of another horse.

* * *

And later that night, Guy grinned across the bed at me, the same smirking smile Spooky does when he's kneading your thigh and knows you hate it. The same grin Melinda did when she'd known that Guy would be off balance and unable to lift my toolbox, but Biff could do it. I should have badgered her to speak up on it. All sorts of words and weird pictures danced around the ceiling of my skull.

"Arielle Blake had a note in her things that Stan Yates found. It said 'Biff C.' and he didn't know who it referred to."

"Biff's last name is Pullara."

"What's his middle name?"

Guy said, "Guys don't ask each other that."

"What's Biff's real first name?"

"I don't know that either."

I thought about Stan Yates and the note Arielle wrote about 'Biff C' and I couldn't peg the right questions and links. "I asked Biff if he knew Arielle and he told me no."

"He didn't. I remember talking when we were on the search party for the sheriff's department. Neither of us had ever heard of her."

"I should have told Melinda about the Biff C thing Arielle wrote."

"Biff had nothing to do with it. And maybe it was Stan Yates who wrote whatever he says he found amongst Arielle's things."

Guy was right, I decided. We couldn't know something was so just because Yates or anyone else said it was. "I thought Vince was the likely person to have fired the shot that rolled Cameron Chevigny's tractor." Guy snuggled, kissed my neck. "Well, Vince had a reason to have a grudge against Cameron Chevigny."

"But Melinda says it couldn't have been Vince that Joby Thurman saw at the water trough by the Chevigny shed. Vince's a big dude. If you can't do that bend over a water trough and lift a concrete block move, then Vince sure couldn't." The lift was about build, I decided. Balance. That's what Melinda was showing.

I realized Hollis Nunn wouldn't be able to do the lift either.

Guy's fingertips worked goosebumps into my spine. He laughed and added, breath in my hair, "We're never going to be tangled up in those triangles like Cameron and Vince were."

"Nope. Not us." I needed to get my mind clear of all this small-town trash, but I thought again of Melinda and Vince's attitudes to each other. "Melinda thinks Pritchard's a scaredy-cat."

"He's picked an odd profession to be in then. I'd think a person would have to be brave," Guy said it like he was ready for us to stop talking.

I shrugged. "I don't know much about being brave."

He smiled then. "You're the bravest person I ever met."

"Meet a lot of weenies, do you?"

Guy snorted. If he was a pony, he'd be saying he was scared or amazed.

Guy made me coffee in the morning, which was not amazing, just regular nice. "Wait for me and I'll go with you to the Buckeye late this afternoon."

I shook my head. "I wouldn't get back before dark if I waited 'til you got off work. I'll be fine. Melinda's probably coming with me.

Anyways, I'm just hauling that tire out and putting it back on the tractor."

* * *

Darby had the tractor tire ready and used his loader to get it aboard Ol' Blue's Brahma topper.

"Watch out for cougars out near that federal land. One of the folks in the Outfitters group rides there, reported sign one time."

"Cougar sign?"

"You packing?"

To Darby, *packing* probably didn't mean getting a suitcase filled up to go on a nice vacation.

Bang! His loader dumped the tractor tire onto Ol' Blue's Brahma topper with a thud that made Charley cower. It's already full of scratches up there but it still made me wince. We set to task with a bunch of spare cord Darby produced, got that tire tied down.

"You got a knife, just in case?" Darby had a wicked way with knots and knew it.

"'Course I've got a knife." I turned my hip and lifted the flannel shirt open over my tank top to remind him who he was talking to. A shoer has tools.

Darby's double take was bell clear. He stared and finally rubbed his jaw, muttering. "It didn't have the engraving when I sold the knife and hammer."

I looked at the Heart R knife in the scabbard on my hip.

Darby wiped his mouth, sealing his lips.

Something like a molasses and manure combo of ideas turned in my brain. I nodded encouragement at Darby, wondering all kinds of things about so many people in Butte County. "You ordered something for Stan Yates? For Biff Pullara? For Hollis Nunn? You ordered something else? A gun?"

He shook his head. "Don't want to add to the gossip."

Chapter 28

O N THE OTHER SIDE OF CHARLEY in Ol' Blue's bench seat, Melinda Kellan eyed Stan Yates's mailbox. I told her about Yates buying the north part of the Buckeye ranch.

"Interesting."

"So we might be fixing Stan Yates's tractor."

"Sweet deal for him."

Yates wasn't outside, weed whacking or otherwise engaged, as I rumbled Ol' Blue on to the ranch. I still thought it would have been great if Yates could have not had it in for a widow who'd done him no harm, but it was still none of my business and I couldn't exactly pull up to his house to give him a piece of my mind. Besides, I needed all my pieces.

Bugs chirred in a golden fall afternoon at the Buckeye ranch. Guy's warning that I not come a cropper in the far fields wasn't much on my mind. Melinda didn't say what was on hers when we dismounted Ol' Blue. The prospect of a ranch ride with a friend—two friends, since Charley was there—finishing my good deed, that's where my mind was.

Slowpoke ran up to greet us, making dust fly, protesting in whimpers when Donna tied him with a lead rope so he didn't follow us out to the back of the ranch.

Then Donna threw me with, "What I said before, the guilt thing . . ."

"Yes, ma'am?" I was surprised she wanted to talk to me in front of Melinda, but I guess she was ready to purge her conscience, and no one was going to get in her way.

"It's not just guilt over not checking on him. It's how I felt. How I still feel," Donna wound up with a resigned breath, like she was some kind of horrible person. "There were days I was ready to be rid of him, I tell you. Days when I could have stood Cameron getting himself killed, bad as that sounds. I was so sick of the shame of him wanting more than me, I . . ."

There in her barn, she wasn't going to cry, she just bit it all back and I was left to say something.

Anything.

But before I could, Donna went on. "I heard a woman say something about the gutter. I thought he was breaking it off with her. He'd had so many."

"You overheard this?"

"On the phone. Cameron had a cellphone—I don't—but it didn't always work out here. He got a call at the house. He didn't know I listened in. It was a woman."

Melinda nodded and echoed, "It was a woman."

I gave Melinda the strange look she deserved, then asked Donna, "Did she sound mad at him?"

"No, she didn't but, oh, I don't know."

It wasn't 'til I'd saddled Skip—one of Donna's best Quarter Horses—and gotten Buster's harness situated that a thought made itself into whole form in one of my spare brain cells. I went to Donna and asked, "Could you have heard talk about something being right under the gutter?"

After a pause, she said, "I could have. I'd heard the word, set the phone back down. I'd guessed maybe it was talk of someone's mind being in the gutter. But maybe that's where my mind was."

More of Donna beating herself, I couldn't stand.

"Perfectly understandable for you to hate him stepping out. He oughtn't to have treated you that way."

Melinda nodded. "I hate that he did that."

Donna's cheeks pinked up. "That's what Hollis Nunn says."

"Guy hates it, too," I added.

"Does he?" Donna asked.

"Yes, ma'am."

"You might have a winner there."

That agreed, I was set to go. Melinda, left out of the loop on account of her not having herself a man worth having or worth getting rid of, felt called upon to mention to Donna how she wasn't a police officer but she wanted it clear that she did happen to work directly for Sheriff Magoutsen, she'd let him know over the radio that she was out here helping me with the tire, and she wanted to make sure Donna was okay with her taking a look at the area where the tractor was.

Donna's sad little smile was wry, looked tried even though she clearly wasn't afraid of anything Melinda wanted to know about.

"I don't know what's what, but I'd like to understand it all better." Donna sounded beat from her stack of chores, the way this winter of her life had turned out.

Not wanting her to mope, I grinned a winner. "Well, how about it, this idea of mine, getting your tractor back up and running, sticking it in the shed?"

Donna looked away, misty-eyed, and I knew not to press another minute. Then she managed a little nod that was my go-ahead, and said, "Well, we can try and see."

Charley followed when I mounted Skip. Melinda straddled Buster like she knew what she was doing, her face firm even after we'd ridden deep enough into the ranch. I knew her legs had to be dying, and I could be the kind of giver who finds a way to distract a friend from pain.

"You think Biff could be a nickname for Bickford?"

"I suppose. Why?"

After I told her about Arielle writing *Biff* C, she asked how I knew that Arielle was the one to write the note.

"Guess you're right," I admitted. The world of police investigations was not one for me. I like horses. Hooves don't lie.

"You really thought Guy's buddy Biff had something to do with Arielle's disappearance and murder? What's Biff's full name?"

"Guy doesn't know." But I explained about Guy mapping runs on TrailTime. "So I guess the website shows when other trail users map runs on the same trails. Guy was running the app off his cell phone when he looked for Arielle and he remembers there being another map around Keeper Lake but it's not there anymore."

"So, why would someone delete a map there?"

"That's the question," I agreed. "Biff says he didn't map, didn't delete. Why'd the sheriff's department have Guy and Biff look around Keeper Lake?"

"Well, this is not public knowledge, but that's where her phone showed as its last point known on the Find My Phone app."

"I don't get that," I said. "I mean, Yates said that, too. But what was she doing there?"

Melinda shifted atop Buster, rubbed her quad muscles. "Who's Hollis?"

"Oh, he's the hay man." I explained about the failed rodeo stock business.

"Interesting," Melinda stopped Buster at the edge of the ravine. "Holy cats, ride him down that?"

"After you. Trust me. And Buster. He's done it before."

Dragging the rock sled down into the ravine was tougher than the travois I'd used to haul it out with, but the rock sled was better for the just-fixed tire. Melinda mumbled encouragement to the big horse the whole way. I figured she was really calming herself. I scratched thank yous to Skip now and again, but the good horse under me had it all under control.

"Good boy, Buster, good boy. That's it. Easy now. Steady. Good boy."

I told Melinda, "You talk as much as your momma."

"Oh, I had an earful from her after she showed the Pritchards and his parents Cowdry property. My mom said it was all her son this and her son that. Retta this and Retta that."

"Who's Retta?"

"Vince Pritchard's wife. Loretta. She's like you, into horses—"

"Give Buster his head. He won't go too fast, you can trust him, but he might need to swing his neck for balance. Holding the reins short hampers him." I'd given Skip all the rein he wanted as we inched down the switchbacks into the ravine.

"Since all the Pritchards are looking at horse property on the west side, they're moving, and if they're moving, he's got the job. He'll be the next deputy."

"Maybe there will be another job opening for you sometime soon."

We hit bottom in no time.

"Wow," Melinda said, gawking at the switchback in front of us. "We're climbing up that?"

"I'll go first this time."

"Why'd you make me go first when we came down here?"

"Same reason I should be ahead this time: In case Buster loses the load."

She craned her head at the tire on the sled Buster was dragging. We'd long since tuned out the racket of the rock sled. "Is he going to lose it?"

"Nope." I nudged Skip up the ravine. In a few minutes, Buster leaned forward with one last heave that hurfed Melinda and the rock sled with the tractor tire cargo clean out of the ravine, up onto the back of the Buckeye ranch. I explained to Melinda all about Stan Yates's land bordering the west end and him telling Donna he had a handshake deal with Cameron Chevigny to buy it in hopes of more wind farming.

"Interesting," Melinda said.

Even with the day dying around us, under the direct sun it was baking, and my old dog panted like he'd raced the miles to the tractor instead of slow-trotted behind a walking horse.

Water and shade were up at the shed.

"Go on, Charley," I said, pointing up the hogback to the shed. "That'll do, wait for me there."

I explained to Melinda how the shed was an open breezeway, not the solid square it looked to be from our angle. She nodded and I watched her squint at the far corner where the water trough was. Maybe we both thought about things that little Joby Thurman saw near the shed during Outfitters weekend a year and a half ago. And what happened that same night.

"Where was the horseshoe?" Melinda asked.

I pointed between the tractor and the hogback spine. "Where was Arielle Blake's body?"

She waved up the rocky hillside on the federal land behind the Buckeye's back fence. "Not too far up there, from what I saw of the crime scene photos."

The notion of looking at creepy photos of a decomposed and murdered woman gave me a shiver.

Melinda's gaze narrowed at the fence separating us from the lease land. "Our detective figured Chevigny killed Arielle Blake after she went Fatal Attraction on him."

I frowned. "And her body was on the federal land. Chevigny would have told her to use the federal land to walk over to meet him, rather than cutting right through his west pasture above the ravine here, just in case the bull was in this west pasture."

Melinda swiveled on Buster to face me. "It's not though, is it?"

I shook my head, absorbing the motion with my back as Skip began to trot. He'd expected to find a dozen ranch horses out here, but I realized Donna had brought them home after all. "The bull should be secure in the east pasture. Only gate is up there at the shed."

"Wonder if this fence is all intact."

"It better be."

"Wouldn't have been hard to get over or through that fence on foot, but with a vehicle, of any kind, someone would have to get from one pasture to the other by going through the gate at the back of the building up there, right?"

"Yep."

"Easy to see if the wire's ever been cut, but that's a bit more like a search, than me just riding along with you."

I explained the standard way to lay down a fence pulling the staples and standing on the wire, stretching it to the dirt. I pointed. "And there's another way to lay a fence down. See, a lot of the posts are just stiffeners in a length of wire."

From Melinda's expression, her face all wadded up, I could tell she didn't see this at all, so I kept trying. "The real, set-in-the-ground type posts are every three or four of those verticals you see out there. A person could literally lay a loose section down, just bend the whole fence ninety degrees, stand on it, then lead a horse over it, drive cattle over it." I pulled Skip up at the pole corral, hopped down and loose-tied him.

Melinda nodded and shrugged and maybe winced just a little as she moved to dismount. "Just trying to think through all the possibilities." She led Buster up to the tractor where he was happy to stand and blow sweetly at us.

The thing with Melinda is, if I tell her plain what to do, there's no one better at doing. I had to say which way to shore up the cribbing, but she eased the wood into place and then kicked it in hard. Working together, we had that tire back on in jig time.

Which didn't mean I could drive it up the hogback. The thing had no intention of starting, which was not too much of a head-scratcher. Would have been smart to figure the battery wouldn't kick after all this time.

Melinda rubbed her eyebrows. "Can't this horse pull that tractor?"

I looked at Buster, Melinda's hand resting on his enormous shoulder. "Sure. You mean up to the shed?"

"No, I mean about ten feet, so we can look underneath it."

"No point in that." The tractor sat on a miniature high rise of packed dirt that was rippled with old use but the ground was clean enough to see nothing was hidden under the tractor, no clothes or blood or something that would raise the four eyebrows of a police clerk who wants to be a deputy and her horseshoer friend.

She asked again. "Humor me?"

Last time I humored her, my Intended about fell on his face. So, for grins, I retied the line from Buster's harness to the tractor and put the transmission in neutral.

"Walk him forward," I said.

She clucked to Buster and he obliged, pulling the tractor clear of its year-and-a-half-long parking spot. Then she dropped his bridle and hustled behind the tractor for a look-see.

"Oh. Oh!"

Twisting around in the tractor seat, I stared down at the ground behind me, thoughts coming too quick to be counted.

"Jeez Louise in a jalopy." I finally got that 'Rielle Blake wasn't Heart R.

Charley perked up at the shed. Was it my imagination, or did his little bit of a fluff tail give a wag?

Melinda was still gawking at the tracks and hadn't noticed my good old dog's concern. I wasn't too sure he had more than a passing quail on his mind anyways, but I could go for a look see at the shed alone if Melinda wanted to stare at the uncovered truth a while longer.

Plus, I needed to pee.

So, with Melinda staring at her prize dirt and all its meaning, I hustled up the steepest part of the hogback in the direct route to the shed.

For the gajillionth time in my life, I wished I'd put things together quicker. The hammer. The TrailTime deletion. The picture Biff took.

Trappy hoofbeats made the *duh-duh, duh-duh* sound so different from other horses.

I should have been thinking faster when the too-even sound of a Paso came in a soft echo through the shed.

Loretta Pritchard stared at me and I stared at her rushing out of the shed, heading for the fence connection at the water trough.

"Hey." I yelled, unable to do more but watch and continue climbing the hogback.

Charley wagged at the horse, at me, shifting about, pleased as ever.

Loretta dismounted and reached quick as a snake for the gate handle, then dropped the tension on the electric wire that was keeping everyone in the west field safe from Dragoon in the Buckeye's east field.

The bull was watching, too. His attention focused past me, to Melinda or Buster.

Buster. Buster, still hitched to the tractor.

Dragoon did a cocky challenge snort that threatened pain.

At the pole corral, Skip snorted, yanked himself free and made dust, galloping for the trail into the ravine. Skip's sprint drew Dragoon's attention even harder. Though Loretta was closer to the bull, she was off to his side, out of sight, through the shed. I knew she'd clear the gate that led to the safety of the lease land.

As bad a spot as I was in, my first sick thought was that a draft horse was no match in speed for a put-out bull. And that's what Dragoon became right then—true to his reputation, fixed on the horse in his line of sight. I whirled and screamed at Melinda.

"Get Buster free of that tractor!"

She didn't. She slapped the horse's chest, tugged his reins back toward his neck, and clucked at him. Buster leaned back into the breeching straps across his haunches and pushed the tractor right back where it had rested all this while, protecting the evidence we'd exposed.

A year and a half, covering the tracks of Loretta's Paso, and Melinda thought she needed to cover them for the next two minutes?

Two minutes might be the rest of our lives.

Then Melinda freed Buster from the tractor. But a draft horse isn't a runner. Dragoon could catch him, gore him. Time that I could have spent running up the hogback, I stood with tears in my eyes watching Buster decide best what to do. The big horse gave an alarm snort and turned tail to run, inspired by Skip. I froze, not wanting to attract Dragoon. Melinda hunkered in a squat on the tractor seat. Guess she didn't want to chance leaving her legs dangling. The bull barreled by her, pegging for my borrowed draft horse, who ran.

Soon as she saw Dragoon's interest was all about Buster, Melinda threw herself off the tractor and charged up the hogback toward me. "Come on, come on! We've got to get to that shed!"

Buster, bless his brave soul, decided he wasn't a runner. He butted his chest against the ragged remnants of the pole corral where Skip was supposed to be. I think he and I were both worried that Dragoon might just run through his back end. After all, Buster would only have the one chance at kicking the tar out of the bull's face. That horse of heart turned himself around before Dragoon got there. He backed himself against the poles and said he'd face all comers.

The bull stopped when he saw the draft horse squared off with pinned ears.

Dragoon should have run into a big tough horse a long time ago. Might have quelled his aggression against God's finest animal. Bile pitched up into my mouth.

Pawing, Dragoon shook his head, snot and sweat flying through the air as his neck lolled, choosing who to crush. He had his pick of anyone in his path with less power than Buster.

"Should we split up? Make him divide his attention?" Melinda caught me on the hill and paused, dancing from one foot to the other, like she was willing me to go with her idea. Us parting ways would certainly divvy up the bull's attention, sealing an escape for the one he didn't pick and sealing the death warrant on whoever he picked for a quick goring and grinding into compost. If there were hiding places in two different directions for us to run to, it would guarantee one of us lived. The shed—once the drainpipe or corner post was climbed—looked to be our only close hope. Beyond the shed, the rocks on the lease land might offer a hiding spot.

"Run for it!" I wished I had a Quarter Horse under my butt. Ahorseback wasn't a good and comfortable way to be around Dragoon but afoot was way worse. Melinda and I pelted up that steep slope.

Turns out, a woman who can run two hours without stopping can also scramble up a hogback a lot faster than a horseshoer. I could do the math well enough, seeing how far I had to go for safety at the shed. Melinda saw that the roof was the place to be, and set to start shinnying up the nearest corner post with a starter boost from the edge of the water trough. The last glance I allowed over my shoulder showed how long it'd be 'til that amazingly fast and enormous angry bull would catch me.

And then my right foot bogged down in a patch of super soft dirt amongst the hard scrabble. In a flash, I slipped to my knees and would need one or two whole seconds to get up.

Never. I would never make it to safety at the shed before Dragoon crushed me with his skull.

Chapter 29

CHARLEY'S LEGS TREMBLED AS THOUGH HE was in seizure. Old dog legs do that. Excited dog legs, too. And sometimes a working dog, who aches to work, will quiver with anticipation. Charley had all three reasons to shake. I prayed his feet wouldn't fail him now as he challenged Dragoon in a series of yipping charges.

Rolling in the dirt as I scrambled up the hogback, I slipped again, knees in the dirt and pushed on without looking back. Behind me, I could hear the bull snort. I could sense Charley's stress.

And his courage.

Playing chicken is a tough game when it's being done for keeps. Probably, both the bull and my dog were willing to take it as far as it could go. Old Charley weighed about thirty pounds. Dragoon weighed in at a near-ton of bad news.

Size matters.

But Charley matters to me, so I matter to him. He snarled at Dragoon, made another run, then jinked around, barely avoiding the bull's crushing head.

Dragoon turned away from me and the hill, tried for Charley again.

Zipping by, Charley gave that put-out bull What For in little growls. Wasted breath, that's what Charley's snarly threats were.

I couldn't watch. And I had to get myself safe to not waste Charley's effort. Melinda beckoned. As I reached the top of the hogback, she yanked my sleeve.

She should have already scrambled for the shed's rooftop, but she'd waited for me.

"The roof." The two words popped out of my mouth as we ran for it.

The gutter downspout came down with a shriek of weak metal, so there was a climbing aid that wouldn't work again.

We had one more chance, with every bit of muscle power. One try. Stretching up with every fiber in my arms and chest, I caught the roof edge in a death grip that felt like I was breaking my fingers. Melinda managed the same and we banged ourselves up in torso-scraping rips until we chinned our upper bodies onto the roof. Then we air-kicked 'til we could swing a leg up.

It's the kind of desperate leap and pull-up that can be managed once in a lifetime, in every way that counts. Muscles shredding, I used every last bit of upper body strength.

We were spent, but we'd made it. I rolled over on the corrugated metal roof, onto my feet, careful to bend all my joints for stability, desperate to see my boy get clear, too.

"That'll do, Charley, that'll do." I screamed his release command at the top of my lungs. Shouting is not the right way to command a dog. High-pitched desperation made my voice sound like a stranger's.

Charley became a fur blur, shooting between the strands of barbed wire back for the relative safety of the federal lease land.

Below us, hoofbeats pounded irregularly amid shouts of, "Whoa! Whoa!"

Then came a shriek, a thud and the sound of a retreating gallop, followed by a shout of terror.

Panic is contagious in horses. My voice, Melinda's urging, our frantic running, it had all signaled urgency and fear. Loretta's Paso had had enough exposure to the infection of terror.

I couldn't place the sound at first but the next noise made sense: hoof beats coming up the hogback, accompanied by the bull's snorts. Those were cloven hoofbeats!

That'd teach Loretta to try to kill us and then hang around to enjoy the show. I realized she'd hung at the back gate, not even closed it.

And as she went to remount, she got dumped.

Beneath us, Loretta screamed again, giving Dragoon focus.

By then, I'd had more than I could enjoy and wanted to tell her to shut up. Loretta having a hissy fit wasn't going to grow any sympathy in me.

Dragoon kept trotting up the hogback, all the way to the shed.

"She's going to get hurt," Melinda said, worrying at the edge of the roof. "That bull's looking for a target."

That didn't seem like something needed pointing out. Loretta's scream was calling Dragoon like a siren.

"You do know she just tried to kill us?" I asked.

"I have to help her."

"You can't."

"Send him," Melinda said, sliding to the edge of the roof.

"Send who what?"

"Send your dog," Melinda snapped. "Send him after the bull again."

Charley was safe now, tucked into the rocks on the lease land, Dragoon's attention all about Loretta. I could hear her in the shed below us. She'd fallen for the false feeling of safety, a roof over her head.

But it was an open shed, even Dragoon could figure that out.

I looked out, north and south. My dog on one side, Dragoon puffing up the other. Loretta beneath me, about to die. Her Paso was gone. Skip was gone. Buster moved away from the pole corral, headed to the ravine trail Skip had taken.

"Rainy, you've got to send your dog before the bull gets Loretta. People before pets."

I didn't want to trade Charley's life for Loretta's. She'd caused all this mess. Swallowing, trying to keep my voice a strong command tone instead of cracking, I half-sobbed and called my tired old dog out of his safety.

"Charley? Away to me."

He popped out of the rocks and loped long, circling in a push that would put him facing the bull, trying to beat him to the shed.

Just before Dragoon got to the shed's opening and the human target hiding there, he snorted, stopped, and eyed the panting old dog.

Then the bull switched course and started a new charge—away from Loretta, bent on smoking my Charley.

Melinda dropped off the roof, hitting the ground as soon as Dragoon turned away. I could hear her bustling about down there, but I watched my dog.

"Charley, come bye!"

Charley reversed direction and I prayed he had enough of a head start as I called his release command again.

"That'll do, Charley! That'll do!"

Dragoon's charge hit top speed.

Charley shot through the barbed wire again and ran for cover in the rocks with barely a few body lengths to spare as Dragoon tried to kill him.

A shovel blade flew up in my face.

"Grab it, Rainy! I'll lift her high enough to hold onto this end." The next sound was Melinda's grunt as she lifted Loretta Pritchard straight up.

I power-yanked on that shovel. Loretta appeared, red-faced and white-knuckled, her grip slipping on the shovel handle.

Bizarre it was, hauling her body up onto the shed roof beside mine. The woman had just tried to get us killed.

"Let go," I yelled at Loretta as soon as I got her fully on the roof.

I pulled the shovel free and pushed it down at Melinda. Leaned over the edge to pull Melinda up to safety.

I braced one foot against the remains of the gutter. I stretched down and held fast. No way I'd let go. Melinda kicked a leg up and I grabbed her waistband. It had been easier to climb up the first time. We were peaked now.

All I could picture from the eyeballs that wanted to be in the back of my head was Loretta putting a boot in my behind and helping me on over, again ditching my buddy and me in the dirt as bull bait.

The barbed wire fence stopped Dragoon from going after Charley, so the danged bull was trotting back up to the shed in search of entertainment. Of course, Dragoon could pass under the shed roof and be on the lease land where my old hero dog waited, but if he did, Charley'd have time enough to scoot back under the barbed wire. They could see-saw who got what chunk of land forever, as long as the bull still respected that wire fence.

And we were safe, atop the shed. When Melinda sat up on the roof, I set the shovel down gently, extending it up the roofline so it might not slide away. Loretta glanced at the shovel we'd used for a rope to pull her to safety. Then she glared at us good and ugly.

Just the three of us sitting on a shed roof with nothing to do but make girl-talk.

The shoe that made that track was in Ol' Blue.

"We know, Loretta," I said. "Your Paso has an odd shoe, makes an odd track. You rode right up to Cameron Chevigny when he was pinned under the tractor. We've got—"

"You've got nothing!" The physical threat of Dragoon was over and the hard work of getting to safety on the shed roof was behind us, but Loretta's chest heaved, inhalations coming faster and deeper through an open-mouthed snarl.

"Rainy can identify your horse's tracks," Melinda said.

I eyed Loretta steadily. "The sheriff's department has the empty shell casing from the round you fired." Had I ever told Melinda about the casing? Had the old Suit Fellow? I couldn't look at Melinda, 'cause I wanted to watch Loretta, but I pointed to my girlfriend. "And thanks to her, they have the bullet from inside the tire.

"You fucking bitch." Loretta glared at me. "Both of you."

"If I were you," I said, "I wouldn't talk that way."

"If you were me," she said right back, "I bet you would."

"Donna heard you on the phone, telling Cameron about this knife you hid for him by this shed's gutter." I twisted my body to show the scabbard on my belt.

Loretta did a double take at the sight of the Heart R knife.

A hammer, Darby had said, bought at the same time as the Heart R knife. I could see a guy like Cameron Chevigny special ordering through Darby instead of going online for his ordering. I could see him pouring over a special tool catalogue with his chippie, Loretta. They'd probably ordered the gifts through Darby so their spouses wouldn't chance to see the deliveries.

"He gave you a dead blow hammer to use in leather working." I figured that before he died, Cameron Chevigny told his latest mistress that she'd never be anything more, and I wondered if he had any idea what happened to that hammer.

"Sweet. You swapped tools." Melinda looked pretty proud of herself, be-smirking Loretta now. "Look, we know you rode out here and tried to shoot him, you missed, hit the tire and it made the tractor roll."

Melinda was like one of those prosecutors, speechifying a final argument. Hey, I'd have voted for a conviction. Even Loretta swallowed at all the truth Melinda spelled out.

"Then you rode right up to him on your horse. You sat there, watched him dying, needing help, and you rode away. The tractor protected your tracks all year. It's plain as day. Your horse makes distinctive impressions. Your horse lost a shoe as you rode out. We have the horseshoe. Your shoer identified it as coming off your horse, too."

"That's not proof of anything." Loretta sounded like a cook-ie-stealing kid who had already swallowed and thought not admitting anything was the way to go.

"We know about Arielle Blake, too," I said.

"Everybody knows about her." Loretta moved up the roof peak.

Where did she think she was going? I glanced at Melinda. She wore a poker face that would have stumped Guy and Biff and their other buddies during card night.

Reloading was all Donna could think of when the detective asked her about a little pile of spilled shot they found back here, but the Chevignys never did any reloading.

"What's your handle on TrailTime?" I asked, "The find-my-phone tracker showed Arielle's phone somewhere around Keeper Lake. You rode out there with her phone after you killed her. Did you kill her with the dead blow hammer? You had to get rid of the murder weapon. But you broke it. Over her head? They found the lead shot spill out here. And the emptied plastic hammer floated on the lake. Guy's buddy Biff photographed it on Keeper Lake. You used your hatchet combo tool to bury her, didn't you? Did you throw that in the lake, too? When you heard people were sent to search around the lake, you had the good sense to delete your ride from TrailTime—"

Melinda said, "Their servers will still have her entry."

The look Loretta gave was one for Lucifer.

"You bitches. You can't prove anything." Loretta snatched the shovel off the roof in less than a blink's time, cocked back and looked to be sizing up the distances between her and Melinda, her and me.

I thought I could prove the theory of gravity and I was willing to give it a whirl in the next breath if Loretta gave us any guff. High time for me to holler some encouragement to Melinda. "Shoot her! Shoot her!"

Melinda gave me a glance. "I don't have a gun."

Loretta dropped the shovel. The clang of the blade striking the tin roof made Dragoon snort beneath the shed. As quick as one thought skidded into my brains—why would Loretta throw down a perfectly good weapon, one with such long reach as a shovel?—a brighter realization kicked it out. Um, because she had something better?

As the shovel blade slid in a slow screech down the roof, Melinda pinned it with one foot. She took her eyes off Loretta as she bent for the shovel, so she didn't see Loretta reaching. Pushing her riding jacket back, Loretta touched the holstered pistol on her right hip.

"It's ok, Melinda," I said. "She's a lousy shot." Well, she was, right?

Loretta straightened up, her hand gripping the pistol, deciding. It hadn't yet cleared leather. Maybe she hadn't unsnapped the holster's retainer strap. It would be awful close to the point of no return. But she stood stiff and I was afraid in that split-second she was choosing to draw.

She's a tall drink of water, taller than either Melinda or me.

Or maybe guns do that to my perception of a person.

So, I went to my butt, then my back, just pressed my sweet self right onto that shed roof.

The nap position may seem like a bad way to have a brawl, but on a shed roof, it's the best way to fight. The winner is the one who stays on the roof and being on my back gave me a one-up on that score. Melinda crouched, low and ready, but waving one hand in a calming kind of way, like she was going to talk Loretta out of doing another desperate thing.

If Guy was around, he'd be singing about a catfight on a hot tin roof, I just know he would.

I inched toward Loretta on my back, hips and knees bent, ready to mule kick.

Melinda talked low. "Look, Loretta, let's not make this any worse."

While she reassured our would-be killer, I got in kicking range.

Maybe Melinda was in shovel-swinging range by then. I couldn't concentrate on anything but that pistol snug between Loretta's hip and hand. If the gun barrel started to move up toward me or Melinda, I was going to kick Loretta right off this shed in one move. The fall wouldn't hurt her much, but Dragoon might entertain himself by killing her.

I said, "You carried Arielle Blake's cell phone all the way out to Keeper Lake, threw it in there with your hatchet tool. You threw the dead blow hammer Cameron Chevigny gave you in the lake too, but it floated up, because you broke it open out here. They found the lead shot. Got pictures of what's left of the hammer. They'll get your hatchet and her phone out of the lake bottom."

Loretta opened her mouth to talk several times while I held forth, but she never came up with a thing to say.

"Raise your hands," Melinda ordered her.

Loretta would not obey.

"Rainy, if she tries anything—"

"I've got this." Cocked and ready, my double kick was.

"Okay," Melinda said, cocking the shovel back with her voice like thunder, "here's what's going to happen. Loretta, I'm going to drop that pistol over the edge and it will fall. You will not move a muscle."

I tightened my abs for booting the bad woman to the back of beyond. I didn't trust Loretta a hair width, not while she was still breathing.

It was the longest split second on record, Melinda stepped forward, drew Loretta's pistol and dropped it over the edge of the roof. Dragoon snorted and trotted out from under the shed, down the hogback, back into the east pasture. I saw Charley perk up out on the lease land, watching the bull move.

Loretta sat down, knees to chest, wrapped her arms around her legs and buried her face in her thighs.

I scooted away from her a bit. Melinda did, too, holding the shovel like a shepherd's staff.

When the sky cracked and it started to sprinkle, Loretta was the first to want to get on the right side of the roof where we were all stuck. She pointed out that Dragoon was far enough away that we could get in the shed, close it off with electric wire to keep safe from him.

"We're staying right here," Melinda said. I was way with her on this. It was stable here, things couldn't get worse.

"But it's raining." Loretta said this like she was explaining things to dummies.

I glared at her. We could shiver on that roof all night if we had to. Donna or Guy would eventually call out the cavalry, so to speak. "You made of sugar? You gonna melt or something, 'Retta?"

"Don't call me that."

I figured the pet name thing was something Cameron Chevigny plied all his chippies with, and they responded in kind. Arielle Blake played with his middle name, calling him Biff. Loretta called him Cam. He called them Rielle and Retta. Wondering what his special name had been for Earl Delmont's sister, I rolled my lips in and clamped my teeth shut, managing for once to not speculate out loud when it would only escalate the mood.

Melinda grinned at me and I flashed a big smile back in spite of the situation. I admired her quick, brave decision to go get Loretta out of danger.

S'pose Sheriff Magoutsen hired on guts? Surely that'd make my buddy Melinda the next deputy. I'd an idea what'd happen when he heard about Almost-a-Reserve Kellan facing Dragoon and thinking to study on those tracks that the tractor had protected all year. It would make Loretta's husband miss the chance to get hired full time if Melinda got the job.

And that might make Reserve Deputy Vince Pritchard cry like a girl.

Chapter 30

WE COULD HEAR HOLLIS'S ENORMOUS HAYING tractor rumbling a mile off and soon we saw the headlights making their slow way through Stan Yates's land and then through the wire fence into the Buckeye west pasture north of the ravine. By now, Dragoon wandered to the lease land, which sent Charley scampering back to the ranch side. The tractor cab was stuffed with the three menfolk—Hollis Nunn driving fast as that big John Deere allowed, with Sheriff Magoutsen and my Guy crammed in next to him.

I was real glad about having asked Guy to marry me.

"Donna must have called Magoo out," Melinda said. When I laughed, she added, "Oh, crap, I shouldn't call him that."

Pointing at Loretta, storm-faced witch that she was, I told Melinda that there was a police scanner in the Saddle-Up shop.

"Oh, then that's how she had a nice head start to get out here so she could sic that cow on us."

"It's a bull," Loretta and I said together, though it was the last thing we'd agree on.

Hollis motored the tractor straight into the shed, which made a big amount of racket, and someone hopped out. The gate banged

241

shut with a reassuring clang, the electric gate over the water trough snugged up. I loved the relief of knowing Dragoon had a fence to stay behind.

My first view of Guy was upside down as I somersaulted off the shed roof.

"What are you doing here?" I asked.

"Donna gave up her spot in the tractor to let me come check on you. Hollis had to take the sheriff and couldn't carry a fourth." He explained how the bid for the third slot in the tractor led to a certain fit pitched by Vince Pritchard, who was having to stand by back at Stan Yates's property with Donna. Guy smirked, liking telling me about Loretta's husband trying to argue his way in, talking big and getting a big black stare from Magoutsen on that account.

Then Magoo heard from Melinda and me on a mess of happenings.

Loretta said, "I want a lawyer."

About Reserve Pritchard, Magoutsen said, "A bully I don't need."

He didn't need a coward either but maybe I didn't need to say so.

Hollis said, "I'm going to have to make two more trips, since that tractor only held a couple of people besides the driver."

It was so dark by then that scaring up some horses was not something anyone but me wanted to do.

"Loretta Pritchard," Sheriff Magoutsen said, "turn around and put your hands behind your back."

"No way." Loretta looked like her mind hadn't caught up to the consequences of all she'd done.

"Way," the Sheriff said. "You're under arrest, Loretta."

Loretta looked good in handcuffs. Guy gave me his coat and Sheriff Magoutsen shed his uniform jacket for Melinda.

Melinda looked good in an official sheriff uniform.

* * *

Melinda and I spent some time under that shed, waiting for transport that night. She finally had a chance to see the water trough, the concrete block behind it.

"That's where the knife was?"

"Yeah." I undid my belt and shucked the scabbard off. Maybe I'd give the knife back to Darby, if the Sheriff didn't need it. I knew I wasn't going to keep it. "So you knew it was Loretta that the kid saw."

"Well, I figured it was a woman the kid saw. In that position, men can't lift, because their center of gravity is near their chest. Women can do it, because our center of gravity is lower."

"Unless it's a really small, light dude? Like Biff."

Our eyes adjusted as night fell. The rain gave up and the stars turned on by the hundreds. There are worse ways to spend an evening than in remote central Oregon, hanging out with a good friend, watching for shooting stars.

When Hollis came back out, he had another deputy who carried cameras and notebooks and looked like he'd be busy for a little while. Melinda talked the deputy through things while Hollis drove Guy and me back to the barn in that loud, lumbering haying tractor that could make the long drive around the ravine. Magoo went back out again on the last trip and I thought about Donna taking the long way around in her life.

Back at the Buckeye barn, things were getting sorted out, Donna and I talked.

This knowing more, knowing the fullness let Donna see some spring even as we both shook our heads at Loretta Pritchard's off-the-map acts. I swear, it was a thing of beauty, her awakening.

Loretta had gone as far as to eliminate her competition—poor Arielle—then point a gun at someone she said she loved. And she pulled the trigger. When she saw him caught under the tractor, she left him to die. To top it all off, she tried to get Melinda and me killed.

"I don't know," Donna kept saying. "I just don't know."

"Makes no sense, does it?" I said, shaking my head and following Donna to the far corner of her porch, wanting to put my hand on her shoulder but just not sure.

Donna was quiet a long time, looking like she'd cry or laugh. "Makes as much sense as falling for your hayman." Her mouth curled. "Makes no sense, does it? Woman my age, taking up with a man again?" Redness glowed under her heavy, working-woman tan.

"I guess it makes sense to me," I told her. "As much as the notion of any great couple makes good sense."

Donna nodded, knowing my meaning, what and all with both of us still being too much of ourselves to say something as mushy as . . . love.

What a notion. I puzzled on it like a business undertaking in the days of loafing I took next. Felt due. I was bushed. The only thing that lightened my load was learning that I wouldn't have to go to court. The man who'd tried to make a piñata out of me last spring took a deal, as Melinda put it. I could only hope that Loretta Pritchard would too. They sent scuba divers into Keeper Lake and found a cell phone, and the hatchet-shovel-combo tool, though the one was dead and the other bad rusted. Melinda told me that Stan Yates identified the cell as the right color and make and model to be Arielle's.

* * *

I brought the Heart R knife back to Darby Ernst.

"I got it for Loretta Pritchard," he said.

"Good trade."

"No, I meant—" He stopped as I handed it over in its scabbard.

"You can resell it or whatever. Donna doesn't want it and neither do I."

* * *

The last thing I wanted settled made me stop at Stan Yates's house on my way to the Buckeye. I faced the man and put it plain. "You have no reason to bear a grudge against Donna Chevigny."

He looked down and away. "That's true."

"You and Cameron didn't have a deal."

Yates shook his head.

"If you go talk to her, it would clear things up," I said.

Could have knocked me over with pony breath and a soft muzzle when he told me he'd already been to see Donna and they'd come to an understanding.

"She even said she'd like to come out and lay some flowers for Arielle," he told me. "I'm going to spread her ashes out there where she loved to walk."

Head bowed, I asked if I could pay my respects as well. Sounds like we're all taking a long walk, 'cause I knew Guy would be beside me.

* * *

Meanwhile, visiting back at the Buckeye ranch, I did many hours of wedding planning.

I'd sit on the porch with my good friend Donna, lacy shade trickling through the last of the maple leaves as winter drew in. A good winter, it'd be.

Some days, my buddy Melinda'd came up to the Buckeye with me. Guy, of course, hung out sometimes, too. Some Sundays, Hollis and his sister brought out enough beef to make a body think they'd rustled cattle and needed to burn the evidence. We had a big old time.

As much as Donna sort of appointed herself an aunty to me, Hollis wanted to uncle me and he was a little stern with Guy sometimes, checking out the intentions of my Intended.

This takes some getting used to, this having a made-up family, but I'd like to try.

"You must hold her high," Hollis told Guy, shaking gnarled fingers at my boyfriend. "Put her above everything else."

Love him, Guy. He took the talking-to with proper seriousness. "Yes, sir."

"Does she come first?" Hollis asked, still stern.

"Heavens, yes," Guy grinned.

I asked about Dragoon.

Donna made a call, a good one. "He's going to Black Bluff, going to sell him."

I perked up. "In California? Always thought that'd be real interesting."

My adopted uncle looked over quick. "You want to see the Black Bluff bull sale?"

I tipped my noggin. He saw my nod and raised me a head cock.

"The Black Bluff bull sale is an area you ought not bother with."

"How's that?"

He put it a little more plain, but not much. "Rainy, you and yours might want to stay clear of there."

Him uncle-ing me to Donna's aunty-ing could get to be a bit much. I snapped my noggin back over to eyeball him, but Hollis was looking away. Somehow, I knew he wouldn't say more. I didn't know if I was being warned off for good reason and if so, I could hardly guess at what that reason might be and I wanted to get back to my own aunty-ing. As I was looking for Abby, my best friend found me.

"They say the Loretta Pritchard case is probably not going to trial," Melinda said. "She'll plead out."

I was mighty grateful for that news and asked how things were at work, what and all with one reserve Pritchard quitting and the sheriff looking to fill the retiring guy's spot and almost-reserve-deputy Kellan having cracked the whole deal in on Cameron Chevigny's non-accident.

Melinda blushed a bit. "Well, there are, you know, thousands of rules about police procedure and maybe there were a couple that I didn't break, but in this case, it seems not to count too bad since I wasn't a cop."

A cop.

"Someday," I told her, this like-a-sister buddy of mine, "you'll get to do your dream job."

Her blush was as real as her ambition. She didn't have words for it, but none were needed.

"So, there's going to be a wedding," I said. "Thanksgiving Day. Isn't that a cool day for a wedding?"

"We might have those days off," Melinda drawled, "I'll be in the dorm outside of Salem by late November." She was truly blushing like this was big news.

"The dorm?"

"At the academy."

"You, you got hired? You're going to be the new deputy at the Sheriff's Department?"

Beaming now, Melinda nodded, her face split into a happy display of her dental property.

* * *

So this year's Turkey Day was for the joining of Donna and Hollis.

They wanted a coming-winter wedding. Donna told me she loves Hollis, that she'd almost been ready to wither but now she was loved by a good man, she wanted only to keep going.

On the day, Donna said she had something for me.

I shook my head. "It's me who gets to give you a gift." Guy and I did all the food for the Chevigny-Nunn wedding, which is to say, I cut and peeled veggies, folded napkins, plated turkey, brisket, and potatoes and whatever Guy said, exactly how he said. Somehow in all this busyness, he made a tiered lemon cake with meringue frosting. Better sweets and savories were never made or chowed down on.

But after eating, Donna took me to the barn and showed me a

saddle, an old, old one, beautifully kept. There's often a good story in old leather.

"It's a Fallis," Donna said. "It was my daughter's and I want you to have it."

That I started crying is not my fault.

"It's what's alive in us, what makes us grow." Donna nodded again.

Seems a much better idea, being alive and growing, instead of giving up. Best Thanksgiving ever.

THE END

A sample from the next Rainy Dale Horseshoer Mystery . . .

FORGING FIRE

Chapter 1

THE KIDNEY-BUSTING DRIVE DOWN THE GRAVEL road to the Buckeye is extra rough in a diesel with stiff suspension like Ol' Blue, but rolling closer to the ranch always makes me smile. My teeth air-dried by the time I eased the truck under the gate header. Charley got up from his snooze, shook his furry, yellow self, and did a chortle-woof in appreciation of our destination.

"No herding today," I told him.

My dog didn't look convinced. The second I opened the truck door, which bears the decal *Dale's Horseshoeing* along with the house phone number, Charley bailed out with hope in his heart, staring at the faraway rangeland like anyone with a working soul does, before he got busy with his sniffing.

"No good, no good." Manuel, the guy who works seasonally for the Nunn Finer Hay Company, was muttering under the hood of the pickup between the main barn and the all-quiet ranch house.

"Hey, Manny." I don't know if he heard my greeting as he continued to commune with the innards of his engine, but I reckoned Skip and Harley, the geldings I planned to shoe, were in the corral at the run-in shed the other side of the house. Soon as I found the horses, I'd move Ol' Blue so I wouldn't have to haul my anvil too far.

"Miss?"

Missing me—instead of calling me by name—is one of Manuel's things, but I try to have the kind of faith my dog does and gave him another chance.

"Rainy," I reminded him.

"Miss, you know a phone number for the Mister?"

I always enjoy when anyone makes the mistake of asking Hollis something about ranch plans and Hollis directs them to Donna, who's Hollis's new wife and the real owner of the Buckeye ranch.

"Mister Hollis, he gave me money to take the bull to the sale down in California, but today my truck, it has problems, and I cannot do it."

"Oh." I sort of got it now. Not due in 'til after this weekend, Donna and Hollis. Ranch folk don't often get to get away. "They're kind of out of town."

"Yes, but you have a way to talk to them?"

"They're not cell phone people." No way, no how was he going to reach the honeymooners anyways. Their wedding was last November. With spring around the corner, the old newlyweds were more than ready to ride off into the sunset. They'd gone so deep in the backcountry with four horses, they'd probably slipped back in time a full century.

"The bull, he is supposed to be there tomorrow," Manuel said.

"The bull's behind the barn," I said, pointing to the huge old gambrel-roofed barn behind him, meaning the sturdiest stock pen on the other side of the building.

Manuel turned for a quick look at the old barn and spun his eyeballs a lap like I was way off, but I knew what I meant. Then he leaned forward like I was the one a little deaf or half-stupid. "The bull is supposed to be at the big sale tomorrow."

"Oh!" Now I got it extra good. Donna's killer bull was supposed to go to the Black Bluff bull sale, down California-way, and Manuel was supposed to haul the blasted beast there.

Suggesting Manuel to Donna and Hollis as a ranch hand had been my doing. They'd needed help, didn't need to be breaking their backs as hard as they do. Donna has given me all the pull to shoe her horses when and how I thought best. Plus, her stock are so well-handled, they stand like a dream, no fussing or yanking away while I work on their feet. I even shoe the ranch geldings in the pasture sometimes. Real well-behaved, old-style Quarter Horses. With most clients, I require a person be there to handle the horse, but I trust Donna and her stock, and she trusts me. I just about love Donna. She's become like another mother to me, and her horses behave so well that I just shoe when my schedule's open.

Fact is, the horses I'd planned to end my afternoon shoeing, they could wait a couple days just fine. Twisting my ponytail around my thumb made the idea come quicker. I've always wanted to go to the Black Bluff bull sale, even though Hollis has said a time or two, kind of weird-like, that I ought not visit there. Now fate was handing me a great excuse to go. I'd be helping out Hollis and Donna by getting a bad news bull off the Buckeye ranch. It'd get me to the best-of-the-west sale I'd long wanted to see—horses, cattle, and herding dogs worth big bucks would compete and change hands at the Black Bluff sale. And tonight, my Guy was going up to Seattle to buy special food at a big market for our wedding next Wednesday.

Rare is the night and day I'm alone, but right now I could make the free time to do Manuel's hauling job. All kind of good could come from me hitching Ol' Blue to Hollis's stout stock trailer, loading that bull, and hitting the road.

If I left right away, I could be back before Guy had a chance to miss me.

My boot heel ground the dirt as I turned for the barn to call home from the landline. I let the phone ring 'til the message machine came on, hung up, thought hard, then called the restaurant. This road trip idea of mine was coming together. I'd put the diesel charges on my debit card, sort it out later with Donna and Hollis. Tomorrow was Saturday. I had no clients scheduled until Monday afternoon. The last day of the bull sale was tomorrow and I could maybe send Charley on cattle at the sale, which everybody knows is cooler than ice. I mean, herding at the Black Bluff bull sale, for mercy's sake? Everyone in the world wants to work their herding dog there someday, it's the cream of—

"Cascade Kitchen," a gal's voice said, sounding rushed over the clink of coffee cups and plates and whatnot.

"Guy still there? This is Rainy." This last bit of information would make sure she didn't just put me on hold. My husband-come-next-week always takes my calls.

"No, he left like a half hour ago. He thought he wouldn't go 'til five or six but he made it out of here earlier even though he thought he'd have to get the dinner rush moving before he could go, but he didn't."

Yeah, that was Sissy on the phone, that server-and-dishwasher Guy hired. She talks funny circles, always. I thanked her and called our house again, this time leaving Guy a message that I was going to take this all-the-sudden road trip to get Dragoon to Black Bluff since Manny couldn't do it. I promised to call him later and be back tomorrow night. The big thing on the list—getting my horses taken care of while Guy and I were both out of town for a night and a day—would need more than a phone message left on an answering machine, but my best friend was probably working right then. I left a message on Melinda's cell. I'd call her again later, go ahead and hit the road now.

It was that simple. Manuel and I got the stock trailer hitched up to Ol' Blue, checked the lights and brakes—the left signal flickered, but mostly worked—then opened the trailer and backed it to the pen gate. That big Brahma gives me the heebie-jeebies. We didn't need to risk getting into the pen with him. We swung the gate open to the inside then hollered and waved around the outside until Dragoon decided the hay in the trailer looked like a better deal than a bare pen being circled by a couple of shouting idiots.

So what kind of an omen is it that as I pulled off the ranch road onto the two-lane highway that would take me to the interstate, a marked deputy's car with a man and woman in the front seat was coming in the opposite direction? I flashed my lights, then eased Ol' Blue and the stock trailer onto the highway's shoulder. The cop car activated the spiffy, flashing up-top lights, did a one-eighty, and came up behind me. The male cop stayed in the patrol car as the uniformed woman left the driver's seat.

Charley thumped his stubby tail as she sauntered up.

"Hey," I said, when probationary Deputy Melinda Kellan stuck her nose in my window just a hair. Ever since she went to police school, Mel's got all these weird habits, like the way she stood just back of my truck's door post and leaned to talk to me.

"Hey, yourself." She nodded at me, then gave Charley a proper howdy. "You being good as gold, pretty boy?"

It's like Melinda thinks she's the funniest thing ever, every time she says that about Charley being gold. True, his long coat is all shades of yellow—not super-common in Aussies—but he's no beauty queen, he's a worker. As though to prove he's come from some school of tough knocks, his ear tips are missing, though the long fringe pretty well covers the flaw. Charley's a fine example, considering he's a stray I picked up along the interstate on my way to Oregon.

When they got done nuzzling each other, both glanced at me. Charley's eyes said I was really the only girl for him. Melinda asked, "What's up?"

"Wondering if you could maybe swing by tonight and tomorrow to feed the horses and Spooky too, if the spirit moves you. Guy's gone 'til tomorrow afternoon-ish and now I'm going to take Donna's bull down to a sale. I'll probably make it back late tomorrow night."

She swung her head the quarter turn it took to squint at the swaying stock trailer Ol' Blue was towing and wrinkled her nose.

Bulls have a more than manly scent, it's true. Dragoon smells like the bad news he is. Manuel and I had put plenty of hay in there and a water bucket tied up that I could fill without having to open the escape door. Not one to turn your back on, Dragoon. I planned to rest the bull's legs by stopping on the three-hundred-plus mile drive, but I wouldn't let the bull out of the trailer until I backed into a waiting pipe corral at the Black Bluff sale grounds.

Melinda stood with her arms folded across her chest, then shifted to rest one elbow on her pistol and the other wrist across a couple of extra magazines on her gun belt.

"You know," she said, "the only reason I ran from that son of a—"

"Bull," I put in, doing my part to keep her from cussing all the damn—oops—all the daggummed time. "Son of a bull, Dragoon is."

She glared at the trailer hitched to Ol' Blue. "I didn't have a gun on me at the time. Now, I could drop him at a hundred yards with a twelve-gauge slug. Or six of them, if that's what it takes."

Carries a grudge, my friend Melinda does.

"At this sale you're going to," she asked, "will there be mules?"

"Not officially. It's a stock dog and beef cattle thing, mostly. Replacement females. And some real nice geldings will be sold. But I'll keep my eyes and ears open for your mule."

She nodded. "You said you'd find him."

One thing that's a little annoying about this buddy of mine is the way she remembers everything. There's that, and the block on her shoulder she packs around.

Melinda glared at me good and hard, up one side and down the other. "Do I still have to wear a dress next Wednesday?"

"Well, yeah. Since I do."

"But you're the one—"

I waved her off. Best she not get started and dig too deep. "I'll find your mule."

"You'd better."

Melinda is sometimes a bit of a jawbone.

Guy says we could be sisters.

* * *

I made good time crossing the state line not too many hours after dark. It's a border I hadn't touched since I found my way into Oregon looking to get back my childhood horse, Red, nigh two years ago. Touching the northern edge of California then had been lucky though, as it's how I acquired—and named, come to it—good old Charley.

He'd watched me as I relieved myself at an unofficial interstate pull-out, wary and tired, though he wasn't in too bad of shape, just alone. I'd known his feeling purely. He'd needed someone. Back then, I wanted to need no one.

"Sorry, Charley." That's what I'd said, crushing the half hope glimmering in his gold-ringed brown eyes. But then, as I'd opened my truck door, something in my soul made me pause, changed my mind. I'd waved the stray into Ol' Blue's cab.

Within a few miles, Charley and I had started calling each other by our first names. What and all with him having no collar, I took that 'sorry, charley' and made it something we could both live with.

Charley wasn't sorry as a dog and he never seemed sorry to have joined me. He's loyal and a good judge of character. He had Guy figured for a keeper way before me. And his herding's solid, fun, and a time saver. When a killer loosed Dragoon on Melinda and me last fall, Charley was a genuine lifesaver.

* * *

At a spot along the dark interstate with an extra wide shoulder, I pulled Ol' Blue over for a snooze, and wrapped myself in the familiar scent and creak of my worn leather jacket. I prefer this kind of rest stop to something full of truckers and tourists and weirdos and whatnot. It swerves on the nerves something fearsome, a lack of space. Here, the interstate is bordered by real ranchland. Charley stared across the freeway, up the steep hill that angled down to the northbound lanes. Stock dogs always want to work, but my good old boy finally settled, curled against my ribs, and we kept each other warm.

Being on the road on my own was a good rinse for my brain. I'm trying not to get too clutched up in the throat about what's going to happen next week. Until the last year of my life, I'd figured I was best off with a good dog as my hot water bottle and general nighttime warmer.

This Friday night alone, my first in forever, was the reason I was able to jump in and get this blasted bull gone for Donna and Hollis. Guy had taken as much time off as he could for the coming celebration, would be back tomorrow night, cooking up a storm. My coming wedding would be followed by a lazy, married weekend, which would make two Saturdays in a row with no horseshoeing scheduled or even contemplated.

* * *

Dragoon woke me in the dark, rocking the truck with his motion in the trailer, but at first, I didn't remember where I was or why. My brain's transmission was stuck two years back, when I'd driven north in search of my horse Red. The warm breath on my neck made my hand reach to feel Charley's fur, remember I had a dog, I'd already found Red, I'd established myself as a horseshoer up in Cowdry, and I'd fallen in love, for real.

"Look how far we've come in two years," I told Charley as I re-did my ponytail.

He wiggled and stared at Ol' Blue's condensation-coated windows. Four a.m.

We went out in the dark and did what comes natural. Dragoon was fine, as was his hay and water. I called Charley back from too much nosing at the hill across the northbound lanes and we got gone.

Interstate 5 is blessedly calmer after midnight. The easy driving gave me thinking time. I need plenty of pause to chew on things, and I don't often get it. Miles zinged past.

The famous Black Bluff bull sale had a canvas banner across the main entrance. The red-haired cowpoke with a gray-flecked moustache at the main check-in gate looked right across Ol' Blue's cab, eyeing my dog instead of me. I like that real well in a person. Given where we were, the attention wasn't unusual. This yearly sale is not just about the bulls and other cattle on the offer. No, the running of the working dogs, one right after the other, moving rough stock with reason is the other big draw of the Black Bluff sale.

I leaned toward the man to be heard over Ol' Blue's diesel engine. "Got a bull here from the Buckeye Ranch up in Cowdry, Butte County, Oreg—"

"Bring it over there." He waved and jabbed his pointer finger toward the heaviest pipe corrals at the back of the sale grounds. He was already making a phone call as I pulled away.

Trucks and trailers of all sorts lined the acres of open fields beyond the many pens surrounding the huge main arena, but I couldn't gawk, had to pay attention to backing in where I was directed. The way it is, is the bull's my responsibility 'til it's out of the trailer, then the sales people have the charge of moving him and handling the auction. But if Dragoon didn't sell, it'd be my job to get him home again. After I backed the stock trailer to a stout corral, the receiving stockman complimented my driving and asked if I minded unhitching the trailer, so he could get Dragoon out when he had a couple more hands at the ready.

"Makes sense," I agreed.

Clear of the trailer, I parked, let Charley out for air and a pee, then hupped him back into Ol' Blue's cab and opened the rear slider window for ventilation.

A good stock dog has to watch his person, has to have access.

One or two fellows checked out Charley and me. Eager to show my dog's skill, I strolled over and asked the most relevant question of the day to a man leaving the check-in booth. "When're dogs working?"

"You got something to exhibit, little lady?" His lop-sided grin gave way to a leer. Flirt Boy seemed to have an idea that he was all kinds of charming, which didn't exactly sugar my grits.

"Maybe so." I spoke gruff enough that he'd rethink whether I was meaning my words, like him, in extra ways. I'm average-plus height or more and made out of trim muscles, nothing little about me.

"Then you're up." He jerked a thumb over his left shoulder to the main arena then pressed a button on his radio to tell someone to release six steers to let a demo run before the official program started.

That's more like it. Ready to run my dog in this thunderdome, I whistled. Flying yellow fur bailed out Ol' Blue's driver window and we slipped into the ginormous arena, first of the day.

The Kelpie that was officially entered downed at the gate with a word from his handler in that way we call honoring. The dog wanted to work but was going to honor Charley and me.

At the far end of the arena, a gate clanged, admitting a half dozen rowdy cattle. They snorted, stamped, and scattered. Near me, two green metal fence panels were set up with a ten-foot gap between them. Charley would have to drive the cattle between the panels.

"Away to me," I told Charley.

Distinctive in his work, my Charley is. Plenty of eye, confident, with a knack of knowing when to use which kind of manipulation to make cattle stop or move where needed. Younger dogs have faster out runs, sure, but Charley possesses the wisdom of experience. He ran to the end of the arena and gave the milling steers the benefit of his glare. They pretty well gathered up and began to move along the long line of the fence. Charley would have to force the loose steers toward me through the panels, then around again and out a gate again at the far end.

One crusty half-breed steer decided he liked the original end of the arena better. He whipped around and charged my dog.

Feinting, Charley whirled and told the steer to get back, told it he wasn't giving up ground. In two seconds of stubborn, Charley further explained that he was fine with either one of them dying over the issue of whether that steer should move along peaceably and join the others.

It went like that. These rough cattle didn't cotton to being herded at all, but Charley wasn't intimidated.

Without a wave of my hand, I verbally directed Charley to bring the stock through the panels. Charley bossed them right and proper, until he could deliver them again to the end of the arena where we re-penned the lot.

The nods we got, well, we'd earned 'em.

"That'll do, Charley," I told my old fellow.

Both our hearts were brimming with pride and love. We thought we were pretty much the coolest thing on the planet. I'd run my dog, my Charley, at the Black Bluff bull sales, first run of the day. Bucket-list life item, check.

It's a herding-dog thing. Maybe everyone wouldn't understand.

A microphone clicked on with a squeal. They were ready to get started with the day's official program. An announcer asked my name, my dog's name, and where we were from. He repeated it all over the loudspeaker to clapping and cheering from the hundred or so early spectators, and he welcomed everybody to the last day of this year's Black Bluff bull sale.

They released more burly cattle, rough enough, barely dog-broke. The first official man up gave me a considered, congratulatory nod, then sent his Kelpie, who spent a lot of air yipping. The tough little dog would need that energy for the extra outruns he'd have to do when his stock scattered. And now Charley had to honor the Kelpie, ignore the fresh steers he wanted to work.

A big fellow across the way looked above the crowd to eye me and mine. Seemed like too much attention. Not a good thing at all. Another feller—this one smaller and dark-skinned with straight black hair and no hat—eyed the one eyeing me and then stared at me way too long. He edged my way and paused, then faded back, 'til I lost him in the milling crowd.

Then I saw him again. I'm not all that given to the heebie-jeebies but that dark-haired wiry man moved toward us in a way that made me not want to turn my back.

It's always a sign when I start to think ill of others that someone around here needs a nap. And I was hungry, having not so much as a stale half-box of Milk Duds to munch on since I'd left the Buckeye. I'd done my road trip in hard hours. If I caught a few more winks, I could maybe unofficially run Charley again during one of the program breaks, take a gawk around, then hit the road. I just needed a small corner of the world, some open space at the end of the sale property. I fired up Ol' Blue and cranked the wheel hard, rumbling slowly through the less traveled parts of the sale grounds to gain a patch to myself.

Shady, without such long grass that the bugs would have me for breakfast, and quiet, way back from the hollers and truck sounds and stock smells of the mighty sale, this was a spot where a gal could catch herself ten or twenty winks before she turned her sweet self around and rolled north again.

I slid out of Ol' Blue then started to ask Charley for an opinion on where we should rest, the grass or the cab.

Crack! Something smacked the back of my skull.